THE WOLF IS MINE

PAIGE TYLER

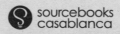

sourcebooks
casablanca

Published by Sourcebooks Casablanca, an imprint of Sourcebooks
P.O. Box 4410, Naperville, Illinois 60567-4410
(630) 961-3900
sourcebooks.com

Printed and bound in the United States of America.
OPM 10 9 8 7 6 5 4 3 2 1

Also by Paige Tyler

With special thanks to my extremely patient and understanding husband. Without your help and support, I couldn't have pursued my dream job of becoming a writer. You're my sounding board, my idea man, my critique partner, and the absolute best research assistant a girl could ask for. Love you!

CHAPTER 1

San Antonio

"WHY THE HELL WOULD ZANE AND ALYSSA COME all the way out here to the middle of nowhere?" Officer Connor Malone, Dallas PD SWAT, asked as he looked around the abandoned condo complex he and his teammates were searching. "It doesn't look like anyone has been here in months."

"And we're nowhere close to the place where the actual murder happened," Officer Hale Delaney, his blond, blue-eyed teammate, added, leaning over to show Connor the screen of his cell phone. Hale had pulled up a map of San Antonio, and the two dots displayed there were a good fifteen miles apart.

"That detective from San Antonio PD said Zane mentioned something about meeting a possible witness out here, but that was two weeks ago," dark-haired Senior Corporal Trevor McCall answered from the far side of the parking lot, where he and Officer Diego Martinez were sniffing around. As in *literally* sniffing around, hoping their enhanced werewolf sense of smell might pick up something to suggest Zane and Alyssa had been here.

"Seems more like a place a cop goes to get ambushed than to meet a witness," the other member of their team, Senior Corporal Mike Taylor, murmured as he tugged on the chain wrapped around the handles of the building's main doors. "If Zane came out here, it was because he and Alyssa were desperate for a lead. Or thought they were onto one worth the risk."

Officer Zane Kendrick and his mate, Alyssa Carson, had come to San Antonio more than three weeks ago to investigate what had been described as "a murder with supernatural and ritualistic indicators," but they hadn't been heard from since.

While Zanc was an alpha werewolf like all the members of the Dallas SWAT team, Alyssa was a human who worked for the Special Threat Assessment Team, an agency that specialized in dealing with supernatural creatures regular law enforcement would never be able to admit existed, much less deal with. Connor's werewolf pack had originally run across STAT when they'd worked together to take down vampires in Los Angeles, but this was the first time one of the Pack's werewolves had gone on a mission without more of the Pack for backup.

The trip to San Antonio was supposed to have been little more than a reconnaissance mission. Zane and Alyssa were here to look at the body of the murder victim and see if there was enough to warrant a more detailed investigation. Considering

Zane was an alpha werewolf and Alyssa an experienced field agent, it should have been a piece of cake. Nothing should have gone wrong.

But something *had* gone wrong.

And now both of them were missing.

In the three days since Connor and his pack mates had been down here, they hadn't found a single clue telling them where Zane and Alyssa were. They'd gotten a look at the autopsy report and confirmed that the knife wounds definitely looked ritualistic, but other than that, they had nothing. Hell, they weren't even sure if anything supernatural was involved.

"Everybody spread out," Mike said, cupping his hands to look inside the glass doors of the building. "See if you can pick up a scent or find anything that looks out of place."

While Diego and Trevor continued around the right side of the complex, Connor headed for the left, Hale following. Connor breathed deeply through his nose, trying to pick up the familiar scents he associated with Zane and Alyssa, while at the same time remaining attentive to other smells that might suggest something unusual had happened there. Like smokeless powder or blood. Even the desiccated stench of vampire.

As for Hale, he didn't bother trying to find anything with his nose. He'd broken it so badly in a fight when he was younger that it had damaged the olfactory nerves and receptors. For some reason, the damage hadn't been repaired when Hale went through his werewolf change. Now, he couldn't smell anything. Sniffing for leads was a waste of time, so he depended on his keen eyesight instead.

Connor and Hale were fighting through chest-high brush and thickets along the side of the building when his phone vibrated in his pocket. Connor didn't even consider letting it go to voicemail. He'd been desperately waiting for one particular bit of news, and he prayed this was it.

"Rachel," he said the moment he answered. "Please tell me you've found her."

"Not yet. Sorry," one of the two female alpha werewolves on the team said softly, and Connor felt despair and anxiety clamp down on his heart like a pair of pliers. "We put up flyers in all the neighborhoods around the SWAT compound and have all the street patrols in the area keeping an eye out for her—sort of an unofficial BOLO. Everyone's looking for her. We're going to find Kat. I promise."

Rachel kept talking, telling Connor what else they were doing in their search for the team's feline mascot, but he was having a hard time paying attention to anything she was saying. The only thing he could think about right then was that Kat had been missing since the morning he and the other guys left to drive down here to San Antonio three days ago. And he was flat-out losing his mind.

Connor was so freaked out that it was actually starting to concern him. He and the Pack had adopted Kat when she'd climbed in one of the SWAT response trucks at a crime scene nine months ago. He'd never thought of himself as a cat person—he was a werewolf for crying out loud—but all of that changed when Kat had shown up in his life and begun following him everywhere he went. He didn't understand it, but he and Kat had bonded so strongly that they spent almost every moment of every day together. Hell, she slept on the pillow beside him in bed every night, too. It wasn't normal to worry this much simply because she'd been missing for a few days, was it? Seriously, he felt like he was about to have a nervous breakdown.

He was able to collect himself enough to at least get Rachel up to speed on what was going on in San Antonio. Not that there was much to tell her in that regard. He gave her the location of the abandoned condo complex, promising to call back once they'd cleared it.

"We're not holding out much hope of finding them here, though," he added. "The place seems deserted."

"Nothing new on Kat?" Hale asked when he hung up, even though Connor knew his pack mate had heard the entire conversation. His nose might be crap, but his ears worked fine.

Connor shook his head. "Not yet. Rachel told me not to lose hope, though."

"She's right," Hale murmured, his voice encouraging even as he gave up fighting through the brush and looked around for a better route. "Kat's too smart to get herself into trouble. She's probably out hunting for mice. That or she's looking for a hunky tomcat to spend some quality time with. Trust me, she'll be back before you know it. In fact, I bet she's on her way to the compound right this second."

Connor didn't say anything. He knew Hale was only trying to help make him feel better, but his buddy was wrong. Kat hadn't gone out hunting for mice. She was the pickiest cat he'd ever seen when it came to food. She turned her nose up at anything in a can, even tuna. No, Kat preferred fresh-caught fish, filet mignon, and lightly seasoned flank steak, all of them cooked to perfection. The one time she'd seen a mouse running across the yard at the compound, she'd gotten this look on her face suggesting someone needed to call an exterminator.

The idea that Kat would be out chasing a tomcat was also ludicrous. While she got along great with Tuffie, the pit-bull mix the Pack had rescued and adopted, she'd never shown any interest in hanging out with other cats.

No. Kat hadn't run off for either of those reasons. There was definitely some other stuff going on, and he couldn't help but think the worst.

"Connor. Hale." Mike's voice sounded in his radio earpiece. "Come around to the east side of the building. We found something."

Connor and Hale exchanged looks, then quickly retraced their steps through the brush. Once clear of the overgrown thickets, they both took off running. Connor didn't have a clue if whatever Mike and the other guys had found was dangerous or not, but he didn't want to chance it one way or another. They'd barely made it a few hundred feet along the east side of the building when he picked up a pungent scent.

"Blood," he said for Hale's benefit. "There isn't a lot of it, and what's there isn't very fresh, but it's definitely not werewolf blood."

Which meant it didn't belong to Zane or Alyssa, thankfully.

They found Mike, Trevor, and Diego standing outside a set of stairs that led down into what Connor assumed was the maintenance level. The smell of blood was stronger now. When he stopped beside his pack mates, he saw something painted in muddy brown along one side of the wall above the steps. It looked like some kind of graffiti. He frowned when he realized that was where the scent of blood was coming from. Someone had used blood as paint.

"What the hell is that symbol?" he asked.

It was a diamond with a long line running

vertically through it. A few slash marks had been added to the top and bottom of the vertical line, like the fletching on an arrow. Connor honestly had no idea what he was looking at.

"I don't know," Mike murmured, staring at the symbol, brow furrowed above his dark eyes. "But I took a picture of it and sent it to Rachel. She'll see if STAT can come up with something on it."

"I'm not sure we can wait for them," Connor said. "Painting a ritualistic-looking symbol on the wall in human blood falls under the category of supernatural indicators. I think we need to see where these stairs lead."

When none of his pack mates seemed to have a problem with that plan, Connor led the way down the debris-cluttered steps to the set of metal double doors at the bottom. He expected to see more chains around the handles, like the ones on the front door, but there weren't any, which was kind of weird.

"I'm picking up some scents," Mike said.

Connor glanced over to see his teammate standing there with his eyes closed, an expression of intense concentration on his face.

"I want to say they belong to Zane and Alyssa, but they're barely discernible," Mike added. "Like they were here months ago instead of days or even weeks."

Connor shared looks with Trevor and Diego to see if they'd picked up anything, because Connor couldn't smell anything other than metal, but they both shook their heads.

"Your nose must be better than ours because we're not even getting a hint of whatever you're smelling," Connor said. "Is it coming from whatever's on the other side of the door?"

Mike opened his eyes. "Only one way to know for sure."

Connor expected the doors to be locked, so he was surprised when Mike pushed them open without any effort at all. He was about to question if maybe this was a trap when he picked up two very familiar scents.

"It's them," Mike said. "I'm sure of it."

Pulling his department-issued weapon from the holster on his waist, Mike stepped through the door and moved deeper into the darkness within. Diego, Trevor, and Hale followed. Connor did, too, not even slowing to consider what might be waiting for them in there. Zane and Alyssa were Pack. That meant it didn't matter what dangers might be waiting for him and the other guys. They'd face whoever they had to face and do whatever they had to do to rescue them.

The basement of the complex was a sprawling collection of interconnected rooms, support columns, and decades' worth of broken wood pallets and assorted junk covered with a thick layer of dust. The only illumination came from the tiny grated vents set up high near the ceiling. But none of that mattered as they followed Zane's and Alyssa's scents toward the west side of the building.

In a puddle of light created by two of the small windows, they found their pack mate and his fiancée leaning against a concrete block exterior wall. Zane and Alyssa were surrounded by dirty plastic bottles filled with even dirtier water and a handful of cardboard boxes and cellophane wrappers—Twinkies and Oreos, he'd guess by what was left of the packaging. But the strangest thing wasn't any of that stuff. It was the two broken pieces of wood lying across their laps. Like they'd been using the makeshift weapons to defend themselves.

To put it bluntly, Zane and Alyssa looked like death warmed over. Alyssa in particular, as she was bleeding through half a dozen rough bandages that had been applied to wounds along her arms, shoulders, and sides. Both their clothes were smudged with so much dirt, it was like they'd been rolling in it. If Connor hadn't heard their slow, shallow heartbeats with his own ears, he would have thought both of them were dead.

After holstering his gun, Diego scooped Alyssa into his arms as Connor dropped to his knees at Zane's side. He cupped his pack mate's jaw and carefully lifted Zane's head to get a better look at him in the darkness.

"He looks like he's lost thirty or forty pounds," he said softly.

Connor had never seen a fellow werewolf look so gaunt.

"That's probably because he almost assuredly gave all the food they had to Alyssa," Mike said as he and Trevor knelt on Zane's other side. "Even if it was only ten days, that's a damn long time for a werewolf to go without food. Especially with whatever the hell it was they had to fight off."

"None of that matters now," Connor said, knocking aside the scrap of wood and picking Zane up in his arms. "We're getting both of them the hell out of here."

Zane came to as Connor and the other guys headed for the door through which they'd come in, his voice hoarse as he mumbled something.

"Don't worry, buddy," Connor murmured. "We got you. We're getting you and Alyssa out of here right now. Promise."

"Can't…leave," Zane whispered. "Won't…let…us."

Connor could only imagine that Zane was delusional from hunger and exhaustion, so he didn't bother to respond to his pack mate's comment. Up ahead, Mike led the way while Trevor and Hale brought up the rear.

It wasn't until they reached the doors leading to the stairwell that Connor began to understand what Zane had been trying to tell them. The doors had disappeared, and in place of them, there was simply a rough concrete block wall.

There was no way out.

They were trapped.

CHAPTER 2

THE GATES OF THE SWAT COMPOUND WERE locked as usual, but it wasn't like that had ever stopped Kat Davenport before. Of course, she normally would have followed the fence around to the left side of the enormous compound and slipped through the small gap that had opened near one of the corner posts. She couldn't do that now, though, since she was quite a bit bigger than she'd been a few days ago. But that was what happened when she started walking around on two feet instead of four. There were lots of places she couldn't fit.

But on the bright side, she had hands now. It was difficult to put into words how stoked she was to be able to wiggle her fingers whenever she wanted. It made using magic so much easier. Not that she hadn't been able to do magic before, while in her cat form, but it had definitely been more complicated.

Taking a moment to calm herself, Kat reached out with her mind and let herself feel the magic around her. She pulled it in, then whispered a simple opening spell—one of the first ones she'd learned when she was a kid—giving her fingers a little wiggle.

She wobbled a little as the magic flowed through her, immediately feeling weak. That wasn't shocking.

She was always wiped out right after her transition from cat to human form. Luckily, she'd found a fore-closed home near the compound where she'd been able to hide. She'd spent the past three days doing little more than sleeping, as well as eating food she'd found in the kitchen cabinets. Thankfully, the people who'd lived there had left some clothes, too, including the jeans, black long-sleeve tee, and tennis shoes she wore. Otherwise, she would have been wrapped in a bedsheet right now.

In front of her, the lock on the gate clicked and fell to the ground with a thud, along with the heavy chain accompanying it.

Success!

Opening the gate, Kat slipped inside. She immediately took note of Connor's Silver Chevy Silverado parked in the lot next to the rest of the vehicles. He and some of his teammates had left days ago to go to San Antonio, but they were surely back by now. A shiver of nervousness skittered through her, and for about the fiftieth time that morning, she wondered if this was a good idea. As she'd laid on a dingy mattress over the past few days recovering from her magical exhaustion, revealing her secret to Connor had seemed like a no-brainer. He was the closest thing she had to a friend in this so-called life she led. She'd found peace and happiness in his presence for the first time in almost four years. Why wouldn't she tell him everything?

But now that she was here, seconds away from confronting Connor for the first time in her real human form, doubts crept in. What if he didn't believe her? What if he thought she was completely delusional and decided to call in the nice people with the wraparound loungewear? What if he *did* believe her but now didn't want to be anywhere near her? What if he liked her more as a cat than a person?

Forcing herself to push those fears away, she headed for the collection of buildings that made up the compound. She'd come all this way. She would see it through.

But halfway across the parking lot, she stopped, looking back and forth between the training and admin buildings, wondering where she should look first. At this time of the morning, Connor was usually at his desk in the bullpen, trying to keep up with the paperwork that seemed so much a part of every cop's life. She remembered spending long hours as a cat watching him hunt and peck his way through the reports on the computer. She smiled at the image of him letting out these adorable little growls whenever he made a mistake, which was frequently.

But on days when the Pack did an extended physical training session, Connor could sometimes be found in the workout room, lifting weights and getting deliciously ripped and sweaty. She suddenly hoped that was where he'd be now. She'd spent several long nights during the past three days fantasizing about running her fingers over his muscular chest. Then again, she'd had that fantasy a few times a week since first meeting him. And now that she had real fingers again, there didn't seem to be anything keeping her from living out that fantasy.

Kat stood there frozen in the middle of the parking lot, still not sure which way to go. For the first time in years, she actually missed her feline form. She'd grown dependent on a nose that always fed her loads of worthwhile information, including the location of her favorite stud-muffin belly-scratcher.

She was still lost in thought when the door of the admin building opened and Officers Landry Cooper and Eric Becker stepped outside. They both wore curious—though somewhat suspicious—expressions on their faces.

"Ma'am, you can't just walk in here," Cooper said. The tall officer with dark hair and brown eyes threw a quick frown at the gate—which was still hanging partially open—like he couldn't figure out how it got that way. "That's supposed to be locked."

Kat gave both werewolves a smile as she walked over to them, trying to appear as casual as she could. "Yeah, I know, but I'm a friend of Connor's. I needed to talk to him and thought I'd stop by."

She almost laughed at the shocked expressions on their faces as she breezed past them and into the admin building. Cooper and Becker followed, but she ignored them, making a beeline for the bullpen. Connor wasn't anywhere in sight, but Rachel Bennett, one of the two female werewolves on the SWAT team, was there, along with a few of her teammates. Even though they seemed as relaxed as they always did, Kat had the sensation that something was wrong.

"Where's Connor?" she asked.

Before anyone could say anything, Cooper and Becker came around to stand in front of her, almost like they were blocking her way.

"He's out on a call right now and won't be back for a while," Cooper said. "If you could give us your name and phone number, we'll make sure he gets back to you as soon as he can."

Mouth tight, Kat glanced at the sign-out board on the far wall. The names of everyone on the team were listed on one side, and there were little colored magnets arranged beside each to let their commander—and alpha of their pack of alphas— Gage Dixon, know who was available for response calls. If Connor and his pack mates didn't keep it updated religiously, Gage would chew them a new one. She'd watched it happen a time or two. It wasn't a pretty sight.

There was a team out on a call, red magnets beside those names. Scribbled in barely legible letters beside their names were the words *University Park*, the location of the call.

There was a black dot beside Gage's name, which meant he was at headquarters.

It was the blue magnets beside Connor's, Mike's, Diego's, Hale's, and Trevor's names that worried her. Blue normally indicated training or schooling, but the Pack also used it when someone was out doing something strange and freaky that couldn't be mentioned to anyone else in the police department. Which was why there'd been a blue dot beside Zane's name for three weeks.

But it was the words beside all their names that really freaked her out.

San Antonio.

How the hell could Connor and the other guys still be down there looking for Zane? It'd been *three* days.

Kat was about to call Cooper out for his lie when something thumped into her leg so hard, it almost knocked her off her feet. She looked down to see Tuffie, her best friend and partner in crime, looking up at her with the most baffled expression she'd ever seen on a dog. The precious pit-bull mix leaned forward and gave her a thoughtful sniff, then regarded her with a look as if to say, *Did you do something new with your hair?*

Even though she wanted to find out what the heck was going on with Connor, she still took the time to drop to a knee and ruffle Tuffie's short fur. Tuffie gave her a big doggy grin in return. She really *was* the sweetest creature ever placed on this Earth.

After Tuffie seemed content that Kat was still Kat the cat—only taller—she turned and walked over to plop down on the big, plush bed to one side of the bullpen.

Kat stood, shooting a glare in Cooper's direction. "I know you're lying about Connor. He went down to San Antonio with the other guys to find Zane and Alyssa. But they should have been back by now, unless something happened. So you'd better tell me what the heck is going on, or I'll turn you into a toad. And trust me, I *can* do that."

The entire room full of werewolves stared at her, which was more than a little disconcerting, Kat had to admit. In retrospect, maybe she should have tried a different tack with them. The toad thing might have been a little much.

"Look," Cooper said, scowling at her as he crossed his arms over his chest. "I don't know who you are or how you're connected to Connor, but you can't walk in here and threaten a cop. It's not cool. And that crap about the toad was just plain weird."

Becker opened his mouth to add his own two cents when Rachel suddenly pushed back her chair and walked over to them. Blond hair pulled back in a neat bun, Rachel stopped in front of Kat, then leaned forward and sniffed her.

Talk about weird.

Kat knew werewolves were all about their noses, but it was still hard not to be offended. Then again, she hadn't had a chance to shower since the change. Well, technically she hadn't showered in about a year. But that was because Kat the cat did not get along with water. Unless it came out of a faucet at a moderately slow drip.

She lifted her right hand, ready to wiggle her fingers, do some magic, and put a little distance between her and Rachel, when the werewolf glanced up sharply, a stunned expression on her face, dark eyes curious.

"She smells like Connor," Rachel announced, not taking her gaze off Kat. "She also smells like Kat. She's obviously been staying at his place—a lot."

The rest of the werewolves got up to crowd around Kat. They tried to be covert about sniffing her, since it wasn't normal to do that to complete strangers—or close friends, for that matter—but she knew that was exactly what they were doing. It was a rather unique experience. Which was saying a lot considering she spent most of her time living as a cat these days.

"You can stop trying to be all subtle," she said as Cooper leaned in to take another sniff. "I know Connor and the rest of you are werewolves. I know Alyssa works with STAT and that she and Zane went down to San Antonio to check out a suspicious murder with supernatural indicators. And I know Connor and the other guys went down there three days ago because you haven't heard anything from Zane or Alyssa in three weeks."

Rachel and her fellow werewolves did a double take, their gazes darting back and forth from one to the other. Like they were silently asking, *Did you know anything about this?*

"Connor *told* you all of that?" Rachel finally asked, giving her a look that was hard to decipher. She seemed stunned and suspicious but also rather amused.

Kat smiled. "Not exactly. I *have* been staying at his apartment, but that's not why I smell like Kat. I smell like Kat the cat because I *am* Kat the cat."

That announcement went over about as well as she'd expected. They all looked at each other again, this time like they were wondering if they should call someone and get her psychological help. She was on the verge of pointing out the hypocrisy of werewolves thinking she couldn't possibly be a cat but stopped herself. She was here to find Connor. She didn't have the time for this discussion to devolve into an argument.

She folded her arms and pinned Cooper with a look. "You have multiple scars along your abdomen from getting shot, another scar in your chest from that time your wife's brother stabbed you, and at least a dozen more from when a friend tried to blow you up with a bomb. Oh, and I also know that you and Everly are expecting your first child any day now."

Cooper opened his mouth to say something, but Kat kept going. "Becker, you have a big surgery scar on your chest and two more directly above your belly button from the wounds that turned you into a werewolf."

He looked as stunned as Cooper had, but she didn't give him a chance to say anything.

"Max, you have scars from bullet wounds on the left side of your rib cage, as well as one on your chest, and another on your right shoulder, which you got saving your wife's life from a group of werewolf hunters." She swept the rest of them with her gaze. "I can keep going, but I think you get the idea."

Rachel frowned, looking wary now. "How do you know about their scars? Connor would never have told you personal stuff like that."

"No, he wouldn't," Kat replied. "And he didn't. I know about all your scars because I watched you guys work out all the time with your shirts off."

"What?!" Cooper and the other guys sputtered in unison.

She shrugged. "Hey, I might have been a cat, but I was still a woman. You can't blame me for looking. And as far as knowing *how* you got the scars, that's easy since all you guys do is brag about when and how you got injured."

Cooper started to respond, but she cut him off again.

"Enough about me and all the things I already know. How about you tell me why Connor and the others haven't come back from San Antonio? It shouldn't have taken them this long to find Zane and Alyssa."

Rachel exchanged another look with the guys, then sighed. "I talked to Connor fifteen minutes ago. They haven't found Zane and Alyssa yet, but they have a lead. They were searching an abandoned condominium complex when they found some kind of graffiti painted in blood on one of the walls."

Kat's stomach clenched. "What kind of graffiti? Did they describe it?"

"I'm not really sure." Rachel reached into her back pocket for her phone. "But just because it was drawn in blood, doesn't necessarily mean anything—even if that blood happened to be human. There are a lot of sickos in the world, you know? They sent me a picture of it, if that helps."

The moment Kat saw the image, her heart started thumping faster, a shiver of fear running down her spine. "Oh, crap. That's an inverted protection rune. We need to get to San Antonio. Now! We may already be too late."

"Inverted what?" Cooper asked, leaning over her shoulder to look at the phone, his gaze darting back and forth between her and the screen, expression doubtful.

"If there'd been one horizontal slash at the top and bottom of the vertical line, this would be a traditional rune for protection," she said impatiently, pointing at the screen. "All these additional lines pervert the entire purpose of the symbol, changing it from protection to confinement. The way it's drawn, this rune will trap anyone who steps into the guarded space. We have to get there and break the rune before whatever else was left in there gets to them."

"Calm down," Rachel said, reaching out to grab her cell. "I don't think there's anything wrong, but if it will make you feel better, I'll call Connor so you'll know that he's okay." She held the phone to her ear for a moment, then frowned. "Huh. It says his phone is out of service. I'll call Mike."

Thirty seconds later, the whole room was full of werewolves frowning and looking more than a little concerned.

"All their phones are out of service?" Cooper said. "How is that possible?"

"It's possible all right." Kat was so exasperated, she wanted to scream. "That inverted protection spell won't let anything—including cell phone signals—in or out of that building. Now, we need to stop talking and start driving. If we don't get to San Antonio soon, Connor and everyone with him will end up dead."

CHAPTER 3

"THIS SHOULDN'T EVEN BE EFFING POSSIBLE," Connor growled for what had to be the dozenth time as he stood in front of the concrete block wall.

He and his teammates had searched the entire mazelike basement for the past two hours and had yet to find a door anywhere. Even discounting the suddenly missing door, there should have been some way to get out of there, like an air-conditioning ventilation system or a trash chute. But if there were any, he and his pack mates hadn't been able to find them. In the end, they had to accept there was no way out of this place.

They weren't only trapped.

They were screwed.

"There's no cell service anywhere in this damn place," Trevor muttered, shaking his head as he stared down at the phone in his hand. "I've walked every square foot of this room and can't get a single bar. I even piled up some boxes and climbed to one of those tiny vents and still got nothing. It's flat-out unreal."

"If I had to guess, I'd say someone is purposely jamming the signal," Hale remarked from across the room, where he and Diego were trying to make

Zane and Alyssa as comfortable as they could. "I'm not sure who that someone is or how they're doing it, though."

"At least why they're doing it is obvious," Mike said, coming back in the room from wherever he'd been searching. "Whoever trapped us down here doesn't want us calling for help. They want us stuck, hoping we end up in the same condition as Zane and Alyssa."

"But our pack mates know where we are," Trevor pointed out. "When they don't hear back from us in a couple hours and can't reach us by phone, they'll come looking."

Connor snorted. "And what's to keep them from ending up stuck in here exactly like us? It's not like we can stand by the door and make sure we don't let it close behind them. We don't even know where the damn door is anymore."

He hadn't realized he was shouting until Zane jerked awake and started mumbling about not making so much noise. Diego immediately leaned down and tried to get him to drink some more of the stagnate water they'd found dripping from a rusted pipe coming out of the wall in the back of the basement, but Zane pushed Diego's hand away, mumbling unintelligibly.

"I don't think we can wait until someone realizes we're in trouble, regardless of whether they can figure out a way to help us," Diego said grimly, his dark eyes full of worry. "Zane and Alyssa are too weak to last much longer."

No one said anything.

Connor's heart thumped harder. He knew Zane and Alyssa were in bad shape, but the idea that they were that close to death was something he had a hard time accepting.

Cursing under his breath, he turned and strode toward the wall. A growl rumbled up from his throat as his fangs and claws extended, the muscles of his arms and shoulders twitching and spasming.

"If we can't find the damn doors, we'll make our own," he snarled, bringing back his arm and clenching his fist as tightly as his claws would allow.

Behind him, Zane muttered something that sounded vaguely like a warning, but right then, Connor was too far gone to listen to reason. All he could think about was getting his pack mates and Alyssa out of this hellhole—by whatever means necessary.

With a roar of barely contained rage, Connor began to punch the concrete block wall over and over. Bones cracked in his hand, but as large chunks of the wall broke off and fell to the dirty floor, he decided the pain was worth it.

He was so intent on pulverizing the wall that he didn't hear the warnings his friends were shouting until a flicker of motion to his right caught his attention. What he saw froze him solid and all he could do was stare at the thing coming toward him.

What the hell?

Connor was still trying to come up with an answer to that question when something that vaguely resembled an arm reached out and back-handed him halfway across the room. He hit the floor so hard, he actually bounced a few feet in the air before sliding the rest of the way and smashing into a wall.

Vision swimming, he pressed a hand to his throbbing head and came away with blood on his fingers even as his pack mates began letting out low, menacing growls. He considered staying where he was for a moment so he could clear his vision, but then he heard gunfire and knew he had to move.

Shaking off the fog, he pushed himself to his feet. And came face-to-face with the thing that had knocked him across the room. Realizing that claws were probably not going to help in this situation, Connor let them slide back in, pulling his gun and hastily taking a step back.

Whatever the creatures were, there were four of them. At first, they didn't seem too intimidating, standing barely five feet tall. But then Connor realized the things were built like frigging tanks, with wide, misshapen shoulders and arms that seemed way too long and too bulky for their bodies. Even in the darkness surrounding the creatures, it was impossible to miss the spikes that seemed to be sticking out all over the things. As the one in front of him moved forward, it stepped into a puddle of light coming in from one of the vents, allowing Connor to get a better look at the thing.

What he saw almost froze him solid where he stood.

The squat creature was humanlike in only the vaguest sense, made of random pieces of splintered wood and jagged shards of metal seemingly held together with little more than wads of wet cardboard. It only took a quick glance around the now-almost-clean floor to realize the thing had been somehow formed from the trash and debris that had littered the place only seconds before. Connor's head spun, refusing to believe this was possible.

What could only loosely be described as a head had spikes of wood in place of hair and a twisted piece of metal buried in the midst of what should have been its face. While the thing had no eyes that Connor could identify, the way it stalked directly at him suggested it could see perfectly fine.

The creature closed the distance between them faster than Connor would have thought possible. One moment, the thing was ten feet away, the next it was swinging one of those long, spike-covered arms toward him again. Connor quickly ducked under the blow, then came up shooting, putting three .40-caliber rounds right through the monster's chest, knocking it backward several steps and sending chunks of wood flying everywhere.

Holes the size of his thumb appeared in the creature's chest, and for a moment, Connor thought the thing was going to fall to the floor. But then the monster stepped forward again as if it hadn't felt a thing, clubbing Connor across the shoulder so hard, it felt like his arm came off.

This time, Connor bounced off the wall before hitting the floor, blood pouring from a wound torn through his skin by one of the rough pieces of wood. He opened his eyes with a groan only to realize the concrete block he'd hit was the same section he'd been punching pieces out of a few minutes ago. Except now the wall was as pristine as it had ever been.

He didn't have any time to wonder how that was possible as the creature closed on him once again. Connor knew he had to move, or the thing was going to beat him to death right where he lay.

Connor slipped under the creature's outstretched arm, its rough wooden fingertips grazing the back of his tactical vest and ripping it open. He spun and put three rounds through the thing's head at damn near point-blank range. Chunks of wood the size of his fists fell to the floor, sparks flying from the metal still embedded in its face.

As half its head disappeared, Connor waited for the thing to drop, telling himself there was no way in hell the creature should have been able to keep going in that condition. But as Connor backed away, all he could do was suck in a ragged breath, cursing as pieces of wood and debris snapped up from the floor and the monster's head began to rebuild itself piece by piece.

"They won't die!" he shouted to his pack mates. "They just keep rebuilding themselves!"

"No shit!" Trevor called from the far side of the room, unloading an entire magazine into one of the creatures, then kicking it in the stomach for good measure. "Help us get Zane and Alyssa out of this room. We can't fight these damn things and protect them at the same time."

Connor couldn't disagree, but he had to bite his tongue to keep from pointing out that leaving the room might not help. What would stop these things from simply following them and continuing the attack, room after room after room? Sooner or later, they'd be pinned, their backs to a wall with nowhere else to run.

But he kept those thoughts to himself, quickly moving over to help Trevor and Diego scoop up Zane and Alyssa off the floor, then slowly moving toward the next room as Mike and Hale protected their retreat.

"What the hell are we going to do?" Connor shouted even as Mike punched one of the things in the face so hard, its head exploded.

"We survive," Mike growled while the monsters continued to advance, even as the one he'd just hit reformed its head, acting as if it simply didn't care what was done to it. "Until we find a way that will work. Or the Pack figures out we're in trouble and finds a way to help us."

Connor didn't say anything. Instead, he put a bullet through the kneecap of the creature closest to him, then wedged a shoulder under Zane's arm and backpedaled as fast as he could. While Mike's plan might make sense—not to mention it was the best they could do at the moment—he had a hard time believing they were going to last long enough for their pack mates to show up all the way from Dallas. Even if they did get there in time, what the hell could a few more werewolves hope to accomplish when these creatures they were facing seemed to be damn near indestructible?

CHAPTER 4

"THEIR VEHICLES ARE STILL HERE," COOPER SAID as he stepped out of the SWAT SUV the four of them had driven down to San Antonio in, glancing around the abandoned and overgrown condominium complex with a worried expression. "Maybe Kat was onto something when she said the guys are in trouble."

Kat had to bite her tongue to keep from saying something rude as she, Rachel, and Becker joined Cooper in front of the main entrance to the dilapidated building. Of course she'd been onto something when she said Connor and his pack mates were in trouble. She didn't simply make up crap to get attention. And she certainly didn't need to manufacture drama. Unfortunately, it seemed to naturally follow her everywhere she went. Put her in the middle of a pack of werewolves and chaos was a given.

She only wished they'd taken her warning seriously enough to bring extra backup with them. The three of them didn't seem like they'd be enough. She hoped they didn't end up regretting that decision.

"Connor! Hale! Where are you?!" Becker called out, wandering around to the left side of the building.

Assuming he was following their scent, Kat went with him. But it wasn't long before Becker stopped in his tracks. She thought it was because the high brush in front of them was too thick for anyone to get through, but then she realized he was studying the ground, like there was something interesting in the grass.

She scoured the ground to see what he was studying but didn't find anything.

"They turned around and started running," he said, motioning for her to go back the way they'd come.

"Like someone was chasing them?" she asked, hurrying to catch up to him as he strode past her.

Before he could answer, Cooper interrupted, his deep voice echoing through the air. "Kat! Becker! Get over here! We found something."

Becker looked her way for a second, then they were both hurrying around to the front of the building. There was no one there, so they kept going around to the right side. It was only a couple hundred feet, but even that short distance had Kat breathing hard. The change from feline to human form had sucked a lot more out of her this time than usual. Not even the two-hour nap she'd taken on the way to San Antonio had seemed to help. Of course, there was also the matter of her being a little behind on her cardio. For reasons that didn't seem to make a lot of sense, she'd never wanted to exercise when she'd been in her cat form. It seemed so undignified, at least to her cat sensibilities.

They found Cooper and Rachel standing near an open stairwell along the side of the building, both gazing at something on the wall to the right of the stairs. Curious, Kat stepped closer to see what they were looking at so intently. A little shiver of fear rippled down her spine when she saw the runic symbol painted there. She'd been right about what it meant. There was no doubt this was a trap.

"They took these steps," Rachel said, eyeing the dirt-and-leaf-strewn entryway. "I guess the bloody graffiti on the wall was enough to make them suspicious."

Cooper and Becker immediately started to follow Rachel down the steps without realizing how dangerous it was. Kat supposed it wasn't their fault. They didn't know what that kind of magic could do.

"Stop!" she called out quickly. "Don't go down there yet, or you'll be trapped like Connor and the rest of them. I need to break the rune first."

The three alpha werewolves stared at her like she was speaking a foreign language. Which, from their perspective, she probably was. Instead of trying to explain it, Kat reached out with her senses and searched for the flow of magic through the rune on the wall.

She grimaced the moment she encountered the energy powering the twisted protection spell. In its raw form, magic was clean and pure, kind of like a crystal-clear waterfall running down a mountain stream. But the stuff she was touching now felt oily, leaving a bitter tingle in her mouth. Like she was chewing on aluminum foil.

Not that the magic itself was actually repugnant, of course. That couldn't happen. Magic simply existed. It wasn't good or evil. But the people who used magic could sure as hell be good or evil. And they could have intent for the magic that would be construed as good or evil, too. That's what Kat felt in the rune spell. It was put there with the intent of trapping and killing people. That kind of act could taint the magic around it for a long time, the same way that dumping a barrel of toxic waste in a clean, pure stream could contaminate it for decades.

She closed her eyes, letting herself see the tainted magic with her heightened senses. It ran all over the building like greasy spiderwebs but was concentrated most heavily over the doors at the bottom of the stairs. The web practically pulsed with the magic they drew on from all across the local area. If she wasn't mistaken, quite a lot of the magic currently powering the spell was coming from inside the building. That meant it was slowly draining the life from Connor and everyone else in there.

The thought suddenly made it hard to breathe, and she had to force herself to focus. To disable the spell, she had to disrupt it. Now, she had to find the least taxing way to accomplish that. Because she definitely wasn't in any shape to channel a buttload of magic at the moment. Not unless she wanted to face-plant right there in the overgrown weeds surrounding the building.

In the end, it wasn't as difficult as she'd feared. Magic could be twisted to do all kinds of unsavory things, but that didn't mean it liked it. Water could be forced uphill, but it would always try and find its way back down. All Kat had to do was reach out a hand toward the bloody rune and wiggle her fingers at the offensive parts of the symbol while channeling a line of clean magic into it, willing it back to its intended protection purpose. While it wasn't sentient, the magic helped her a little bit since that was what it was supposed to be doing in the first place.

She still got a little weak-kneed from the effort, but the results were exactly what she'd been going for, if a bit more dramatic than she'd expected. The pulsing, tainted spiderweb began to ripple, visible sparks and embers cascading down the walls and doors at the bottom of the stairs. When the spell finally collapsed completely, it was with an extremely loud snap that sounded like a gunshot.

"What the…?" Cooper started to say before being interrupted by the cacophony of real gunfire from inside the building, along with shouts and more than a few fierce growls. For a moment Kat wanted to say *I told you so*, until she remembered Connor was down there among all that commotion.

"Go! The spell is broken," Kat yelled even as Cooper, Rachel, and Becker raced down the steps.

She'd seen how fast werewolves could run, but even she was surprised they were a blur as they slammed through the double doors at the base of the stairs.

A little voice in the back of her head suggested waiting until the werewolves could check out the situation and get a handle on things. But then her heart pointed out that those could have been shouts of pain she'd heard from beyond those doors. What if one of those shouts had come from Connor?

Kat ran down the steps into the darkness without thinking further, weaving around piles of trash and stacks of boxes as she moved deeper into the basement, following the sounds of gunfire, shouts, and growls. She liked to believe she could recognize Connor's growls from among all the others, but maybe that was simply wishful, romantic thinking.

In the darkness her feet hit something that made a metallic clatter as it bounced across the floor. She was certainly no expert, but she thought the things she'd almost stumbled over were bullet casings. A lot of them.

Her heart pounded like a drum as she tried to move faster. After she'd run through a dozen rooms, each one dirtier and more cluttered than the last,

Kat finally stumbled into a large open area where Connor and his pack mates were, along with...well, hell...at first, she wasn't sure what it was. It looked like nothing more than a pile of moving debris. But then she made out the vaguely human forms and realized she was looking at some kind of simulacrum—a collection of random debris shoved together to look like a person and then magically imbued with movement and behaviors meant to imitate true life.

She'd never had a reason to try and make a sim like this herself, but what else would be made of wood, metal, and trash, running around, trying to kill a pack of werewolves?

It took several seconds for the reality of that last part to sink in—along with the image of Connor standing over the unconscious bodies of Zane and Alyssa with blood soaking his uniform—before she started running forward to help.

One of the sims was plodding ponderously toward Connor and the two injured people he was trying to protect. As she watched, her favorite belly-scratcher put a bullet through the thing's head. As expected, it didn't do much. Then again, shooting something in the head when it didn't have a brain was a waste. Why did people want to treat every supernatural thing they met like a zombie? It was almost offensive.

Then she realized Connor seemed to be out of

bullets and had dropped his weapon to extend his extremely long claws. While she had to admit they looked good on him, Kat felt the urge to point out that if putting a bullet through the creature's head didn't do anything, a set of claws probably wouldn't be any more effective.

Wiggling her fingers, Kat solidified the air around the sim and sent it flying toward the nearest wall as fast as she could. Channeling that much magic in her exhausted state damn near knocked her off her feet, but it was still nice seeing the thing explode into chunks of kindling as it impacted the concrete wall. Unfortunately, as soon as the wood, metal, and cardboard stopped drifting to the ground, the sim began to re-form. That positively sucked. But seeing the bits of cardboard fluttering around abruptly reminded her that there was a way to end this before anyone got hurt.

Or at least, more hurt than they already were.

"There's a stone token in the center of their chest!" she shouted, taking another wobbly step forward on legs that were suggesting she sit down right where she was. "You need to rip them apart and find the token. Once I destroy it, they can't reform."

Connor and the rest of his pack mates who'd been trapped there all turned and stared at her. In between fighting the sims, of course. Kat could see the doubt on their faces and had no idea how to resolve the situation in the short amount of time they had.

"Do what she says! She knows what the hell she's talking about!" Cooper yelled before turning on the creature closest to him and unloading an entire magazine of bullets straight into the thing's chest.

While painfully loud to Kat, the hail of bullets was effective, wood bits flying as the creature's upper torso turned into Swiss cheese. The sim was close to completely breaking in half and stumbling backward when Cooper surged forward and shoved his clawed hand into its chest and started rooting around. A few seconds later, he came out with a flat, round piece of stone two or three inches in diameter, dozens of bloodred runic symbols carved into both sides. Cooper studied it for less than a second before turning and tossing it in her direction.

Kat didn't pause to think about the possibility of being too weak to do it but simply reached for the magic around her, then pushed it out toward the token.

"Perdere," she murmured softly.

With the simple destruction spell, the air between her and the fast-approaching piece of stone began to ripple and swirl with darkness, thickening until it slowed and then stopped, hanging there in midair. It began to vibrate as Kat poured more magic into the stone even as her vision started to dim.

A moment later, the token shattered into a

hundred pieces, the remains drifting to the ground, leaving little more than dust on the floor. Half a second later, the sim who'd been trying to re-form collapsed into pieces, the chunks of metal inside it making a loud clanking sound as they struck the concrete.

The rest of the werewolves went after the three remaining sims, the violence they displayed almost terrifying. But then stone tokens came flying at her all at once, and she stopped worrying about how dangerous werewolves could be.

Kat considered asking if anyone maybe had a sledgehammer, but her pride wouldn't let her do that. So she sucked it up, channeled as much magic as her exhausted body would allow, then destroyed the three spell-worked pieces of stone before they reached her.

Her legs turned to complete jelly from manipulating so much magic in her condition, and her insides weren't far behind. She would have dropped to the floor, but the thought of needing to use more energy she didn't have to get back up was too exhausting to think about.

The three remaining sims disintegrated, wood flying everywhere, but she was too tired to care. At least until Connor appeared in front of her, concern clear on his face. There was confusion there, too, but she ignored that. The same way she ignored all the other werewolves who were gathering around the two of them. They weren't important right then.

Connor was so damn gorgeous, it was sinful. Regulation-cut dark-blond hair, hazel eyes, a strong jaw with the perfect amount of scruff, and the sexiest dimples any man could possess. Yes, he looked tired and more than a little bloody. But she knew he was okay— and oh so scrumptious.

Taking a few careful steps forward, Kat threw herself into his arms, dragged his head down, and captured his lips with hers. Connor seemed a bit surprised at first, but he figured out the plan soon enough and started kissing her back. And like she'd always imagined, damn, could the man kiss. And the way he tasted should have been illegal.

Kat wasn't sure how long they made out, but she was vaguely aware that she was getting a little dizzy. Purely from all the magic she'd been using, of course. Nothing to do with forgetting to breathe.

When she finally pulled back from Connor's perfectly magical mouth, she couldn't hide the smile crossing her lips, even though she was definitely starting to swoon now. "I've been waiting to do that for nine months, and it was just as good as I imagined."

"Um, don't take this the wrong way," he said slowly, his arms still wrapped around her, "but do I know you?"

A part of Kat was disappointed he didn't recognize her. But then again, she *had* looked a little different the last time he'd seen her. Taller now, for sure. No tail. And hairstyle definitely different.

"I would certainly think so," she said with a lazy smile. "It's not like I let anyone rub my belly, you know."

When Connor looked even more confused, she decided to cut him a break.

"I'm Kat."

Her big guy didn't have a chance to answer as Trevor chose that moment to appear at their side, leaning in close and messing up the moment.

"Sorry to interrupt," Trevor said, an expression halfway between amused and pissed. "But what the hell were those things, what the hell did you do to them, and how the hell did you know how to do it?"

Kat opened her mouth to answer but then closed it again as everything around her started to get fuzzy. Wow, she really was out of it. Taking a breath, she tried to settle herself, only partially succeeding. Her vision cleared a bit but stayed dim at the edges.

"Those were simulacrum—or sims for short," she said softly, looking from Trevor to the rest of his pack mates. "Magical constructs that follow simple instructions imbued into them with an empowered token. When I destroyed the stones, I removed the intent and purpose that powered them. As for how I knew how to do that or how I knew how to break through the binding rune outside, it's simple. I'm a witch."

She would have said more—a lot more—about

how she'd gotten to this point in her life, how she'd ended up at the SWAT compound, and why she'd felt the irresistible need to come save Connor's life, but unfortunately, at that particular moment, the dizziness decided to make a reappearance. She swayed and slumped into Connor's arms, her eyes fluttering closed.

Any more answers would have to wait until she had a nap.

CHAPTER 5

KAT JERKED AWAKE AS THE SUV BOUNCED OVER a pothole. She felt the arm around her shoulders tighten a little, and for a moment, she thought it was Connor. The disappointment she experienced when she realized it was Rachel who'd been holding her while she slept was enough to almost break her. She blinked, fighting the tears that threatened to well up and run down her cheeks.

Straightening, she pushed her long hair back and looked around groggily. Cooper was driving, but Becker was nowhere to be seen. Connor wasn't with them, either. After they'd kissed, she naturally assumed he'd ride back to Dallas with them. So much for the romantic reunion she'd been hoping for.

"We're getting close to the SWAT compound," Rachel announced softly, as if she could somehow tell how befuddled Kat felt. "You were out cold for the two hours we hung around San Antonio and the entire drive back. We had a paramedic take a look at you and she said you were okay but really exhausted, so we let you sleep. I hope that wasn't the wrong thing to do?"

Kat shook her head. "No. The paramedic was

right. Though I'm dealing with magical exhaustion more than anything physical. But the recovery process is the same. I just need something to eat and drink and a lot of rest. That nap definitely helped."

She wanted to ask where Connor was and why he hadn't ridden with them, but wasn't sure she wanted to know the answer. Or maybe part of her already did. So, instead, she settled on the next most obvious question.

"How are Zane and Alyssa?" she asked, casually turning to gaze out the side window so she could covertly wipe away a traitorous tear before Rachel could see. "I didn't get a chance to get a close look at them in the basement, but they seemed like they were in pretty bad shape."

"STAT arranged for a medical airlift from the parking lot of the condominium. Mike and Becker flew back with them," Rachel said, her voice heavy with concern. "They're already at a private hospital in Dallas, but we haven't heard anything yet. We're hoping there's an update on their condition by the time we get back to the compound. Gage has called a pack meeting, by the way. Everyone is going to want to hear your story, I'm sure."

Kat sighed. She should have expected that, she supposed. But damn, she'd really been hoping to talk to Connor privately before discussing anything with the rest of the Pack. Her *story*, as Rachel called it, was going to be hard enough to get through without having an audience. Then again, it wasn't a given that Connor would even want to talk to her. So maybe having his teammates around for the explanation of why she'd been a cat but wasn't a feline at the moment might actually be a blessing in disguise.

Rachel fell silent after that, giving Kat some much-needed time to collect herself. Her first instinct was to run away the moment they got to the SWAT compound. Bailing on bad situations had worked for her many times in the past, so why not do it now, too? It would almost certainly be easier than attempting to explain everything. The idea of finally sharing the trauma of what had happened to her with people she'd already come to think of as family should have made her feel better, but it only terrified her more.

Sooner than she would have liked, Cooper pulled into the parking lot of the compound. Kat took a deep breath. If she was going to walk away, now was the time to do it: before she saw Connor again and lost her courage.

But the moment she stepped out of the SUV, Khaki Blake came running out of the training building, a bewildered expression on her face, and Kat knew her chance to escape—if she even wanted to—was gone.

"Kat, is that really you?" Khaki asked, slowing her steps. Dressed in her SWAT-issue dark blue tactical uniform, the werewolf had her dark hair back in her signature bun, like she always did when she was on duty. "The guys told me it was, but I didn't know if I should believe them."

Khaki stopped a few feet away, her nose working a mile a minute as expressions of curiosity and confusion slid back and forth across her face. The next thing Kat knew, she was in Khaki's arms, pulled close for a warm hug she hadn't realized how much she needed until that moment. Kat damn near broke into tears as she wrapped her arms around the other woman and hugged her back. A second later, Rachel was right there with them, her arms going around both of them. Man, did that feel good.

True, she'd spent most of her time with Connor, going for long drives in his truck, curling up on the couch watching TV with him, even sleeping on a pillow right next to him in his big bed. It had been those little private moments when she'd essentially fallen for him. But sometimes a woman—even when she was a cat—needed to hang out with other women. That's where Rachel and Khaki came in. The three of them had spent hours and hours sitting around, engaging in girl talk. Kat had cherished those moments, even if she hadn't been able to join the conversation.

"The guys have already told Gage the basics," Khaki said after pulling back to gaze at her. "That you're the same Kat who'd been hanging around the compound since before Christmas and that you're a witch. But it goes without saying that he's going to want to hear the whole story from you. Because you have to admit, it's a bit much to take in."

Kat could only nod, not trusting herself to speak. Taking a deep breath, she fell into step beside Rachel and Khaki as they headed for the training building. If she could survive getting turned into a cat, she could handle anything. At least, that's what she told herself.

Kat had walked into the training classroom more times than she could count over the past nine months, but this was her first time doing it on two feet, and it felt drastically different. Even though no one was staring or anything, she felt more exposed now that she was a person than she ever had as a cat.

A therapist would have a field day with her, she was sure.

There were trays of sub sandwiches on a table along one wall, along with bags of chips and a cooler filled with ice, bottles of water, soda, and iced tea. Kat couldn't help smiling. No matter what was going on, werewolves had to eat—a lot. She grabbed half a turkey and cheese for herself, along with a bottle of water, then took a seat near the front.

Connor strode in a few seconds later. He stopped in front of Kat, locked eyes with her for what felt like forever and yet not nearly long enough, then walked over to get something to eat without a word.

She thought he might sit beside her, but instead he took a seat on the far side of the room, as far away from her as he could get. She swallowed hard and tried to tell herself it didn't mean anything, but damn, it hurt all the same.

Tearing her gaze away from Connor, she looked down at the sandwich on the plate in front of her but couldn't bring herself to eat regardless of how hungry she was. Instead, she took a long drink of water, nearly downing more than half the bottle. Out of the corner of her eye, she saw Gage walk into the room. Dark-haired, he was as tall and muscular as the rest of the guys and could stop every alpha werewolf in the Pack in his or her tracks simply with a look if he wanted to.

"Before we start, I want to personally say thank you to Kat for everything she did today," Gage said. "It goes without saying that things in San Antonio would have ended a lot worse than they did if it weren't for her help."

Kat blushed as everyone hooted and clapped their hands. Well, everyone except Connor. He simply sat there in his seat, gazing at Gage with that damn unreadable expression on his face. Like he was present and accounted for but not *truly* there.

When the cheering finally stopped, Kat looked up to see Gage smiling at her in a way that did more to relax her than she would have thought. Gage was the alpha of a whole team of alphas. That meant he had to be sort of intense sometimes. Well, most of the time. But the way he was looking at her now, it was like he wanted her to know she was welcome here. She couldn't put into words how much that meant to her.

"First and foremost, I want everyone to know that Zane and Alyssa are going to be okay. Becker and Mike are still with them, and Zane is already starting to come around," Gage continued. "STAT got them into a private hospital with some of their own doctors providing care. They'll both be in recovery for a while but will be out of action for several weeks. And before you ask, the doctors have asked that we wait a few days before we inundate them with visitors."

Everyone grumbled at that, but Gage silenced them with that patented look of his. "While I'm glad that Zane and Alyssa are doing well, right now I'm concerned about what the hell did this to them and the poor kid who was murdered down there in the first place." He turned dark eyes on her. "That's where I'm hoping you come in, Kat."

She wasn't surprised that was the topic of conversation he wanted to start with. On the bright side, at least they weren't talking about her first. She supposed that was the best she could hope for right now.

"I wish I could tell you exactly who did both of those things, but I can't," Kat said, looking around the room at everyone. "All I can say for sure is that it was obviously a magic user of some kind. That means we're dealing with a witch, warlock, mage, or one of a dozen different supernatural creatures that are known to manipulate magic. Though it could be a combination as well. Witches, warlocks, and mages frequently come together in covens; the other supernaturals, not as much."

Gage frowned at that, but before the Pack's lead alpha could say anything, Trevor interrupted.

"Wait a second. You said *warlock*." Trevor regarded her over his bottle of iced tea curiously. "Is that the same thing as a wizard, or are they different?"

Kat snorted. "It means the same to most witches, but guys can be so twitchy about titles. I think the whole Tolkien description of wizards as dudes in robes with long, gray beards sort of made men shy away from using that word. Most male magic users I know prefer to be called warlocks because they think it sounds more badass. Some people prefer a nongendered term, so they use mage. I've always been comfortable with witch, so that's what I use."

"While I'm sure the proper form of address for a male or female magic user is drastically important to some of you," Gage said, scowling at Trevor with an expression that clearly indicated he wasn't one of those people, "I'm more concerned about whether we have to worry about whoever these people are coming after Zane and Alyssa again."

Everyone looked at Kat expectantly, waiting for her to answer.

Like no pressure or anything.

"I don't think you have to worry about Zane and Alyssa being targeted again," she finally said after thinking about it for a bit. "The murder they were down there investigating happened over a month ago, and there's no indication the people hung around after that."

Connor frowned. "What about the trap in that basement? Doesn't that imply they were there watching Zane and Alyssa the whole time?"

"I don't think so," Kat answered. "The trap Zane and Alyssa walked into had been set weeks ago, probably at the same time as the murder. The killers simply left a trail of false breadcrumbs for anyone who might come after them as insurance. The trap didn't require anyone to watch it. It would have been triggered by anyone who walked down there. That way, their unsuspecting victim or victims wouldn't be able to ever get out and track them down."

"How did they know it wouldn't be a bunch of kids who walked in there?" Trevor asked. "Or a maintenance crew?"

She shrugged. "They probably didn't care one way or the other. As a witch myself, I hate to say this, but trust me when I tell you, there are some witches and warlocks out there who will do anything for power. I think what Zane and Alyssa stumbled across down in San Antonio was a coven of horrible people willing to sacrifice an innocent kid simply to make their ability to use magic stronger. With people like that, is it any wonder they'd leave behind a trap that would kill anyone who walked into it?"

Kat glanced at Connor out of the corner of her eye to see what effect her words had on him, but he was staring down at his sandwich, like it was more interesting than anything she had to say.

In the front of the room, Gage regarded her thoughtfully. "Were you born a witch?"

She couldn't help smiling a little at his question. Gage was nothing if not direct.

Instead of answering right away, she got up and helped herself to a bottle of soda before going back to her seat. While the water was great, she needed something with sugar in it right now.

"I've known I was a witch since I was four years old when it came as a shock to me that not everyone could make their stuffed bunny hop around their bedroom," she explained. "Since then, I loved magic, not for what I could do with it but simply because it exists. I think it's because there's something so amazing about never having to give up that sense of wonder that comes with believing in magic."

She opened her soda and took a sip, stifling a moan. There was nothing quite so wonderful as that first gulp of a cold soda, especially when she hadn't tasted it in forever. The sweetness of the syrup, the tickle of the fizzy bubbles. Damn, she'd missed little things like this.

"I had a nice little coven in my hometown of Kennewick, Washington. Just north of the Oregon border," she continued after a moment. "We weren't the largest coven in the country or even in the Northwest, but we were definitely powerful. Not that we cared about any of that. We spent our time collecting and studying old magic tomes and developing our bonds as a coven. It made us stronger together than any of us were apart."

She glanced at Connor again to see him studying her intently before he quickly looked away. She wished she knew what he was thinking.

Then again, maybe not.

"Our combined strength is what got us noticed by a warlock named Marko Kemp," she said, going back to her story. Merely saying the name made her want to shudder. "Powerful covens with limited members can be easy targets for other covens interested in boosting their memberships. It's kind of the magical version of a hostile takeover. Marko came to us with the normal sales pitch, telling us how we could be part of something bigger, become stronger than we ever thought possible, and accomplish things we'd only dreamed about."

"What kind of things?" Connor asked.

"The usual," she said. "Fame, fortune, power,

undying devotion of anyone we chose, control over the world. The kind of things that vain, shallow people always seem to want. Marko was a smooth talker to be sure, but my coven wasn't interested in anything he had to offer, so we turned him down."

"I'm guessing Marko didn't take that very well?" Trevor asked.

Kat frowned, replaying the particular moment when Marko had dropped the charming veneer and revealed his true self. His face had become a twisted mask of rage, his lips curling in disgust, eyes hard as ice. It had given her nightmares ever since. "Honestly, I think he knew we'd say no before he even asked. In his mind, it justified everything he did after that."

"And what did he do?" Connor asked when she didn't say anything more. He sounded a little wary, like he wasn't sure he wanted to know the answer.

She tightened her grip on the bottle of soda, trying hard to keep from completely losing it and crying right in front of everyone as one horrible memory after another flashed through her head. Even now, she could hear her friends' screams, could see them writhing in pain. There wasn't a week that went by without her waking up scream-ing—or yowling—in fear from the dreams she had about that night. It had been four years ago, but the pain was as strong as if it had happened yesterday.

Kat doubted she'd ever be able to truly put that night behind her.

"Marko forced me to watch as he killed every member of my coven," she said quietly. "He sacrificed them in some bizarre scheme to make himself more powerful."

"That's awful!" Rachel said. "How did you get away?"

Kat offered her a wan smile. "To this day, I'm still not sure how I did, especially since he turned me into his familiar." When everyone looked at her blankly, she added, "In the form of a cat. Terribly cliché, I know, but Marko is nothing if not traditional. But before he was able to finish the binding portion of the ritual, I managed to break free of the protective circle holding me and escape. Without the final binding part of the ritual, Marko never gained access to my coven's magic, which he transferred into me after he killed them."

"Doesn't that make you stronger than he is, then?" Rachel asked.

"Unfortunately, no." Kat sighed. "Marko performed a spell that won't let me access any of it. I can barely access my own most of the time. Not that I can use a lot of magic when I'm trapped in my cat form anyway, which is most of the year."

"Most?" Hale echoed. "How much is most?"

She shrugged. "I get to be human somewhere

about seven to fourteen days out of the year. From around the first week of September until the fall equinox, which is on the twenty-second this year. That means this year I get about ten days to walk around on two legs. Unfortunately, I wasted three of them trying to recover from the change. After that, I'll be the cat who's been living with you for the past nine months."

"So, when you disappeared earlier in the week," Connor said slowly, "that was so you could change back into a human?"

She nodded glumly. "I felt the change coming the night before you left for San Antonio. I was afraid I'd change right there in your bed."

Kat ignored the barely hidden smiles from Connor's pack mates. For some reason, they all seemed amused at the idea of him letting a cat sleep in his bed. She could only imagine what they'd say if they knew she spent most of those nights curled up squarely on his chest. Which was damn near the best thing in the world as far as she was concerned.

"When you and I came to the compound that morning, I ran," she added, looking at him. "I had no idea where I was going, but I was lucky enough to find a home not too far from here that had gone into foreclosure. The family must have left in a hurry because there was some food in the kitchen and a mattress in one of the bedrooms. That's where

I stayed until the change finished and I recovered enough to come back here."

No one said anything. It was like they were too stunned at the thought of her changing from a cat to a person to even comment. Which was ridiculous when she thought about, especially since half the Pack could shift back and forth from human to wolf on demand.

"Is your name really Kat?" Rachel asked suddenly, her expression curious. "I mean, Connor seemed like he pulled that name out of his butt."

Her lips curved. "No, it's really my name. Katya actually, but everyone's called me Kat since I was a kid. My grandmother is the only one who ever used my full name."

Rachel turned to Connor. "How did you know her name is Kat?"

He gave his pack mates a sheepish look. "I tried a bunch of different names, and that was the one she seemed to like when I said it."

Kat almost laughed as she remembered the list of suitable "cat" names Connor had come up with and how she'd kept vetoing them by batting at his arm with her paw. For some reason she still couldn't understand, she'd wanted him to call her by her real name.

"You said you could do magic while you were a cat, right?" Trevor asked.

The question caught her a little by surprise.

"Yeah. It's much more difficult and wears me out for days afterward, but I can do it. Like that time you locked me in the arms room because you didn't want me going on that call with Connor and the rest of you. It wasn't that difficult to open the lock from the inside with magic, but I was still furious with you for weeks."

Trevor was still laughing at that reminder when the other questions started coming at her so fast, she had a hard time keeping up with them, each sillier than the last. She did her best to answer all of them, but when Hale asked if she had problems with hairballs, she knew things were getting out of control.

"Why did you run away and hide without letting us know what was going on?" Connor demanded, his voice low and so gruff, it was nearly a growl, silencing the whole room.

It wasn't until that moment that Kat realized Connor hadn't been taking part in the joking going on around them. In fact, he hadn't said a word. The silence following his question quickly became awkward, and as much as Connor was trying to hide it, Kat could tell he was truly angry at her.

"And how exactly would I have done that?" Kat shot back, not bothering to hide her own anger. "Spin around in a circle and meow three times like I was Lassie trying to tell you that Timmy fell down the well? Or maybe I should have typed it out on your laptop with my paws? Trust me, I considered it but figured you'd think I was possessed or something."

That seemed to give him pause, and he flushed under his tan. "Okay, I get your point. But why leave at all? You could have stayed here in the compound, where you'd be safe. We're werewolves. Did you really think we'd care if we saw you change from a cat to a person?"

Kat sagged in her chair, letting out a long sigh. She'd honestly considered staying at the compound, but ultimately, it was the difference between her shift and theirs that made up her mind. For werewolves, going from human to wolf and back again was natural, beautiful. Her change was unnatural and about as far from beautiful as you could get. She refused to apologize for doing what she'd had to.

"When I change, it's nothing like the wolf shift some of you can do. It's slow, agonizingly painful, exhausting, and to be honest, it's mortifying," she said softly. "It starts with hours of shaking, sweating, and feeling like I'm going to be sick. By the time the change actually comes, I'm so exhausted that all I can do is lie there, yowling in pain. Then I spend hours upon hours stuck in various stages partway between cat and human form. It's repulsive. I didn't want anyone seeing me like that. I didn't want *you* to see me like that."

If the room had been quiet before, it was like a

tomb now. Kat sat there, gaze locked on Connor's, holding her breath as she waited to see how he'd respond. But he didn't say anything. Instead, he continued to look at her, his expression unreadable.

Gage's cell phone rang, breaking the painful silence. Taking it out of his pocket, he held it to his ear. "Dixon."

After a few moments of listening to whatever the caller had to say, he hung up and looked at Connor.

"It's obvious that you and Kat have a lot to talk about, but I'm afraid it's going to have to wait. While you were in San Antonio, something happened that the chief wants our help with, and since you have the most experience working missing persons, I want you to take lead on it."

CHAPTER 6

"WELL, YOU GUYS DO THAT SWAT THING YOU DO, while I go take a shower," Kat announced, getting to her feet. "I haven't been able to clean myself in nearly a year, and trust me, tongue baths do *not* count."

Connor heard the words Kat said, but his head was still spinning too fast to comprehend them. He could barely think straight. Truthfully, he'd been completely off balance since she'd kissed him in San Antonio, then introduced herself as Kat before promptly passing out in his arms.

It had only gotten worse since then, as every time he'd opened his mouth, stupid shit had come out. After hearing her story, Connor knew he didn't have any reason to be mad at Kat, but he couldn't help feeling that she'd been lying to him for all these months. It was stupid and childish, but he couldn't seem to stop.

He supposed part of it was the fact she was human now. He'd be the first to admit he was having a hard time dealing with that. The last time he'd seen her, she was ten inches tall, furry, and liked to have her belly rubbed. Now she was five eight with long, silky dark hair and a perfect body, and gave off a vibe suggesting that anyone who touched her stomach without permission would be turned into a toad. Or maybe obliterated like she'd done with those stone tokens down in San Antonio. It made sense now why she'd never eaten cat food, or played with the toys he'd gotten her, or bothered with catnip. She'd been a person the whole damn time.

It was an awful lot to get his head around.

Of course, there was also the issue of Kat being the most beautiful, distracting woman Connor had ever seen. Perfect porcelain skin, kissable lips, and mesmerizing hazel eyes that seemed to pull him in and trap his soul. There was no other way to describe her but to say she was an angel come to earth.

On top of that, she smelled like an absolute dream. Like cinnamon spice cake with a hint of something vaguely feline. Connor abruptly realized she'd smelled like that even when she was a cat, although it'd been much more subtle then. Even now, in a room full of werewolves, chips, and sub sandwiches, he couldn't smell anything but her. It was messing with his head!

Connor was so distracted that even after Kat left to go take that shower she'd mentioned, he had a hard time paying attention as Gage filled them in on what happened while they'd been gone.

"Last night, two teenagers disappeared from their home," Gage was saying. "A patrol unit responded and checked out the residence but saw no obvious signs of struggle or foul play. No broken windows, no jimmied lock or even a ruffled bedcover. When the officers suggested the boy and girl might have simply slipped out on their own to see a movie or something like that, the kids' parents insisted that wasn't the case and that their teens would never do that. The officers humored them and called the kids' cell phones. When they rang one, they realized the sound was coming from outside the house somewhere.

"They found the girl's phone in a flower bed on the edge of the property. The glass was cracked, and there was some blood on it. When her mother unlocked it, there was an unsent text saying they were being forced to leave the house and couldn't get away. That's when they brought in the Missing Persons Unit and forensics. They scoured the home and surrounding property for hours and didn't find a single damn clue to indicate that anyone besides those two kids had been inside or out in the backyard where the phone was found. That's when the girl's mother started calling in favors and asking for SWAT's help."

Connor frowned. "I understand better than anyone how freaked out parents can be when a child goes missing, but why would they specifically want our help? That's not exactly our specialty."

"Because the parents of these two particular teenagers have trusted their children to our care before," Gage said grimly. "It's Addy Lloyd and Ben Sullivan."

On the other side of the room, Rachel gasped. "What? Why didn't you lead with that?"

Connor remembered the mission back in February, when Rachel and some of their pack mates had provided personal protection for the Lloyd family. Rachel had ended up risking her life multiple times to protect Addy and Ben.

"This can't be a coincidence," Rachel continued, not giving Gage a chance to answer. "The only question is whether Addy's father and that a-hole he was in league with are behind the kidnapping or if it's that *thing* we all thought was dead."

Addy's father was a dirtbag millionaire who'd gotten involved with crime boss Alton Marshall, a man Addy's mother, a Dallas assistant district attorney, had been in the process of sending to prison on multiple charges related to his organized crime operations. Dirtbag Dad had actually sold out his own family on Marshall's orders. Both men were in prison now, but that wouldn't necessarily stop either of them if they wanted to get revenge.

As scary as that sounded, the idea of them reaching out from behind bars paled in comparison to the other possibility Rachel mentioned—that *thing* everyone thought was dead.

While protecting Addy and her mother from an organized crime boss and his goons, Rachel had also been tormented by something called a *nacht-mahr*, a malicious spirit that feeds on its victim's fear. And Rachel had been that victim. Rachel and her werewolf mate had killed the thing. But how could any of them be sure the spirit was dead?

Gage shook his head. "I don't know the answer to that question. All I can say for sure is that Addy and her boyfriend, Ben, were in her bedroom doing homework, and now they've disappeared. It's been close to sixteen hours with no contact or ransom demand from the kidnappers. Not even the standard threatening call not to involve the cops. That's why the chief wants us involved. Her gut is telling her this isn't a normal kidnapping for money."

Connor had to agree with the chief, mostly because nothing in this city ever seemed to happen the normal way these days.

"Rachel, since you have a connection to the kids—and because I know you'd ignore me if I tried to keep you off the team—you'll work with Connor on this. Trevor and Hale, you two are backup," Gage said. "I've arranged for the four of you to meet with the parents and the detective in charge of the case this afternoon."

Gage sighed. "I know what I'm asking you to do is outside most of your wheelhouses. But if nothing else, dig around and determine if there's any supernatural involvement, then we'll go from there. Maybe this really is a ransom grab or an attempt to extort something out of Addy's mother, and the kidnappers simply haven't made contact yet."

"Either way, we're going to find those kids and get them back safely," Rachel vowed.

Connor silently agreed. And while he liked the idea of working this with Rachel, he was concerned about how personal it was for her. She'd bonded with those kids while she'd been protecting them and had talked to them regularly ever since. That connection might be helpful, or it could make this job damn near impossible.

———

When Connor and his pack mates left the training building, he was surprised to see Kat leaning against one of the SUVs. She had on the same clothes she'd been wearing earlier, though he noticed they looked cleaner. Maybe she'd magically washed them or something. She'd definitely washed her hair. It was all shiny and blowing lightly in the breeze, and he suddenly ached to run his fingers through it. It was strange, part of him wanted to still be upset at her for not somehow letting him know she was human, while another part was just irrationally thrilled that this beautiful woman was here in front of him.

She turned to look his way as they approached, and his heart seized as his feet got a little tripped up in the gravel. She was so beautiful, it took his breath away. And rather than mute her scent, the shower had only enhanced it.

Connor threw a covert glance at his pack mates, wondering how the hell they could pick up her delicious cinnamon-spice-cake scent and not remark on it. But none of them were even reacting. He could understand Hale not smelling it, but Rachel and Trevor? That made no sense.

It was only as he stepped closer that Connor realized the feline part of the scent he'd picked up earlier was starting to fade, like Kat was settling into her human form and the cat part was disappearing. He'd never experienced anything like it.

"We have to head out on a call," Connor said as he stopped a few feet in front of Kat. A part of him wanted to be completely up in her personal space so he could inhale that magical scent. But the other part was still miffed at her for leaving and making him worry, so he didn't. "When I get back, we can figure out someplace for you to stay."

Something that looked like hurt crossed Kat's face. He replayed his words, trying to figure out what he'd said that had bothered her.

"I'll go with you," Kat said, looking at him with that slightly haughty expression she'd always displayed when she was in her cat form. Despite the feline scent fading into the background, she was still all cat, all the time. In retrospect, on some level, maybe he'd known she was Kat the cat from the moment she'd walked up to him in that basement in San Antonio and kissed him.

"You can't come with us on a call," he said.

She folded her arms. "I always went with you on calls. It never bothered you before."

"That was when you were a cat," he said, nearly growling as he realized Rachel, Trevor, and Hale were watching them with amusement. His pack mates were eating this whole thing up, weren't they? "Things are different now."

When Kat didn't say anything, he walked around her toward the front passenger seat of the SWAT vehicle. With a snort and a shake of his head, Hale unlocked the doors with the fob in his hand, then headed for the driver's seat, leaving Trevor and Rachel to take the back seats.

Ignoring the urge to look over his shoulder at Kat, Connor grabbed the door handle and tugged. It didn't open. He glanced at Hale, realizing his door wouldn't open either. His pack mate looked confused as he thumbed the unlock button on the key fob again.

Connor tried the door, but it still wouldn't open. He was about to suggest Hale grab the keys for one of the other response vehicles when he realized his pack mate was staring at something behind him.

Kat.

Connor spun around to find her still standing exactly where she'd been a moment earlier, an expression on her face that made her look like the proverbial cat that got the cream. *She* was behind this.

"Unlock the doors," he said.

She arched a brow. "How could I possibly unlock the doors? Hale has the keys."

When he only scowled at her, she rolled her eyes and casually waved her right hand in the air. Behind him, he heard his teammates open their doors.

"Thank you," he said.

Connor climbed into the SUV and buckled his seat belt. He was keenly aware of Kat standing there but refused to glance over at her. When Hale didn't start the vehicle, he glanced over to see what the holdup was. Hale was sitting there with the keys in his hand, an amused look on his face.

"What?" Connor demanded.

"I can't start the vehicle because there's nowhere to put the key," he said. "The ignition is missing."

Not sure what the hell that meant, Connor leaned over to look at the steering column to see there was, in fact, nowhere to put the key. Which was insane, because the ignition sure as hell had been there earlier, when they'd driven this same vehicle back from San Antonio.

Kat.

"You've got to be kidding me," he growled.

Rachel sighed. "You might want to give up while you're ahead. You could make her return the ignition, but it's obvious she could come up with a hundred different ways to keep us from ever leaving this parking lot if she wants. Just let her come with us."

"We can't bring a civilian on a call," he said firmly.

He knew he was being obstinate. He knew why, too, even if the reasoning was more than a little petty. But he couldn't deny that he felt like he'd been used and lied to. He couldn't say what he expected Kat to have done differently. It wasn't like she could have played charades or something and let him know she was actually a witch trapped in a cat's body. And if she had started typing stuff on his laptop, he probably *would* have thought she was possessed. But logic wasn't really in play here. He was pissed off, and he had every right to be, dammit.

"You used to bring a cat on the calls," Trevor pointed out from the back seat. "You never even tried to explain it, either. Not even when IA complained."

Connor was tempted to argue about how that was different, but he stopped himself. He knew this was a fight he couldn't win. He'd never been able to keep Kat the cat from coming on one of their calls when she wanted to go. Trevor locking her in the arms room was a great example of that. Why the hell did he think it would be any easier now that she was walking around on two legs instead of four? Truthfully, it was probably more impossible now, especially since she could simply do magic with a wave of her hand. It was equally clear that his pack mates were more than ready to call him on the hypocrisy.

"Look," Trevor said. "It's your call, but if anyone asks, we can say she's an observer from another police department here to review our procedures. No one will even think to question it."

Connor blew out a breath. "Okay. Rachel, can you let her know she won without making it obvious that she did?"

"On it."

The moment Rachel undid her seat belt and stepped out of the SUV, Kat strolled over, graceful as a feline. A few seconds later, she was sliding into the back seat and settling herself between Rachel and Trevor like it was the most natural thing in the world.

"Do you think we could stop at Krispy Kreme on the way back from wherever we're going?" she asked as she wiggled her fingers and made the ignition reappear. "It's been a year since I had one, and I'm aching for a warm glazed donut. You wouldn't believe how hard it is to get someone to give you junk food when you're a cat."

Connor glanced at Hale as he started the SUV to see his pack mate's mouth twitch. There were four Krispy Kreme shops that he knew of in the Dallas area, and none were on the way back from Addy

Lloyd's house. But from the way Hale exchanged looks with him, his pack mate thought Kat could make driving back to the compound more of an adventure than it needed to be if she didn't get her way.

He guessed they were stopping for donuts.

CHAPTER 7

CONNOR GOT KAT UP TO SPEED ON THE CASE AS they drove to the Lloyd family residence. The *new* Lloyd residence from what Kat understood, since the original version had burned to the ground back in February, courtesy of a jerk of a husband, a crime boss, and a malicious spirit.

As Connor filled her in on everything, she realized she vaguely remembered some of the story. But since she was a cat at the time and, thus, easily distracted, she'd missed some of the details. The highlight that mostly stuck out to her was that Lloyd and Marshall were both looking at decades in prison. Meaningless revenge aside, she wasn't sure what kidnapping two kids would do to change that, but it seemed likely that detectives from the Missing Persons Unit were already looking into it.

"Rachel, what about this malicious entity you tangled with?" Kat asked, remembering distinctly that when she'd been a cat, absolutely no one had talked about the subject after the fact. Other than to give thanks that the thing was dead. "It was a clown or something, right?"

"Yeah, it was a creature that feeds on its victim's fear," Rachel said quietly, the expression on her face suggesting she didn't like talking about it. Kat couldn't blame her. "It creates that fear by scaring the crap out of them, appearing to each victim as whatever terrifies them the most. In my case, it was a psycho clown."

Kat nodded. "But you killed the creature, right? So there's no way it could have come back to get revenge."

Beside her, Rachel didn't look very confident. "We're pretty sure we killed the creature, but these kinds of things can get weird, you know? What if it simply went away for a while and now it's back? If it wants to get revenge on me, hurting Addy and Ben would certainly be a way to do it."

Kat couldn't disagree. She was even more glad she'd pressed the issue to come with them. If the nachtmahr showed up, her magic might come in handy. Ever since meeting Connor, she'd felt this indescribable need to be with him and protect him, as irrational as that was considering he was a were-wolf and practically indestructible.

The Lloyds' driveway was packed with cop cars when they got there. Dozens of people, some in uniforms and others in suits, came and went from the main entrance of the brick two-story home. The young uniformed officer at the door took down the names of Connor and his pack mates, as well as their badge numbers, on a piece of paper attached to a clipboard before they went inside. He seemed a little lost as to what to do when he learned that Kat didn't have a badge number, but after Connor told him she was a consultant, that seemed to satisfy the man.

The moment they walked into the spacious living room, Rachel hurried over to hug a dark-haired woman with red-rimmed eyes that could only be Addy's mother. That meant the couple sitting on the leather couch, looking as exhausted as any two people Kat had ever seen, must have been Ben's parents. His poor mother looked like she'd cried so much, there simply weren't any tears left.

There were ten cops in the big room, with an even mix of uniformed officers and detectives in suits. None of them seemed happy to see Connor and his SWAT teammates. Trevor immediately approached one of the older detectives and shook his hand. After spending so much time as a cat that was ignored and frequently out of earshot of what people were talking about, Kat had gotten exceptionally good at reading body language. It was obvious Trevor was busy trying to soothe ruffled feathers. If the annoyed expression on the guy's face was anything to go by, it didn't seem to be working.

While Rachel and Trevor did their things, Connor made a subtle head motion toward the door that led out of the living room. A second later, he and Hale casually wandered in that direction. Kat followed, reaching them as they headed up the steps and into a big bedroom halfway down the hallway. A colorful combination of pink and purple with blue accents here and there, the room reminded Kat of her own when she was a teenager, right down to the four-poster bed and posters of teen heartthrobs.

She took in the schoolbooks sitting on the carpeted floor surrounded by notebooks, loose pieces of paper, pencils, and well-worn erasers. Math homework with the last few problems on one of the pages wasn't finished. It seemed like the kids had left in a hurry.

Glancing around, it was clear that the cops had already thoroughly searched the room, with drawers and closets rifled through, clothes, books, and knickknacks pushed around. Kat didn't imagine the police had even known what they were looking for other than something to indicate who had taken the kids and how they had convinced them to leave the house without telling anyone.

"You picking up any unusual scents?" Hale asked, poking his head into the closet for a second, then pulling out a drawer on one of the bedside tables.

Connor sniffed around the room before answering. "No."

Kat closed her eyes and reached out with her own senses. Since she was still wiped out from her cat-to-human transition, she had to push a bit harder than she normally would.

"You okay, Kat?" Connor asked.

"Yeah," she said without opening her eyes. "I'm just trying to see if there's any indication that magic was involved. But picking up remnants of residual magic isn't as straightforward as smelling a scent left behind on a pillow or a piece of clothing. Magic is all around us, in every living thing and everything that's ever been alive, and to a lesser extent, those things touched by the living. The bed, desk, curtains, carpet, even that closet full of clothes carry leftover magic. Residual energy like that can easily hide minor spell work, especially if it's subtle."

"Can it hide the kind of magic that could force two teenagers out of a house in the middle of the night without leaving a trace?" Connor wondered.

"Possibly," Kat said. "Time can blur any spell that was used, and it's been nearly a full day since Addy and Ben disappeared. On top of that, there are spells that witches and warlocks can use to obscure the magic. But I'm hoping I can pick something up."

As Kat stood there trying to feel the magic around her, she wasn't surprised she couldn't come up with anything concrete. She opened her eyes with a sigh.

"Unfortunately, I'm not picking up much in the way of residual magic."

She walked over to the desk and opened the center drawer. Along with the requisite pens and pencils, there were a few ponytail holders, a calculator, and a pack of gum.

On the other side of the room, Hale pushed back the curtains to reveal an open window. He leaned out to gaze at the ground. "The grass looks like someone rolled around on it down there. I think Addy and Ben jumped out the window."

Kat hurried over to join Hale even as Connor did the same. The distance to the ground made her stomach clench. Crap, she hated heights.

"That's got to be at least a thirty-foot drop," she said, yanking her head back inside. "There's no way those kids jumped that far."

Beside her, Connor looked thoughtful. "That text from Addy said she and Ben were being forced to do something. Maybe she meant someone forced them to jump out the window."

Kat supposed that was possible, but it still seemed like a stretch.

"Let's check outside," Connor suggested.

Downstairs, Trevor was still talking with the same detective he'd been speaking with earlier, but when Rachel caught sight of them heading for the door, she quickly followed. As they made their way around to the back of the house, Kat filled Rachel in on Hale's theory.

Kat didn't know much about investigating a crime scene, but when they reached the part of the yard underneath the window in Addy's bedroom, even she could tell that something—or someone—had landed on the grass there. Maybe Hale was right.

Connor went down on one knee to sniff the deep impression in the grass. "This is where Ben landed when he jumped."

"Addy landed right here beside him," Rachel said as she got to her feet after sniffing the ground. She turned and stared up at the window above them, a frown creasing her brow. "What the hell could have convinced a girl as smart as Addy to jump out a window that high off the ground?"

Kat didn't have an answer to that question. Neither did Connor or Hale.

She followed Connor and his pack mates as they used their noses and keen eyesight to track where Addy and Ben went after they'd jumped out the window. The trail led them to the back of the large tree-lined yard.

"These marks make me think someone dragged Addy and Ben across the yard, but there are no other shoe prints anywhere," Hale murmured, pointing at a section of grass that had been scuffed up. "There was no one out here by Addy and Ben, so who the hell was dragging them?"

When they reached the edge of the property, they found the flower bed where Addy had dropped her phone and the low stone wall the kids had climbed over.

"This is going to sound crazy, but I think Addy

and Ben dragged themselves across the ground," Connor said, kneeling in the grass to trail his fingers along a groove in the sod deep enough to reveal the dark brown dirt underneath. "There aren't two gouges side by side anywhere. That means they were dragging the toe of one shoe, while walking forward on the other. It's like they were fighting themselves every step of the way."

Hale and Rachel exchanged confused looks but didn't say anything.

"So what does that mean?" Kat asked.

Connor shook his head as he got to his feet. "It means we're almost certainly dealing with something supernatural."

CHAPTER 8

KAT WANDERED AROUND CONNOR'S ONE-bedroom apartment, taking in everything she'd previously only seen from the perspective of a feline. The one-bedroom place with the sand-colored walls and plush tan carpet seemed so much different now than she remembered it. Smaller and a little less welcoming somehow. She supposed it could be because she was taller now. Then again, maybe it was all the barriers Connor had put up around himself since discovering she wasn't truly a cat. It made any room he was in feel smaller.

Of course, if it were up to him, she'd be staying at a hotel right now. Or sleeping on one of the cots on the second floor of the compound's admin building.

The knowledge that Connor didn't want her around brought a rush of hot tears to her eyes, making it hard to breathe. After living with him for nine months, this was not how she'd imagined the situation would play out when she finally turned back into a human. Maybe it was a little naive, but she'd thought Connor would be thrilled to finally see the real her. She'd dreamed of him sweeping her into his arms and spinning her in a big circle, laughing as he kissed her.

Yeah, that definitely hadn't happened.

She suspected he'd only given in and agreed to let her stay here because the rest of the Pack had started to berate the hell out of him. She wasn't too sure how she felt about the fact that he only let her come home with him out of guilt. But really, what else was she going to do? Where was she going to go? She liked everyone in the Pack, especially Rachel and Khaki, but staying at the apartments they shared with their mates would be all kinds of awkward.

She smiled a little as she admired the various knickknacks and framed photos scattered around the living room and along both sides of the hallway that led toward the bedroom. She'd seen them before, of course, but it was cool looking at them again with human eyes. The colors were more vivid, with a lot more reds and pinks than she remembered.

Kat glanced at the watch on her wrist. It was a gift from Rachel, who'd quickly figured out that she didn't own anything except the clothes on her back, which weren't technically even hers. It had been fifteen minutes since Connor had dropped her off at his place, then left, saying he wanted to talk to some people he knew about Addy and Ben before calling it a night. She was sure that was merely an excuse so he wouldn't have to spend any more time with her than absolutely necessary.

Crap, that hurt like hell.

Back at the Lloyd house, Connor hadn't wanted to give up looking for Addy and Ben. None of his pack mates had. Kat had searched the streets and woods behind the Lloyd residence for two hours along with them, but they'd come up with nothing. They'd all finally decided that until the detectives from the Missing Persons Unit talked to Anton Marshall and Conrad Lloyd to see if they were involved in the kidnapping, the investigation was at a standstill.

On the bright side—if there was one—Rachel hadn't gotten the feeling that the nachtmahr had been anywhere near the house. From what Rachel said, the creature that had gone after her had always left a remnant of fear behind that was enough to raise the hairs on the back of her neck.

Sighing, Kat turned her attention back to the photos on the wall. Some of the pictures were of a younger Connor with his fellow cops, wearing a patrol uniform. Others were of him in a suit and tie. Kat couldn't help smiling at those. While Connor looked dashing in a suit, it was obvious he was one of those guys who simply didn't feel comfortable wearing it. A little farther down the hall were photos of Connor and his pack mates. He seemed the happiest in those. His smiles were broader, and there was a relaxed vibe about him.

But of all the photos spread around the apartment, the ones that drew her in the most were the pictures of Connor's family. He'd never said anything about them to Kat. Then again, telling a cat about your family would have been a little weird, she supposed. Connor was a teenager in some of them, making it almost impossible to connect the kid with the werewolf she knew him to be now. Except for that gorgeous smile of his. That was the same in every picture, regardless of age.

There were four people in the grouping of photos along one wall that Connor had apparently set aside for family. The middle-aged man and woman were his parents, obviously, and the two girls had to be his younger sisters. Kat ran her gaze over each of the framed photos, trying to figure out what was bothering her about them. Then it hit her.

While there were nearly a dozen photos of one sister, ranging in age from early teens to midtwenties, there were only a few pics of the other, and those were all when she was a kid. Kat was afraid to wonder why there weren't any pictures of her after that.

The door of the apartment opened, interrupting her thoughts. Kat turned to see Connor walking in, three pizza boxes balanced in one hand and a six-pack of diet soda in the other. Since he hated diet anything purely on principle, she could only assume he'd gotten them for her. It was silly, but the thought still loosened a little of the tightness in her chest.

"Sorry that took me longer than I thought. The pizza place was packed," he said. "You want plates, or are you good eating out of the box?"

Crossing the living room, he walked into the cozy adjoining kitchen and set the boxes on the table, then grabbed two glasses from the upper cabinet beside the fridge.

"I've eaten pizza out of worse places than a box when I was a cat," she said, pulling out a chair and sitting down. "No need to dirty plates."

Kat was surprised at the expression of pain that flickered across his handsome features. Or maybe it was revulsion. She couldn't be sure. Perhaps she shouldn't be so bluntly honest with him about what her life as a cat was like. He might have all these fairy-tale visions of her living large as some rich person's pampered pet.

Silence descended on the kitchen as Connor filled their glasses with ice from the dispenser on the refrigerator door, then joined her at the table. He popped the top on a can of soda, filling her glass first before taking care of his own. While he did that, she opened the pizza box on top of the stack, almost swooning as the aroma of marinara sauce and pepperoni wafted across her nose. The mozzarella cheese covering it was so thick and gooey, it practically made her drool.

"How long have you been dealing with this curse?" Connor asked as they ate.

Kat wondered if she should correct him and explain that she wasn't under a curse. That magic didn't work that way. But she decided not to bother. It was complicated, and she doubted he'd be interested in the subtle nuances of the spell that had been used against her. Besides, from his point of view, the spell probably seemed like a curse.

She finished the bite of pizza she'd been savoring, then took a sip of soda. "Four years."

Connor winced. "Damn. Where did you stay all that time? Did you find someone to take you in?"

She gazed down at the half-eaten slice of pizza in her hand. After four years, the memories shouldn't cause so much pain anymore, but they did.

"Right after my coven was killed and I realized I truly *was* trapped in a cat's body, I kind of lost it for a little bit." She winced. "Okay, to be honest, I completely lost it. I ran without even slowing to consider where I was going. I knew that if Marko got his hands on me, it would all be over. I'd be his familiar, and my coven's deaths—my friends' deaths—would have all been in vain."

"What about after that?"

"I was constantly on the move for the first week or so, sleeping in the crawl spaces of houses, under cars and bridges, eating out of trash cans and dumpsters," she said quietly, trying not to shudder—and failing. "I was sure that every person I saw, every figure in the shadows, was one of Marko's coven members, there to drag me back to him so he could finish the ritual. Either that or kill me for ruining it in the first place. I was a complete mess."

On the other side of the table, Connor stared at her in shock. "That's how it was the whole four years? You were always on the run, hiding and scavenging for food?"

"Not the whole time," she admitted. "After the initial terror of being a cat wore off, I started working on a plan to reverse the spell. My first idea was to get help from another coven near Spokane, one I'd worked with several times before. I hoped that with their help, it would be a simple process to reverse the binding Marko had placed on me. But apparently, he knew I would try that and had already threatened all the covens in the area with what would happen to them if they helped me. They called Marko the second they realized who I was, then tried to hold me captive until he arrived. Luckily, I got away. I tried a few other covens after that, but they all did the same thing."

His eyes went wide. "They betrayed you? All of them?"

Kat reached for another slice of pizza even as she eyed the other two boxes they hadn't touched yet. Even with Connor's werewolf appetite, that was more than they could eat at one time.

"I guess I can't honestly blame them," she said. "After hearing how Marko had wiped out my coven, who would be dumb enough to stand against him? Why risk angering him when it's easier to simply look the other way?"

"I guess," he said, popping the top on another can of soda and filling both their glasses before grabbing another slice of pizza for himself. "Still sucks, though."

"True," she agreed. "But at least I was able to get away. I was also able to figure out exactly what I was up against. I truly realized that I was on my own and that anyone who even thought about helping me or even loosely connected to me would be in terrible danger. From that point, I kept to myself, even when I was in my human form. I disappeared off the grid and lived in any homeless camps I could find. I can't even come close to explaining what it's like to live like that, feeling as if you're always alone, even when there's other people around. I couldn't trust anyone."

Connor stopped eating and stared at her sharply. "What about your family? They're magic users, too, right? Couldn't they protect themselves?"

"Magic doesn't always work that way," she told him. "The ability to perceive and channel magic can sometimes skip a generation, which is what it did in my family. While my grandma was a witch, my mom isn't."

He considered that. "Huh. How does your mom feel about that?"

Kat was a little surprised at how precise he was in his assessment of the family dynamic that had so greatly affected her life growing up.

"Mom has always been a little hurt by the fact that I'm a witch and she isn't, especially since Grandma spent so much time teaching me magic that it kind of took away from the time that my mom and I spent together. But that's how it is with witches and warlocks. The older generation teaches the younger. I mean, it isn't like we can go to college for this stuff."

Kat would be lying if she said she hadn't loved spending so much time with her grandma. The long walks in the woods near their home, staying up late reading the family books on magic, even simply baking cupcakes and brownies.

"Even as a kid, I noticed Mom and Grandma weren't close," she continued quietly. "I could never understand the distance between them. Between Mom and me, as well, to be honest. I tried to play peacemaker because I wanted everyone to be happy, but ultimately, it didn't work. At the end of the day, there was always a separation there, no matter what I did, simply because I could do magic and my mom couldn't."

"Any brothers and sisters?" Connor asked.

She smiled. "Yup. The twins, Jarrett and Rebecca,

are ten years younger than me. Sometimes, I think Mom had them as a replacement for me, so she could have kids that were really hers, instead of half hers and half Grandma's. I love them like crazy even though the distance between Mom and me ended up creating a gulf between the twins and me, too, no matter what I did. Mom never told them I'm a witch, so they both simply assume I'm a little odd."

Connor chuckled at that, and Kat realized it was the first time she'd heard him laugh since she'd turned into a human. "So the twins don't know you're a witch, but what about your dad? I assume you couldn't hide it from him, right?"

She looked down at her pizza again. "Dad knew."

"I'm sorry," Connor said quickly. "I didn't realize..."

Kat shook her head. "Dad's fine. My whole family is okay. At least, I hope they are."

"What do you mean?"

She sighed. "Once I realized the lengths Marko was going to, I knew that sooner or later, he'd track down my family to use them as leverage against me. So after figuring out that I was never going to get help from any of the other covens in that part of the country, I went home to do whatever I had to in order to protect them."

"What did you do?" he asked, taking another big bite of pizza.

She hadn't been counting, but while they'd been

talking, he'd opened the second box and already inhaled three slices.

"I didn't genuinely consider how difficult it would be to warn them in my feline form until I got home," she admitted. "Since I couldn't talk to them and explain the situation, I finally had to use a glamour and spells to make them forget about me and convince them to leave Washington. It took a while since my ability to use magic is severely constrained when I'm a cat, but when I was done, my entire family had forgotten about me and moved away. I don't know where they went, and I don't want to know in case Marko ever catches me. He'd use them against me even after he'd won out of pure spite."

Connor let out a breath, shaking his head. "That's tough. I'm sorry you had to go through that."

She gave him a small, sad smile. "Me, too. But it's worth the pain to keep them safe."

"What did you do after that?"

"For starters, I knew I had to get out of the Pacific Northwest," she said. "I crisscrossed the whole country and up into Canada. I went anywhere I could get by train or hitching a ride with someone. You'd be amazed how nice people can be to a cute kitty if you play your cards right. They'll feed you, give you a warm place to sleep, and take you wherever they're going. On the flip side, there are some nasty a-holes out there, too, but they're easy to recognize and avoid."

"So you were constantly on the go and never able to completely trust anyone for four years?"

"Pretty much," she said softly. "I did my best to never spend more than a few days in any one place because I was afraid that if I did, Marko would find me. I never stopped moving until I met you. It's a horrible way to live, and at times, it felt like I had completely lost my humanity. But all I could do was keep going."

Connor regarded her thoughtfully. "That's something I've been meaning to ask you. Why *did* you stay when you got here to Dallas? What made you take the risk when you'd never stopped before?"

"I have no idea," she said, though that wasn't entirely true. But it wasn't something she wanted to talk about at the moment, especially not with Connor. "Maybe you seemed like someone I could trust. Or maybe I simply got tired of running."

That confession seemed to catch him off guard, and silence descended over the kitchen again as they ate. There was so much she wanted to say to him right then, a hundred questions she wanted to ask. While she'd lived with him as a cat, she'd collected and stockpiled a laundry list of things she wanted to know about him. But right now obviously wasn't the time, if for no other reason than it was getting late and both of them were tired.

She was mostly exhausted thanks to the magic she'd used during the transition from feline to human form and her body's attempt to recover from the experience. But she was also still worn out from the magic she'd used to take out the sims in San Antonio.

And yet, as she sat there nibbling on a slice of pizza, she knew there was something else weighing on her way more than all the magic she'd been using lately. It was the fact that Connor was keeping her at arm's length. Being rejected by him physically hurt. Unfortunately, she had no idea what to do about it, especially since it seemed clear that he wasn't going to change the way he felt about her anytime soon.

"I think I'm going to get some rest," she announced.

Not because she needed sleep—though she did—but because right then, she needed to be anywhere else other than this tiny kitchen with a man who made her feel things she'd rather not.

"Yeah, of course," he said, and she wondered if that was relief in his voice. "You can take the bedroom. I'll sleep on the couch."

Kat didn't fight him on it, but when she finally climbed under the blankets a little while later, she knew that sleep was probably a long way off. The only time she'd ever slept in this bed, Connor had been in it with her. Right now, he was out on the couch, and all Kat could think about was how badly she wanted to curl up on his chest and snuggle like she'd done every night since moving in with him.

CHAPTER 9

CONNOR WOKE UP TO THE SOUND OF HIS CELL phone ringing, the *Doctor Who* theme jarring in the late-night silence. He instinctively reached out in the darkness to grab the phone and promptly fell off the couch. The thump of his shoulder and elbow hitting the carpeted floor did a bang-up job of knocking the rest of the sleep out of his head. Cursing, he picked up his cell from atop the uniform tee and pants he'd folded and left on the overstuffed chair last night.

"Dude, it's the middle of the night," he said softly, running his hand through his hair and abruptly remembering why he was on the couch and not in his comfortable king-size bed. "What's up?"

"There's been another kidnapping," Trevor said. "Detective Sandoval from Missing Persons called and said it's damn near the exact same MO as Addy and Ben. A sixteen-year-old girl disappeared out of a locked condo while her parents were downstairs watching TV. The window in her room was open, and based on what we told Sandoval we found at the Lloyd residence, he's sure that's how this kid got out, too. No signs of a struggle, no recent calls or texts on her cell, and no emails, tweets, or DMs on her computer or social media. He asked if we could take a look."

Connor was pretty sure Sandoval was the older detective Trevor had been chatting up while he'd been upstairs with Kat and Hale in Addy's room. "I knew you were good at schmoozing, but what the hell did you say to the man to get him on our side? The way he looked when we first showed up, it was obvious he wasn't thrilled to have us involved in his case."

"He isn't," Trevor said, his voice as casual as always, even at this time of night. "But that unlocked window in the condo I mentioned is on the fourth floor of the building. Sandoval doesn't know what's going on, but he's been doing this job long enough to know when he needs help. And he'll take that help from anywhere he can get it at this point."

Meaning Sandoval was probably aware there was something unusual going on and was willing to look the other way if SWAT could come up with something he could use. Which wasn't as strange as it seemed. There were a lot of cops in Dallas who'd run up against the supernatural over the years, even if they'd never admit it to anyone. And those cops were aware that SWAT seemed to have a knack for dealing with the strange and unusual.

"Text me the address and I'll meet you there," Connor said. "I assume you've already called Hale and Rachel?"

"Yeah, they're on the way now," Trevor replied.

"You going to bring Kat? Her ability to sense magic might come in handy."

Connor threw a glance at the closed bedroom door, pausing to listen, hoping his ringing phone hadn't woken her up. She'd been exhausted last night, yet he'd heard her tossing and turning in his bed for hours after she'd gone to bed. He knew because he'd been awake even longer, tortured by Kat's delicious scent wafting under the door in endless, intoxicating waves, paired with visions of her half-naked body kicking the sheets off as she fought for sleep.

He'd been seriously tempted to go in there and suggest something that would tire them both out enough to get some rest. He hadn't, of course, because he was a stupid dumbass.

Connor was baffled by the thoughts that kept popping into his head. Earlier, he'd been mad at Kat, but now, he was having a harder and harder time remembering why. He'd already accepted there was no reasonable way she could have let him know she was a human. There was even a point in the middle of the night when he wondered if maybe he was upset that Kat had essentially "taken" his cat away. But that was just plain stupid—and weird. Kat was still his cat, only in human form. How could he be upset about that? After everything she'd told him about the life she'd been living for the past few years, it was difficult to feel anything but empathy...and respect. Kat had gone through more than anyone should ever have to endure. Pure and simple, she was amazing. "Kat admitted she's been running on fumes since her shift back into human form," he told Trevor. "And that fight in San Antonio used up whatever reserves she had left. She only got to sleep a couple hours ago, so I'm going to let her rest for a while."

"Okay," Trevor said after a long pause. "If that's what you think is best. Just be sure you're doing this for the right reason, huh? Because you know she won't take it well if she thinks you're trying to leave her behind again. She might decide to do that toad thing Cooper told us she threatened him with."

When Connor refused to comment on that, Trevor gave up, saying he'd text with the address of the latest kidnapping before hanging up.

Since he couldn't go into his room for a fresh uniform without waking Kat, Connor had no choice but to pull on the one he'd worn yesterday. He slipped into the bathroom to brush his teeth, leaving his boots off so he wouldn't make any noise, but when he came out a minute later, he found Kat standing in the middle of the living room, looking more exhausted than before she went to bed but fully dressed.

"I heard the phone ring, and then you jumped up and started getting your clothes on," she said. "Did something happen?"

He considered telling her to go back to bed, but

the expression on her face practically screamed *Don't even think about trying to lie to me.*

"Another kid is missing. Same MO," he said, deciding that lying wasn't going to get him anywhere. "Trevor and the others are going to meet me there. And before you ask, I know you want to go, but I think you need to stay and get some more sleep. You look tired."

Her expression softened. "I appreciate the thought, but I wasn't sleeping well as it is, and it won't get any better if you leave, so I might as well go with you."

Connor wanted to know what she meant by that, but there wasn't time. His pack mates were waiting for him.

The drive in his truck was silent, except for the rattle of foil as the two of them ate the chocolate Pop-Tarts he'd grabbed for them on the way out. He almost asked Kat why she hadn't been able to sleep but couldn't find a way to bring it up. So, instead, he sat there in the confined space of his pickup, breathing in her glorious scent, trying not to lean over so he could take in even more of the scrumptious cinnamon cake she smelled like.

It might have been four o'clock in the morning, but the condo was a veritable zoo of a crime scene. He counted at least twenty sleepy people in pajamas wandering the hallways of the fourth floor with their cell phones out as if they expected a movie star to come walking by any second. Or maybe they were all hoping for some footage they could sell to the local media.

Trevor and Rachel were over on one side of the crowded living room talking to Sandoval. Connor eavesdropped for a moment, hearing Rachel asking questions about where Cheyenne Owens went to school and who her friends were. While asking about school and friends was Missing Persons 101, Connor doubted they'd be lucky enough to find such an obvious connection between their latest kidnapping victim and the first two. Things never worked out that easily.

Cheyenne's parents were too distraught to notice two more people wandering around the large apartment, and the other cops acted like Connor and Kat didn't even exist.

They found Hale in an upstairs bedroom, a teenage girl's given the colors and decorations. He looked up and smiled when he saw Kat.

"Hey! I didn't think you were coming with Connor," he said. "Trevor mentioned you were too tired."

"I thought I could help out," she said, walking past the bed and over to the open window.

Kat flinched a little when she glanced out and no doubt saw how far they were above the ground. But instead of immediately pulling back from the window, she instead stood there with her eyes closed, like she was meditating. Connor supposed she was trying to pick up residual magic. She swayed a little on her feet, and he instinctively moved to steady her, but Hale caught his arm.

"Let her do her thing."

Connor definitely didn't want her doing her *thing*. Whatever her *thing* might be. She'd been too exhausted to do it ten hours ago in Addy's bedroom, and she sure as hell hadn't slept enough since to get back to 100 percent. Actually, Kat looked worse now than she had earlier. He wouldn't be surprised if she passed out.

But then her eyes snapped open. "Someone used magic in this room. The residue is strongest right here around the window. Cheyenne put up a hell of a struggle."

"Against what?" Connor asked, moving closer to Kat and the window. He fought the urge to place an arm around her, focusing on the task at hand. "Does that mean a witch or warlock was involved in the kidnapping?"

"They used a compulsion spell to force her to jump out," Kat answered, looking out the window again, as if she expected to see something in the darkness. "And while it could be any kind of magic user, I'm almost certain it was either a witch or warlock."

Connor closed his own eyes, trying and failing to pick up any sense of the compulsion spell she mentioned. But he did pick up a faint trace of blood. Opening his eyes, he leaned in to look out over the sill. That's when he saw a few tiny beads of dark red blood along one of the sharper sections of the frame.

"We got blood trace here," he said. "I'll let the detectives downstairs know. It's not much, but they can at least check and confirm it belongs to the girl. That will tell us for sure she climbed out the window."

"I can get better results out of it," Kat said, reaching out to rest a hand on his forearm. "There's not much here, but if it's fresh enough, I might be able to use it to track down the girl. Especially if she cut herself fighting against the compulsion spell. Her efforts to resist it will make the magic inherent in her blood even stronger."

Connor didn't have to think about whether this was the right thing to do. He simply nodded and stepped back, giving Kat space to do her *thing*, as Hale called it.

He and Hale watched as she hunted around Cheyenne's room, coming up with a glass jar with a screw-on lid filled with the girl's hair barrettes and ponytail holders. Kat dumped the contents on the desk in the corner, then grabbed a paper clip, untwisting it and reshaping it into an elongated triangle.

After moving back over to the window, Kat used the tip of the paper clip to scrape up some of the blood from the sill, then dropped the clip in the jar and closed the lid. Without a word, she sat cross-legged on the floor in front of the window, one hand on top of the jar and the other cradled underneath. Then she closed her eyes and silently began to move her lips. The inside of the jar immediately began to glow with a soft green light even as Kat started to sway. Connor had to once again bite his tongue to keep from telling her to stop. Why the hell was she pushing so hard? Was she trying to hurt herself?

For a while, he thought nothing was going to happen, but a minute later, the paper clip began to dart around in the jar, clinking against the sides like a living thing trying to escape. By the time Kat finally stood up, her slow movements betraying obvious weakness, the paper clip was thumping constantly against the side of the jar closest to the window.

Damn.

It was magic.

Real frigging magic!

"Let's go," Kat said, heading for the door of the bedroom. "This is a simple spell, but with the limited amount of blood I had to work with and how exhausted I am, it's doubtful I'll be able to hold it for more than an hour. So let's not waste the opportunity we've been given."

Kat hurried down the steps so fast that Connor

had to take her hand to keep her from running and gathering too much attention. As they crossed the living room, he caught Trevor's attention, making a motion toward the door, slowing down so he and Rachel could catch up with them just as he, Kat, and Hale left the Owenses' condo.

"Kat has a lead on the kid's location," Connor said, jerking a thumb toward the jar in her hands. "We'll take point in my truck while you guys follow. Try to keep up, huh? Kat can only hold the spell for a little while, so we don't have time to waste if we get separated in traffic."

CHAPTER 10

HALE HAD DECIDED TO JUMP IN THE BACK SEAT of Connor's Silverado and ride with them, saying he didn't want to chance getting split up by a light. Rachel had driven with Trevor for the same reason, though it was also possible that she simply liked riding in his mint-condition 1957 Ford Thunderbird. Candy-apple red, of course. Looking in his rearview mirror, Connor could see Trevor's car right on his tail, keeping close as the morning commuter traffic started to fill the highway.

Keeping one eye on the road, he glanced at Kat and the jar in her lap. She kept her eyes on the thing the entire time, occasionally calling out to turn left or right. In the dim interior of the truck, he saw that the soft green glow he'd seen when she'd first started the spell—or whatever it was called—was still there. The illuminations rippled and grew brighter every now and then, and the paper clip would thump the glass a little more energetically, but he had no idea what the thing was trying to tell them. He left that for Kat to translate.

"Does that thing tell us how much farther we have to go?" Connor asked.

He wondered if maintaining the spell was as

taxing on her as it appeared. Because she was looking more exhausted by the minute. He'd come damn close to telling her to shut it down half a dozen times already. He wanted to find Cheyenne, but not at the cost of Kat's life. The only thing that held him back was the knowledge that she'd probably tell him to pound sand if he tried to dissuade her. So short of chucking the jar out the window, there wasn't anything he could do.

"It's a paper clip in a jar with a Find Me charm stuck on it, not a GPS tracker," she said with a soft snort. "We'll know we're close because the clip will start going haywire trying to get out of the jar. That's all I got for you."

Connor wanted to ask exactly how it worked but decided not to bother her with the question right then. It seemed like she needed to maintain her concentration. So, instead, he focused on driving, turning the truck in whichever direction Kat told him to go. At least she did it calmly instead of shouting at him to cut across a highway divider or anything crazy like that.

They reached Las Colinas, east of the airport, before turning due north on a lonely stretch of road called Olympus Boulevard. The area opened up, with large stretches of green spaces in between new subdivisions currently under construction. Connor knew there was a big lake up ahead with lots of isolated and desolate shoreline, and he couldn't stop his inner cop from whispering that they were going to end up at a body-dump site. He'd seen this situation play out too many times.

"Kat, does that charm of yours still work if the person is dead?" he asked slowly, almost hating himself for going there, paranoid that might jinx the entire situation.

He only felt worse when Kat slowly nodded without saying anything. Oh hell, why had he even asked?

They were moving closer to North Lake when Connor heard the paper clip start going crazy. He glanced over at Kat to see her holding the jar up, gazing at the twisted piece of metal as it attempted to smash its way through the right side of the glass container.

A quick look in that direction had Connor slowing the truck and pulling to the side of the road, his eyes locked on the large two-story farmhouse about a quarter mile off the road with a small metal shed to one side. The old home seemed out of place among the neat and orderly subdivisions that were going up all around it, yet the dim light glowing from one of the windows confirmed that the house was definitely occupied.

But by whom?

Had the people who'd grabbed Cheyenne brought her here?

Were Addy and Ben there, too?

"That the place?" Rachel whispered from outside his driver's side door, and Connor jumped a little, realizing he'd been so focused on the farmhouse and the few vehicles parked randomly around the front of the place that he hadn't even heard his teammate approach his truck.

It only took a few minutes to come up with a basic plan. Connor would do a recon of the farmhouse with Rachel while Kat, Hale, and Trevor would hang back and let Gage and the rest of the Pack know what was going on. The idea was that Connor and Rachel would confirm whether Cheyenne or any of the other kids were present, and if so, how many suspects they were dealing with. If the numbers were against them, they'd wait for Gage to get there with backup.

Connor hadn't said it out loud, but a good portion of his plan involved keeping Kat safely out of the way, with Hale and Trevor there to keep an eye on her if things went sideways. He knew his pack mates would get her out of danger if it became necessary.

There was a wide stretch of open ground to cross, and Connor was grateful that it was still dark. An hour from now, when the sun was up, this approach would be damn near suicidal. As it was, he still felt completely exposed as he and Rachel crossed a field that had only been recently tilled after a summer harvest.

He and Rachel had just reached the edge of the field surrounding this side of the house when Connor picked up the smell of blood. It was faint, but definitely there. A glance Rachel's way confirmed she'd picked up the scent as well.

They moved closer, sticking to the heavy shadows along the back side of the house, well away from the single illuminated window they'd seen earlier. This direction gave them the advantage of being downwind of the place, so they were still twenty feet away when a low growl slipped from Rachel's throat.

"Addy and Ben are in there," she hissed, already moving toward the closest door. "That's Ben's blood we're smelling."

Connor didn't consider for a second that Rachel might be wrong. She'd never forget those kids' scents. It's like they were her own children.

He could tell from the tremor of tension running through her that Rachel was ready to go charging right into the farmhouse without a second thought, but he stopped her with a hand on her shoulder. "Calm down," he whispered. "The scent of blood is faint, meaning it's something minor, like a cut lip. No one is in danger yet. We have time to be smart about this."

Rachel's shoulders remained stiff and tense for another few seconds before she finally nodded and took it down a notch, a ragged sigh slipping out as she relaxed. "Okay, but we have to get them out. I can smell their fear from all the way out here."

"We will," Connor promised. "Let's get a better idea of what we're up against, then we can come up with a plan."

As they cautiously moved closer, Connor quickly realized they were probably dealing with more bad guys than the four of them could easily handle. "There are at least ten heartbeats coming from inside," he said softly. "Even assuming that one of them is Cheyenne, that still leaves seven bad guys that we don't know a damn thing about. They could be heavily armed, or magic users, or something completely different. We need to wait for backup."

Connor could tell that Rachel hated the idea with every fiber of her being, but she nodded, because it was the best thing to do if they wanted to get those kids out of there alive. After he and Rachel pulled back to the edge of the tilled field and crouched in a shallow ditch, he called Trevor to bring him, Kat, and Hale up to speed.

"Gage is on the way with backup," Trevor said. "He's less than thirty minutes out with half the Pack."

Connor glanced at his watch. It should still be dark by the time they got here.

He and Rachel had settled into their comfortable ditch, ready to wait out the next thirty minutes until

Gage showed, when half the windows on the first floor of the farmhouse suddenly lit up bright as day.

Crap.

"Trevor, the house just lit up like a Christmas tree," he said into his phone. "We have to assume the bad guys are getting ready to move the kids. We're not going to have time to wait for Gage and the others. Rachel and I will try to slow them down. You and Hale get here as fast as you can."

Connor quickly headed toward the front of the farmhouse, Rachel covering him as they approached the gravel parking lot and the vehicles they'd seen there earlier. There were sounds of movement from inside the house, and a lot of it, along with a few high-pitched yelps of complaint. The bad guys were rushing the teens, and the kids weren't happy about it.

He heard soft thudding sounds behind him, and he turned to see Trevor and Hale approaching at a run. Connor cursed under his breath when he realized Kat was right behind them. She looked exhausted enough to fall over any second. His heart started to race at the thought of Kat being this close to danger. His head might still be a little confused about all these feelings he was developing for her, but the mere thought of her getting hurt was enough to almost push him into a shift.

It was scary how important she had become to him in such an amazingly short period of time.

"Don't start," Trevor growled at Connor as he stopped and let Kat catch up. "She refused to stay behind, and she would have followed on her own if we left her at the truck. Argue with her about it later if you want."

Regardless of Trevor's advice, Connor would have started arguing with Kat on the spot, but just as he opened his mouth to tell her to go back to the safety of his truck, the front door of the farmhouse burst open. He growled low in frustration as a group of people in dark cloaks came out the door. Connor grabbed Kat and pulled her with him behind a dark SUV. The rest of his teammates barely got out of sight before seven adults and three teenagers stepped onto the gravel, heading toward an unmarked panel van. Connor picked up four distinctly masculine scents, three that seemed to be feminine. Nothing he could smell suggested any of them were supernatural, which he wanted to think was a good thing.

The kids had sacks pulled down over their heads, but even then, Connor could tell they were terrified. The scent of fear was rolling off them in waves as their captors shoved them toward the van.

Connor gestured at Kat to stay behind the SUV, even though he had little hope that she'd do it. Then he started moving around the vehicle, motioning to his teammates as he went, knowing the only way they were going to save those kids was to hit the bad guys before they realized anyone was there.

He reached the rear of the SUV, pulling his weapon from its holster as he poked his head around to get a good look at who they were up against. He relaxed a little when he noticed that none of the people were carrying weapons that he could see. But then again, all of them were wearing heavy cloaks that hung down almost to the ground, some with cowls pulled up to cover their heads. They could be hiding almost anything under those cloaks. He stepped out from behind the SUV, quietly closing the distance between him and the people about to herd the three teenagers into the van.

Connor was still a few yards away when one of the cloaked figures suddenly spun around, almost as if they'd heard him coming, as impossible as that seemed. He had a second to realize the person was a woman before her hand came up in a blatantly aggressive move that could only mean a gun barrel would soon be pointing his way.

Connor lifted his own weapon, ready to shoot, only to hesitate when he realized the woman's hand was empty. But then she thrust her palm toward him, sending him flying backward across the parking lot and feeling like he'd just been kicked in the chest by a horse the size of a truck. He had a single heartbeat to wonder what the hell had happened, then he was smashing into the side of the metal shed and hurting way too much to worry about anything else.

Shouts and gunfire filled the air before Connor hit the ground. He rolled over, groaning in pain as his ribs creaked, looking up to see that everything had gone to crap. Trevor, Hale, and Rachel were trying— and failing—to reach Addy and the other teens.

As he shoved himself upright, checking to make sure he still had his gun at the same time, he saw Hale being picked up and thrown through the air, without anyone ever physically touching him. If Connor's trip across the parking lot hadn't been a dead giveaway, then seeing the same thing happen to Hale confirmed it. The people in the cloaks were magic users like Kat.

Connor couldn't say he was surprised. He supposed a part of him had expected something like this from the moment Kat had dropped her big secret on them.

He started to move in Hale's direction, wanting to check and make sure his pack mate was okay, but then he saw one of the cloaked figures heading straight for Kat.

Instinct made Connor turn and run in her direction as fast as his battered body could take him, his weapon coming up to point at the center of the big man's chest. But before he could even consider squeezing the trigger, the man turned his way and gestured with his hand, ripping Connor's weapon out of his grip and sending it disappearing somewhere in the darkness.

Connor didn't slow down. Instead, he let his anger and concern for Kat wash over him, claws and fangs extending, the muscles of his body twisting and spasming so hard, he thought for a moment that he would drop onto his hands and knees and start the full shift into his wolf form, something he'd never come close to doing before.

He had a second to wonder why the hell his body had chosen that particular moment to try a full shift when a loud roaring sound made him jerk his head up to see a ten-foot-high wall of flames rolling toward him. He barely had time to dive to the ground, burying his face and hands in the gravel as the fire raced over him like a living thing, grasping and tearing at him before billowing up into the sky.

Connor rolled over, expecting another wall of flames to be coming his way, but instead he found Kat standing between him and the big man in the cloak, her hands up and that wall of fire he'd been worried about writhing in midair mere inches away from her outstretched palms.

For a moment, he was too stunned to move as he watched the raging, roaring flames obey Kat's unspoken commands. But then he saw how fast she was waning, exhaustion quickly overtaking her. She'd been wiped out and dizzy before getting here. He had no idea how she was even keeping herself upright.

With a snarl, he charged the big warlock, closing

the distance between them in a few strides and not slowing in the least before slamming into the man at full speed. He doubted the body-jarring impact hurt the guy very much, but it definitely distracted him enough to force him to break off his attack on Kat, the flames disappearing into thin air.

He and the warlock tumbled over and over, Connor twisting around until he was on top of the man, clawed hand swinging back to strike. But he never got a chance to deliver the punch before a savage thump of pressure to his chest sent him flying backward once again. When he hit the ground this time, he was sure he'd cracked some ribs. Well, more ribs, actually, since the impact with the work shed had probably damaged a few already.

By the time Connor got to his feet, the big guy he'd tackled was gone, the three kids were already in the van, and the door was sliding closed. Rachel and Trevor charged in from the side to run after them only to get tossed aside, too. Both of them ended up going right through the windows of the farmhouse and slamming into a few interior walls by the sound of it.

The van kicked up gravel as it spun out of the parking lot. Even though Connor knew he was too late, he ran after it anyway.

Then Kat jumped in front of it, raising a hand and staring down the driver like she honestly thought that would do something besides get her killed.

The van didn't slow.

Cursing, Connor changed direction, heading straight for Kat instead, getting there when the van was only inches away and tackling her before she got run over.

He tried to protect Kat as they landed, but he'd been running at full speed when he hit her, and the impact was vicious. He heard the air *whoosh* from her lungs, and he was sure he'd hurt her. When they rolled to a stop, he cradled her as gently as he could in his arms, looking for obvious injuries.

Kat waved him off, pushing his hands away as he tried to check her ribs. "Go after the kids. They're getting away." When he hesitated, she gave him a shove. "I'm okay. Go!"

Connor didn't want to leave her, but he did, forcing himself upright to sprint after the van as fast as he could.

The van with the teens inside had been joined by two of the large SUVs that had been parked in front of the farmhouse, and now, all three were tearing across the rough farm property, heading for the road near the place where he and Trevor had left their vehicles.

Movement to his left let him know one of his pack mates had caught up to him. He didn't have to look to know it was Hale. Connor assumed that Trevor and Rachel were still trying to extricate themselves from the inside of the house.

The rough terrain of the open field slowed the three vehicles a bit, allowing Connor and Hale to close the gap between them. The two SUVs suddenly slowed then, and Connor could only guess that he and Hale had been spotted. The SUVs were probably falling back to serve as a rear guard, purely to keep them from getting at the van and the kidnapped teenagers.

"We'll have to take out those SUVs first before trying for the van," Hale yelled. "And we need to make it fast. If they reach the highway, we'll never be able to keep up."

Connor didn't say anything because he knew Hale was right. A partially shifted werewolf could run thirty to thirty-five miles an hour over open ground, but even they couldn't keep up with a vehicle on a clear stretch of road.

He and Hale were only about twenty feet from catching up when one of the back windows of the SUV on the left opened and a hand came out, pointing in Hale's direction. There was a cracking sound as loud as a gunshot, then Hale cried out in pain and went down hard, tumbling across the rough ground. Connor ground his jaw. He was pretty sure the bastard had just broken Hale's legs.

"Go!" Hale shouted. "Don't let them get away!"

Connor growled in frustration but kept going even as he had to throw himself to the side in a roll to avoid a hand pointed out the window in his direction now. It was bizarre, diving to avoid a threat he couldn't even see. By the time he was on his feet and back up to full speed, all three vehicles had reached the road and were gaining ground.

He considered continuing the chase on foot but knew it was worthless. So, instead, he turned to the right, heading for his own truck. It would take a few seconds to get it started and then turned around, but if he floored it, he might be able to catch up. He'd improvise from there.

He'd nearly reached his pickup when all four tires blew out at once. A split second later, the same thing happened to the tires on Trevor's Thunderbird.

"Dammit!" he roared.

The precious seconds he'd wasted racing to his truck would be nearly impossible to get back. But since he didn't have any other option, Connor turned and began sprinting down the road toward the three sets of taillights already a few hundred feet away. He didn't like his odds of being able to catch up to them now.

Connor was running faster than he ever had in his life when the unexpected happened and the two SUVs actually slowed down so much that he was forced to swerve in order to avoid running right into the back end of one of them.

Before he could recover, the other SUV swung sideways, slamming into Connor and knocking him off the road. The impact from the vehicle was bad, but tumbling and bouncing across the ground was worse. He curled into a ball to protect himself but still bounced for another hundred feet across the plowed field.

When he finally came to a stop facedown and feeling like he'd broken half the bones in his body, he knew the chase was over. Lifting his head, he watched the taillights of the three vehicles slowly disappear into the distance.

Connor sat up slowly, cataloging the myriad aches and pains spreading through his body. But as much as the physical damage hurt him, it was the mental wreckage that wounded him worse. They'd failed to get Addy, Ben, and Cheyenne back. On top of that, they'd gotten their asses kicked. He and his pack mates had faced so many unbelievable threats, coming out on top every time. It was stupid, but he'd started buying into the idea that there was nothing and no one they couldn't handle. But after tonight, he was forced to accept the reality that when it came to these witches and warlocks, the Pack was simply overmatched.

Trevor showed up a few seconds later to help him up. Back toward the farmhouse, Connor saw Kat and Rachel kneeling beside Hale. His friend was sitting up but making no attempt to stand. His legs were probably too badly damaged to allow them to work right now. It would take a while for them to heal.

Connor and Trevor slowly made their way over to them. Kat didn't look like she'd gotten hurt in that tumble they'd taken, and for that, he was immensely grateful. She still seemed tired as hell, though. That knowledge tore a hole in his gut. It was his fault she'd had to fight again in the first place.

"Is there any chance you can do that Find Me charm again on Cheyenne?" Connor asked.

Kat shook her head as she sat beside Hale. "Now that they know that I'm with you, they can obscure all the kids. I won't be able to find them that way. If it helps, I don't think they're planning to kill them, at least not yet, or they already would have done it."

Trevor glanced at his Thunderbird sitting on the side of the road with four blown-out tires, then looked at them. "I suppose it goes without saying that those were witches and warlocks, right?"

Kat nodded, looking lost and broken. "Yeah. I recognize some of them from when Marko attacked my coven years ago. The big guy who tried to kill me is Tatum Graves. He's Marko's right-hand man. He pretty much runs the coven when Marko isn't around."

Sighing, Connor dropped on the grass beside Kat, wrapping an arm around her. Well, at least now they knew who—and what—they were up against.

CHAPTER 11

IT WAS NEARLY TEN IN THE MORNING BY THE time Kat and Connor got back to his apartment. She was so exhausted by then that she thought falling asleep on her feet was a distinct possibility. The moment they walked through the door, she headed straight for the sectional couch and collapsed onto it.

Connor disappeared into his bedroom, then came out a few moments later with sweatpants and a T-shirt. "I figured you might want to clean up."

She was too tired to do anything more than sit there, but a glance at her clothes confirmed she was a mess. There were rips and scorch marks on her jeans and long-sleeve shirt, along with dirt and mud stains. She shoved herself off the couch and took the clothes he held out.

"Thanks," she said.

The shower revived her more than she would have thought possible. In fact, she felt almost like the human she now was by the time she stepped onto the fluffy bath mat and dried off. As she ran the soft towel over her damp skin, she replayed the events that had transpired last night and this morning. Finding the kids, then losing them again, had been heartrending. Then watching Connor almost get smashed flat by that SUV had nearly torn her already fragile heart right out. Realizing that Marko was not only behind the kidnapping but also now knew Kat was in Dallas was beyond terrifying. For a moment, she'd frozen up completely, unable to function at the thought, that after all these years, she'd finally been caught.

And yet, feeling Connor's arm around her as they'd sat there on the ground after everything had almost been enough to make up for all the horrible things that had happened. In one simple gesture, it had seemed like the distance between them had closed drastically. Not completely perhaps, but it was so much better than it had been.

Kat eyed her bra and panties, shuddering at the idea of putting the sweaty things back on after stepping out of the shower. Instead, she pulled on the sweatpants Connor had given her, glad there was a drawstring in them, or they wouldn't have stayed up. Even then, she had to roll up the waist a few times to keep the wide bottoms from dragging the floor. A smile tugged at her lips as she slipped on the T-shirt and got a good look at the words on the front. *Property of SWAT*. Nope, she shouldn't like that, but damn if she did anyway.

Luckily, the T-shirt was loose enough to not give away the fact that she wasn't wearing a bra. Leaning forward was probably out of the question, though, unless she wanted to give Connor a free show. Which, now that she thought about it, might not necessarily be a bad thing.

She ran Connor's brush through her hair, put some toothpaste on her finger and ran it over her teeth, then swished with mouthwash and called it a day.

Connor was in the kitchen when she came out and climbed back onto the couch. He walked into the living room a few moments later with two plates piled high with a collection of sandwiches and two glasses of diet soda. There was ham and cheese, turkey and cheese, and if she wasn't mistaken, peanut butter and cheese. Okay, that was different.

"I didn't know what you wanted, so I made a little of everything," he said, and Kat didn't miss the way he eyed the bits of bare skin at her shoulder and collarbones exposed by the T-shirt's big neckline. "I'm going to shower off real fast, but if you're hungry, feel free to go ahead and start eating without me."

Kat considered nibbling on a sandwich while she waited but then decided she was too comfortable where she was. She relaxed back on the couch, figuring it wouldn't take Connor long to get cleaned up. As she waited, her thoughts once again turned to Addy, Ben, and Cheyenne. She wasn't sure exactly what Marko had in store for them, but there was no way in hell it could be something good. She hadn't wanted to make any assumptions about the ritualistic murder in San Antonio, but she had a nagging suspicion the kidnapping of the three teenagers was somehow connected to that. She didn't want to say anything until she was surer, though.

Connor came back into the living room less than five minutes later, which was technically impossible by the laws of showering physics as she understood them. He was dressed in a pair of jogging shorts and a T-shirt similar to hers but a lot tighter. And yeah, he made the outfit look good.

"You could have started eating," he said as he flopped down on the couch beside her.

After picking up one of the glasses, he took a long drink, then gestured at the plates of sandwiches. Kat took the first sandwich off the top of the stack and checked the condiment-to-bread-to-meat ratio, happy with what she found. She hated dry sandwiches.

Kat didn't realize how hungry she was until she started eating. She stifled a moan. Connor knew how to make a turkey and cheese sandwich, that was for sure. There was even the perfect amount of mayonnaise and a touch of mustard on it. After finishing the first, she washed it down with some soda, then helped herself to another.

Sitting there with a relaxed Connor, talking about everyday things like what constituted the perfect sandwich, reminded Kat of when he'd put his arm around her at the farm earlier. Those had been the best moments she'd experienced since first being turned into a cat, and she wanted more of that. But soon enough, they'd finish devouring the sandwiches he'd made, and she knew he'd suggest she get some rest.

She sipped her drink, desperately trying to think of something to say when she caught sight of the framed photos on the wall. Specifically, the pictures of his family and the sister who didn't appear grown-up in any of them.

"What happened to your sister?" she asked before she even realized what she was saying. She bit the inside of her cheek the moment the words were out of her mouth as she realized how insensitive she was being.

Connor froze in mid-chew, his hazel eyes locking on hers and making her feel about two inches tall. She opened her mouth, ready to apologize and tell him it was absolutely none of her business, but he spoke before she could.

"How'd you know?" he said, sounding curious rather than upset. "I don't remember ever talking about her in front of you."

"You didn't." She pushed her hair behind her ear, giving him a sheepish shrug. "I noticed that all the photos of her were taken a while ago and that there aren't any of her as an adult, like you have of your other sister."

Connor regarded her for a long moment before nodding. "That's pretty good. Not many people notice things like that."

Being observant seemed to go hand in hand with being able to do magic. Maybe because witches and warlocks tended to be more aware of things around them. But something told her that she'd have come to the same conclusion about his sister even if she weren't a witch. When it came to Connor, she wanted to know everything there was to know about him.

"Where were those pictures taken?" she prompted when he didn't say anything, hoping maybe that would be a better way to ease into the conversation.

"In Los Angeles. That's where I grew up." He glanced over his shoulder at the photos on the wall, as if to remind himself of which ones she was talking about, then turned back to her with a snort. "Back when my big plan was to become an actor. All I wanted was to be an action hero and star in dozens of blockbuster movies."

Kat smiled at the thought of Connor being a Hollywood celebrity. She could definitely see him in the heartthrob role.

"But that was before my sister went missing," he said softly. "Acting and being a fake hero in the movies seemed kind of silly after that."

"How old were you when it happened?" she asked.

"Eighteen," he murmured, focusing his attention on the sandwich in his hand. "It was a month or so before graduation. Hannah and my other sister, Jenna, went with some friends to see a movie at the local theater. Hannah was sixteen, Jenna had just turned thirteen, and the two of them slipped in to see some scary monster movie that would have given my parents a hissy fit if they'd known. But Jenna loved monster movies, and Hannah loved her. So that's the movie they went to see."

Kat waited patiently, not wanting to push. This had to be hard for him.

"There was a glitch with the movie, and it ran late, so they missed their ride home. They didn't want to call Mom or Dad or me, so they walked home." He picked up his glass and took a long drink, then set it down on the table again. "It wasn't that far from where we lived and we'd all made the trip before a hundred times, even at night. But that night was different. They never made it back."

Kat had to force herself to keep from reaching out to take his hand. "What happened?"

He shook his head. "My parents freaked out when they realized Hannah and Jenna weren't home, so they called me, and we all started looking. I got help from a bunch of my friends, while my parents got the cops involved. We found Jenna the next morning in a completely catatonic state behind a dumpster near the movie theater. There was no sign of Hannah."

"Was Jenna ever able to tell you what happened?" Kat asked, aching for Connor and feeling his pain as if it were her own.

"She claimed that Hannah was kidnapped by a monster, but the way she described it was too outlandish to even fathom, and no one—not my parents, not the cops, not me—believed her," he admitted. "Jenna took the fact that no one put stock in what she said really hard. She pulled into a shell and wouldn't so much as speak to anyone for a long time after that. When the cops couldn't find any signs of foul play and no leads on the kidnapping theory, they finally wrote the whole thing off as a runaway teenager and stopped actively looking." He shrugged. "It wasn't their fault. That's how it works with missing kids. You try and find them at first, but there are so many that, after a while, they simply become another poster on a website."

"Knowing what you know now about the supernatural world, have you ever thought that maybe Jenna did see something?" Kat asked.

"Yeah." He nodded. "I've thought about that over the years, but you have to realize, Jenna had always been a little out there. Even as a little kid, her imagination frequently got the best of her, and it was difficult sometimes to tell what was real to her and what wasn't. If you had heard what she said about that night, I'm not sure you would have believed her, either."

Kat sighed. "I'm sorry. Not knowing what happened to Hannah must be tough."

She expected Connor had heard lots of platitudes over the years. He didn't need any more from her, but she would do anything right then to make him feel better.

"You could say that," he murmured. "It would probably be more accurate to say that losing Hannah was like dropping a nuke on my family. Jenna had to go to a therapist for years, and my parents ended up getting divorced. Jenna and my parents all still live in LA, but none of them ever see each other, much less talk. Hell, Mom and Dad can't even be in the same room now without a major fight, which means visiting either of them, even separately, is full of so much drama, it isn't worth the cost of the plane ticket. I see Jenna more often, but our relationship isn't like it was when we were kids. She never forgave me for not believing her. I'm not sure I even forgive myself."

Kat tried to imagine what she would have done in Connor's position. Granted, it was easy because she was a witch and knew all about how strange the world really was. But if she hadn't been fortunate enough to know all of that, how would she have treated Jenna?

"Gage mentioned that you had experience

working missing persons," she said. "Is that what you did in LA?"

He nodded. "Yeah. It took a little while to get into the unit, but I kept pushing until I got there. I never wanted anyone else to go through what I did, to have someone they love disappear and never know what happened. At times, it could be a heartrending job, but it's difficult to describe the sense of satisfaction you get after finding someone that everyone thought was gone and bringing them home."

"You sound like you really loved it," she said. "What made you move to Dallas and join SWAT?"

Without answering, he lifted his shirt, showing a series of scars along the left side of his torso. "Considering how often you've watched me shower, I'm guessing you've seen these before, huh?"

"Yeah." She didn't even blush as she gave him a nod. "What happened?"

He lowered his shirt again, regarding her thoughtfully. "Do you know where werewolves come from?"

She had to admit she was still a little distracted by the flash of skin, so the sudden change in direction caught her a little off guard. She hadn't known there was going to be a test.

As a witch, she'd learned a lot about the different supernatural creatures in the world. There were books on that kind of stuff, and her grandma had been all about the books. Since hanging out at the SWAT compound, she'd learned a lot more, especially during all the girl talk with Rachel and Khaki.

"I know you have to be born with a certain gene for the werewolf change to occur and that a bite or scratch won't do it," she said, replaying everything she knew and had pieced together over the past nine months that she'd been living with the Pack. "And I know that you have to go through some kind of adrenaline-inducing traumatic event to trigger the change. From listening to some of your pack mates, I get the feeling that the traumatic experience is usually pretty horrible."

"I don't think I've ever heard anyone describe the werewolf process so succinctly," he said, clearly impressed by her knowledge. "And that includes a few doctors and scientists who have tried their hands at trying to help me understand all of it."

She wasn't quite sure she believed that. Connor was a smart guy. "So those scars you just showed me," she said, her stomach already aching at the thought of what she was about to ask, "are they from the traumatic event that turned you?"

"Yeah," he said, his expression thoughtful. "It happened five years ago. I was tracking down four runaway kids who'd been living on the streets of LA for months. They'd all gotten away from shitty situations that were so terrible, they'd rather be homeless in a city as dangerous as Los Angeles than go back to them. Unfortunately, they ended up on the radar of a group of human traffickers, who looked at those four desperate kids and saw a hell of a lot of dollar signs."

Kat had spent a little time in Los Angeles while on the run from Marko. Admittedly, not much because LA had way too many cars for a cat like her. But she'd seen enough homeless kids there to understand what Connor was talking about. The worse part was, for all the people out there, it was like no one really ever saw each other. Like everyone was invisible.

"The kids had taken to hiding in the tunnels below the city, hoping to lose themselves in the darkness among the other homeless. Unfortunately, it didn't work."

"The traffickers found them?" Kat asked, horrified, when long seconds passed with him staring into the distance, obviously reliving old memories. She felt bad for making him do that, but as afraid as she was to hear what happened to them—and him—she needed to know.

"I didn't expect to run into trouble, so I didn't even think of calling in for backup," he said quietly, his deep voice rough. "Once I got underground and realized what I was up against, it was too late to do anything about it. There was no cell reception down there in those tunnels."

There was another long pause, but this time

she didn't push him to continue, knowing he'd get there on his own.

"There were six guys," he finally said, his hand coming up to rub along his side through his shirt in an unconscious movement she'd seen many times before. "All of them were armed, and not one blinked at the prospect of killing a cop. One of them hit me here with a shotgun loaded with buckshot at nearly point-blank range. I was wearing a lightweight tactical vest, but it was meant to protect against a frontal attack. The side was completely open. I knew I was dead the second the weapon went off."

Hearing Connor say those words made Kat's stomach twist into knots so badly, she thought she might be sick. The scars were bad, and she'd instinctively understood that whatever had caused that much damage must have been horrible. But hearing the words out loud did something painful to her soul. It hurt so badly that she felt like she'd been shot herself.

"The first thing I wanted to do was drop to my knees and pass out until it was over, but I couldn't," he continued. "Not with those kids down there depending on me. So I shot the man who'd shot me, got those four kids moving ahead of me, then ran."

He shook his head. "I'm not even going to try and describe what it was like down there, mostly because I don't remember much of it. Even now, when I try and replay it in my head, all I get are brief glimpses of running through mazelike tunnels with no idea which way to go, muzzle flashes from guns going off in the darkness, the kids screaming, and pain. So much pain, I swore every step would be my last. Somehow, I took out all six of those traffickers. I don't even remember doing it, but ballistics later confirmed it was my weapon that was responsible, so I guess I did."

"You got all the kids out?" Kat asked.

"Technically, no," he admitted. "We were a couple hundred yards short of one of the tunnel entrances when I passed out from blood loss and shock. But those four kids—none of them older than fourteen—dragged me the rest of the way to the surface and called for help. They stayed with me the whole time, too, even though it put them at risk. Even when there seemed no chance that I'd make it."

"But you did make it," she said firmly, her stomach still clenching, even knowing that everything had worked out okay in the end despite the nightmare he'd gone through.

"Yeah, I made it," he agreed. "I coded out three times on the operating table and even got pronounced dead the last time. But the trauma of the injury started the change, and my newfound inner wolf wouldn't let me go, so I survived. Against all possible odds, I lived."

If she'd thought her body had reacted badly at the

idea of him getting hurt, it was nothing compared to realizing that Connor had actually died. She thought her own heart was going to stop beating.

"Regardless of my miraculous recovery, the LAPD wanted to medically retire me," Connor added with a shrug. "I can't say I blame them, not with the way my behavior changed in the weeks and months right after the change. I'll be the first to admit, I went a bit off the rails during that time. But in my defense, I had no idea what was happening to me. My claws and fangs started showing up at the worst possible times, and my nose picked up scents no human should be able to smell. At first, I thought it was PTSD, but after a while, I figured I was going insane instead. You have no idea how many times I came damn close to committing myself for psychiatric evaluation."

"What happened to convince you not to?" Kat asked.

"Gage happened," Connor said simply.

Kat smiled at the mention of his commander. The pack's alpha was special. Even though she'd been a cat instead of a person when they'd first met, she knew there weren't many people in the world as caring and supportive as Gage.

"He showed up around a year or so after the change," Connor explained. "He said he'd figured out I was a werewolf after reading the press clippings from my various law enforcement exploits.

He helped me finally understand what was going on and then asked me to come to Dallas and be part of his pack. I agreed and never looked back."

"Was it hard not working missing persons anymore?"

He frowned a little as he considered that. "I went down into those tunnels after those kids with no backup and no plan. Some people might say it was admirable, but it was also stupid. And truthfully, it wasn't the first time I'd done something like that. It took almost getting killed, becoming a werewolf, and an honest conversation with myself to realize I'd gone into missing persons for all the wrong reasons. The biggest reason I was there was some misguided attempt to atone for my sister's disappearance. Once I got through all that, I was able to step back and accept there were other cops working missing persons in LA—damn good cops— and that it was time I let my sister go and move on with my life."

She let out a sigh, thinking about all the years she'd spent trying to come up with ways to get revenge for her coven members, feeling like a coward when she'd run away to save herself. How long had it taken her to accept there was nothing she could have done? In all honesty, she wasn't sure she'd gotten there yet.

"I can't imagine that was an easy conversation to have with yourself," she said softly.

Connor grunted in what she assumed was agreement but didn't say anything.

They finished eating a little while after that. Connor had devoured all the sandwiches on his plate and half of hers, but that was cool. He'd made way more than she could eat anyway. And she didn't regret not giving the peanut butter and cheese sandwiches a try one bit. As far as she was concerned, those were two great tastes that were never meant to be together.

"I know it's barely noon, but you didn't get much sleep last night," Connor said. "You should try and get some rest."

Kat knew he was right. After that fight at the farmhouse, her magical core was on the verge of total collapse. If that happened, she'd be wiped out and have to sleep so much that before she knew it, she'd turn back into a cat and waste all her time as a human.

"I can't sleep," she admitted. "No matter how exhausted I am, I can't seem to relax."

He frowned. "I know for a fact that you slept fine when you were a cat."

She wasn't sure what to say to that except the truth. Then again, in a few days, she was going to be a cat again, and with Marko aware she was in Dallas, she'd have to go on the move. Why not be honest with Connor?

"I could sleep fine because I was sleeping with

you," she said softly. "Connor, you're the reason I stopped running in the first place. You're the only thing that makes me feel safe."

Connor didn't answer. In fact, he didn't even react. He simply sat there regarding her with an unreadable expression. She held her breath, waiting for him to tell her that there was no way in hell he was going to sleep with a woman who'd been a cat up until a few days ago. But to her surprise, he stood and held out his hand toward her. She took it, allowing him to pull her to her feet. Then, without a word, he started walking toward the bedroom. Once inside, he led her over to the bed she'd tossed and turned in the night before, then moved to the far side of the room to close the curtains, casting the room into semidarkness.

Kat felt like she should say something, but instead she reached over to pull down the sheet and blanket, sliding into the bed and across to the far side. After she was settled, she pushed the sweatpants over her hips and down her legs, then dropped them on the floor beside her. She turned back around to see that Connor had stripped off his T-shirt and was climbing into bed with her. Now that her eyes were adjusted to the dim light, she could clearly see the exceptionally well-done tattoo of a wolf head on his chest. All the guys on the team had them, and while they were all identical, she'd always been partial to his tat.

She noticed that he kept his eyes to himself. Not that it mattered. She still had the long T-shirt on, so it wasn't like she was naked under the blanket.

They lay there, side by side, quietly for a while, a foot or so of space in between them. But that didn't work for her, and after a moment, she slid closer, putting her body against his and resting her head on his bare, warm chest. He wrapped an arm around her shoulder, and just like that, she could finally relax.

Kat smiled as she listened to his heart beating steadily under her ear. She could stay here the rest of her life. Unfortunately, that thought only reminded her that she would once again be a feline soon.

She lifted her head to look at him. "In less than a week, I'm going to turn into a cat again. I don't want to waste what little time I have left in this body. I could sleep here on your chest and be happy, but truthfully, there are other things I'd rather be doing."

"Such as?" he asked in a soft voice that did crazy things to her.

Kat climbed up a little higher on his chest and kissed him. His lips were warm on hers, his taste enough to drag a moan from her throat.

"Such as that," she whispered, pulling back to gaze down on him.

Connor's hazel eyes glowed gold at her words. It was so unbelievably sexy, she promised herself that she'd never forget the image. Then he pulled her in for another kiss, taking the lead this time as his tongue slipped into her mouth to tangle with hers. If she'd thought he'd tasted good before, it was nothing compared to this.

This was absolute heaven.

CHAPTER 12

KAT THREW ONE OF HER LEGS ACROSS HIS HIPS, never breaking the kiss as she slid her bare inner thigh back and forth across the hard-on bulging under Connor's shorts. He groaned, and Kat would have let out a laugh if her mouth hadn't already been busy. She couldn't help but be thrilled to know Connor was as excited about this moment as she was.

Then again, she wasn't sure how he could be *quite* as excited as she was. But that was only because she'd been waiting for this moment since the day she'd met Connor. And yeah, she was fully aware how weird it was for a cat to lust after a guy, but the truth was she'd been hot for him even while trapped in a feline body and walking around his apartment on four legs. Not that she'd ever admit that in a million years.

Slightly distracted by those thoughts, she barely noticed when Connor reached down to wrap his fingers around her waist and drag her on top of him so she was straddling his hips. The feel of his erection pressing against her was delicious beyond belief. Even if he *was* still wearing his shorts.

The urge to wiggle was impossible to resist,

especially when he slid his hands down to catch the hem of her tee, pushing it up as those warm fingers traveled up her thighs. When he reached her hips, those strong hands squeezed a little bit more firmly as he guided her movements against him. She let out an audible sigh of pleasure.

Breaking the kiss, she slowly pushed herself upright, her hands planted firmly on Connor's chest as she ground down on him in a circular motion that did absolutely magical things for her—pun intended. It felt so good, she wasn't sure she ever wanted to stop.

Connor gazed up at her, his eyes glowing so brightly now that Kat swore she could feel the heat of his smoldering gaze warming her entire body. He was looking at her as if he might eat her up like a piece of apple pie. And damn if she wasn't looking forward to that.

She didn't even realize she was digging her fingernails into Connor's bulging pecs, first one hand and then the next in an extremely familiar kneading motion, until he groaned. While the catlike behavior was comforting to her, it was apparently arousing for him, if the hardness pressing against her was any indication.

They gazed at each other for a long time as she casually rode his hips, getting lost in each other. She suspected she could orgasm if she moved a little faster, but she didn't allow herself to speed up.

She wanted to enjoy the moment as long as possible, teetering on the edge of climax and letting the pleasure build.

She lifted her arms to help when Connor pushed her T-shirt up and over her head. The moment he flung her shirt across the room, she placed her palms on his muscular chest again, gradually moving her hands a little lower so she was rhythmically kneading his rippling abs this time. The move made him pulse against her even harder.

Connor cupped her breasts in his hands, gently massaging as he captured her nipples between thumb and forefinger and squeezed them with the perfect amount of pressure, which sent little lightning bolts of pleasure zipping back and forth through her body.

Kat would have been content to ride him like that for hours, but Connor must have had other plans, because he suddenly flipped her onto her back. The move was so smooth and graceful, she barely realized what happened until she looked up to see his huge body above her. She'd always known he was strong—it was part and parcel of being a werewolf—but she hadn't known until that moment just how fit he was. She also hadn't known until that moment that she liked powerful guys. It definitely did something for her, that was for sure.

Who knew?

After making quick work of his shorts, he looked

every inch the predator as he gazed down at her. She quivered at the sight of him bending his head to press his mouth to her inner thigh, the hunger in his gold eyes impossible to miss. She knew exactly what he was planning to do, and the anticipation was killing her.

When she felt his fangs graze the tender skin on her leg, she caught her breath. She'd obviously seen them many times over the past few months but had never imagined them coming out in this kind of situation. Shockingly, she wasn't bothered at the thought of those razor-sharp canines so close to her skin. Actually, she was kind of turned on at the idea that he might nip her a little.

Obviously spending a good portion of the past four years in a cat's body had rendered her much kinkier than she'd ever imagined.

That was her story, anyway.

And she was sticking to it.

When Connor slid his big hands under her butt and buried his face between her legs, Kat arched her back and let out a long, low moan. His tongue traced a warm path along her folds over and over again until she was dizzy from it. She swore it was like he could read her mind because he seemed to know exactly where she needed to be touched. Never too much pressure, never too light.

With all the riding she'd done on his lap earlier, Kat was already close to orgasm. She weaved her fingers into his hair, trying to urge him upward, knowing that a little bit more attention to her clit would push her over the edge. But he refused to obey her directions, continuing to lazily swipe his tongue along her folds, staying away from that one place that would allow her to come.

"Stop teasing me," she pleaded, tugging on his hair.

Connor chuckled and slowly slipped a finger inside her, sliding in deep and then curling until he found that perfect spot.

"Yes!" she gasped, arching her back even more and clamping her thighs tightly around his shoulders as he slid a second finger in. "Right there. Don't stop. Please don't ever stop."

When his warm mouth finally found her clit, that was the moment she exploded, screaming so loud, she worried the neighbors might hear. Not that it stopped her.

The orgasm she experienced right then was probably the longest and most powerful of her life. Connor was the best ever, and that was that.

When she could finally see straight again, Kat lifted her head to look down between her legs, finding Connor lying there, his chin resting comfortably in the palm of one hand, molten eyes still smoldering. After pushing himself upright, he moved off the bed and pulled open his nightstand. She knew that was where he kept his condoms because she'd caught a peek a while ago, when he'd dug in the drawer for his phone charger. She also knew for a fact that he hadn't used any since she'd moved in with him.

They'd better not be expired.

Connor seemed satisfied with what he found, making quick work of the foil package and then getting back into the bed, his cock hard and ready. Kat pushed up on her elbows, watching as he worked his way up her body. She was more than ready for the main event, but she couldn't find it in her to complain when he took his time to nibble his way up her stomach to her breasts.

If the feel of those fangs on her inner thigh had been amazing, it was nothing compared to how they felt on her nipples. It was practically mind-numbing—in the best possible way, of course—and for a moment, Kat almost forgot about what they'd been about to do. At least until she felt the head of his thick shaft nudging her wetness. That reminded her quickly enough.

"You aren't going to tease me again, are you?" she asked as his arms came down on either side of her body, bracketing her in walls of muscle on every side. "I don't think I can handle that after waiting this long."

His eyes glowed vivid gold as the corners of his sensuous lips tipped up in a smile. "And just how long have you been waiting?"

"Too long," Kat murmured, wrapping her legs around his waist and pulling him closer.

The feel of him inside her took her breath away. It was unlike anything she'd ever experienced. It really *was* like he'd been made for her.

He moved slowly at first, pulling almost all the way out before sliding back in deep. But even if he wasn't moving fast, each thrust made her entire body go into little spasms of pleasure.

"You don't have to take it so easy," she whispered as she pulled his head down and traced her lips across his ear. "I might still be tired, but I'm not made of glass. I won't break. Promise."

Kat felt the shiver run down his spine, though she wasn't sure if it was the feel of her lips on his skin or the fact that she'd asked him to take her harder. Either way, it was thrilling to know she could cause such a reaction in him.

Regardless, Connor must have decided to believe her, because after a long, scorching kiss, he started thrusting a little harder. Her whole body shook as his hips slapped against the inside of her thighs.

She went back to kissing and nibbling on his ear, her fingers twisting in his hair as she whispered another endless chant, begging him to *go faster, harder, never stop*. Connor gave her exactly what she wanted, low, rumbling growls coming from deep in his chest as he began to pound into her harder.

Those growls had to be the sexiest sounds Kat had ever heard.

She tilted her hips up so the head of his cock glided across that one perfect spot inside her, the one that sent little tingles of pleasure rippling through her body with each thrust. Her breath caught in her throat as the heat that had been pulsing deep in her core began to build rapidly, blooming inside her like she was on fire.

"Don't stop," Kat gasped, sliding her hands down from his hair to his back, her nails digging in as she yanked him tighter to her body, wanting… needing…to feel his weight pressing her down into the mattress. "I'm so close."

That feeling of heat and pressure deep inside continued to build until she was almost hyperventilating in anticipation of the climax she felt approaching. She knew it was going to be huge. Just like she knew she would never experience anything this perfect with another man.

Connor let out a low growl, his fangs grazing the sensitive skin of her neck. That was the thing that pushed her over the edge, and just like that, the world went white, and ecstasy coursed through her.

Kat buried her face in the junction of his neck and shoulder, clamping her teeth down on the muscles there out of pure instinct. Then she squeezed tightly with her arms and held on for dear life as her orgasm washed over her in endless waves that threatened to push her under and never let her back up. Connor groaned hoarsely in the middle of her climax, and knowing they were coming together made everything that much more exquisite.

She was so addled right then that she was barely aware of Connor rolling them over so she was resting comfortably on his chest. She lay there, listening to his heart thumping hard and fast under her ear, letting it slowly lull her to sleep. Right before she dropped off into slumber, she felt him pull up the sheet and blanket and then press a soft kiss on the top of her head.

Part of her agonized over the fact that she wouldn't have this for very long before she would become a cat again, but she resolutely pushed that thought aside, deciding to enjoy what she had while she had it.

CHAPTER 13

"I talked to Detective Sandoval and let him know we have solid suspects that have no connection to Conrad Lloyd or Alton Marshall," Gage said. "I obviously couldn't tell him about the supernatural angle, but at least he and the other detectives aren't wasting time looking for clues they'll never find."

"I've put out BOLOs on the people we fought at the farmhouse," Trevor added, pointing at the drawings on the conference table in Gage's office, which Rachel had helped the forensic artists come up with. "But so far we don't have anything on them. Not even an ID."

"Considering they can do magic, I'm not surprised," Connor murmured from where he sat in a chair on the other side of the table. "I'll ask Kat if it's possible, but those faces we saw might not even be theirs."

That announcement earned him a mutter of discontent from Hale, who was sitting beside him.

Rachel would have been there for the discussion, too, but she and Khaki had taken Kat shopping for clothes. The fact Kat had nothing to wear but his sweats and T-shirts apparently bothered his female pack mates. He couldn't understand why. He thought she looked sexy as hell in his workout gear. Of course, she looked even better out of it.

He was abruptly interrupted from his thoughts of yesterday afternoon…and last night…and this morning by Gage going on about something else related to the witches and warlocks they'd fought at the farm.

"I talked to Davina, and she's going to do some research to see if she can figure out what Marko might be planning to do with the kids he's been kidnapping. Fortunately, she's already familiar with the guy, so she knows what kind of psycho we're dealing with."

Davina DeMirci was a witch who ran a club out in Los Angeles that catered to the supernatural crowd, and she'd helped SWAT on a few cases involving strange creatures before. There wasn't much the woman didn't know about things that went bump in the night. They could definitely use her expertise.

"Did Davina have any idea whether Marko and his coven are done grabbing kids, or do we have to be worried about him kidnapping more?" Hale asked.

Gage shrugged. "She isn't sure yet."

Connor frowned. The mere thought of Marko's coven grabbing more teenagers and the team having no way to stop it was infuriating. And terrifying, if he was being honest. He didn't want to think about what might be happening to those poor kids right this minute.

"Did you bring up Kat's situation to Davina?" Connor asked. "She seems to know a lot about how the supernatural world works, so I was hoping she'd be able to help Kat find a way to stop from turning back into a cat."

"Yeah, I mentioned Kat and what Marko did to her," Gage said, regarding Connor with an expression that could only be described as pity. "Davina has never heard of a familiar spell like Marko put on Kat, but she's looking into it. Do you think Kat would be willing to talk directly with Davina and share some of the details?"

"Definitely," Connor said.

They spent a few more minutes talking about what their next steps in the investigation would be. There were a few things they could do, like continuing to dig for a link between Addy, Ben, and Cheyenne, and looking for some connection between Marko and the farmhouse his coven had been using. But they all knew the deal. Until Kat or Davina came up with some clue about what Marko was up to, which would give them some idea of where to look next, there wasn't much they could do.

After the meeting ended, Connor headed outside with Trevor and Hale to watch other members of the SWAT team run through the obstacle course that filled the center of the compound, climbing up one side of the training house and rappelling down the other. As usual, the whole thing turned into a competition within minutes, complete with shouting, trash-talking, and random bouts of angry snarling. At some point, the fangs would come out and somebody would try and bite somebody else. Or shove them off the building. He chuckled. That was simply the way the Pack played.

"How come you're not heading back to your place?" Hale asked. "Gage told you to spend as much time with Kat as you needed."

His pack mate moved a little slower than normal because his legs were still healing—and hurting. For werewolves, broken bones usually repaired themselves within an hour or two. The fact that Hale was still dealing with the pain was an indication of how seriously those magic users had messed him up. They hadn't merely broken the bones. They'd shattered them. Which didn't exactly bode well for the next time the Pack ran into those bastards.

Before Connor could say anything, he felt a thud against his leg and looked down to see Tuffie staring up at him, giving him the sweetest puppy eyes on the planet. Damn, the pitty mix could melt the polar ice caps with that gaze.

"What's wrong, girl?" He dropped to a knee at her side to ruffle her ears, then ran his hands along the dog's side, giving her a good rubdown. "You're missing Kat the cat, aren't you? You're used to her being your full-time wingwoman and partner in crime."

Tuffie looked at him, and Connor swore the girl nodded, like she was totally agreeing.

"Well, as I'm sure you're aware of, Kat is dealing with a lot right now," he told the dog seriously, gently cupping her furry face and looking right into those intelligent eyes. "She's getting used to her human form again, and on top of that, she just found out that the guy who turned her into a cat is probably here in Dallas. He might even be looking for her. So you need to give Kat some time. I promise I'll let her know you want to see her, okay?"

Tuffie let out a soft bark of agreement, then licked his face, confirming once again that dogs are smarter than people. And way cuter.

After giving him a doggy grin, Tuffie turned and ran toward where the rest of the Pack was hanging out at the far end of the compound, happily barking the entire way.

"That was incredibly adorable," Hale said. "But it brings me back to my original question. Why aren't you home right now instead of hanging out with us? You could be spending your free time with Kat, helping her reintegrate into the land of walking on two legs if nothing else."

"And before you answer that," Trevor added,

watching Tuffie follow their teammates around the obstacle course, "I should probably tell you that we know you and Kat are sleeping together now. Her scent is all over you."

"Speak for yourself, dude," Hale said with a chuckle. "I had no idea you two had gotten together. In fact, I got the feeling you were attempting to keep Kat at arm's length for some dumb reason. What changed?"

Connor opened his mouth to answer but then closed it again, unsure of what to say. "I honestly don't know what changed. I've been trying so hard to maintain my distance from her, but I guess I got tired of fighting it."

Complete silence settled over the compound at that. He looked up to see that everyone out on the obstacle course and the rappelling building had stopped what they were doing and were looking expectantly at him. That was the obvious drawback to working with a pack of werewolves who could hear a penny hit the grass on the far side of a football field. Especially when dealing with a particularly nosy pack of werewolves.

After he glared at them for a while, his teammates turned their attention back to what they were doing. Not down with the idea of continuing his conversation with Trevor and Hale out here in the open, he jerked his head toward the training building, then headed in that direction.

Once inside, Hale immediately made a beeline

for the boxes of donuts on the conference room table. They'd been rifled through, and Connor heard his pack mate mutter something about people always eating the cream-filled donuts first and leaving behind the plain and the stupid sprinkle-covered ones. The complaint didn't stop him from grabbing one of them though.

"You obviously like Kat," Trevor said, picking up their conversation where they'd left off. "Hell, I think we all know it's gone way beyond *liking* her. There isn't a person on this compound that doesn't know she's *The One* for you."

The One was that one special person supposedly out there in the world for each and every werewolf who could accept them for who they were—fangs, claws, and all.

For years, everyone in the Pack thought the whole thing was an urban legend until Gage stumbled across *The One* for him two years ago, proving the myth true. Since then, one pack mate after another had found the person they'd spend the rest of their lives with. That was twelve soul mates in the past two years.

As each of his friends found *The One* for them, Connor couldn't deny hoping there'd be someone for him someday. At the same time, he'd been terrified he'd be the one wolf in the Pack left out.

"You're right. And I *am* crazy about her," he said. "Why wouldn't I be? She's beautiful, graceful, smells like a dream, and is strong as hell. The crap she's been through would destroy most people ten times over. But she keeps getting up every time she gets knocked down. And yeah, I think it's obvious she's my soul mate."

"Great, so you're capable of seeing what's right in front of your face," Trevor said. "But if that's the case, why do I get the feeling you're fighting this thing between you and Kat?"

"Because it's complicated," he growled.

He knew that sounded lame, but there was no other way he could think to describe it.

"Doesn't seem all that complicated to me," Hale murmured, most of his attention focused on flicking the yellow, pink, and white sprinkles off a chocolate-covered donut. Apparently blue, red, and green sprinkles were acceptable since he wasn't bothering with them. "She's great, you're hot for her, and you're soul mates. What's the problem?"

"I'd like to say that the problem is that I spent nine months giving belly rubs to a furry black cat," he said in exasperation. "That I bought her fresh tuna and cooked her tiny little portions of Wagyu beef night after finicky night. That I laughed along with everyone else when she liked to hang out in the weight room, watching raptly as we worked out. Or maybe the problem is simply that I'm pissed she didn't even try to come up with some way to tell me that she was a woman trapped in a cat's body."

"But?" Trevor prompted impatiently, looking like he thought Connor was being a moron. Which was entirely possible.

Connor sighed. "But that would be a lie. The real reason I'm fighting this thing with Kat is that I'm falling like a rock, and she doesn't even have a week left before she turns back into a cat again. And if I'm being totally honest, I don't think I can handle seeing my soul mate turn into a cat, knowing she'll be trapped like that for another year."

"You haven't even talked to Davina yet," Hale pointed out. "You don't think she'll be able to help?"

"She might," Connor said, though his first thought was pointing out that Kat had been trying to find some way to stop turning into a cat for four years and had all but given up. "But what if she can't? What do I do then? Just stand there and watch her run around the compound on four legs so I can have a few days a year with her?"

Trevor crossed his arms over his chest with a scowl. "So what are you going to do? Turn your back on the best thing you've ever had because it's not enough for you?"

Connor stared at his teammates. He'd expected some supportive words out of them, not anger. His inner wolf bared its teeth even as it whimpered in anguish. "What the hell do you expect me to do? What *can* I do?"

"You can hold on tight to every second you're

given like it's all you're ever going to have," Trevor said firmly. "And you fight with everything you have for more."

Connor didn't say anything. That all sounded well and good, but he knew deep down that all he was doing was setting himself up for one hell of a heartbreak. More than he could live through. Because while everyone in the Pack had been dreaming about finding *The One* for them, none of them had ever thought about what it would mean to lose them.

———

"I don't need all these clothes," Kat complained, looking at the three pairs of jeans and as many tees, a flirty sleeveless dress, a pair of strappy black sandals, a set of pink sweats, running shoes, underwear, and even some sexy lingerie she, Rachel, and Khaki were holding in their arms as they stood in one of the department stores in the fancy Galleria Mall. "I'll be back in my feline form in less than a week, and then all of this will be a waste of money."

"Don't say that! There has to be a way to fix this," Rachel said, her expression so desolate and sad that it was all Kat could do not to cry. "You're a witch. Isn't there something you can do to stop the change and break the spell?"

Kat took two pairs of jeans from Khaki's arms and

put them back on the rack, then studied the sandals dangling from Rachel's fingers, debating whether she should forget about them, too. They were cute but not very practical. Neither was the lingerie. When would she even have a chance to wear them between now and turning back into a cat?

And yet, she couldn't help thinking about how much Connor would enjoy seeing her in them. She smiled a little as she imagined the way his eyes would glow gold when he saw her in the cute dress and sandals, his eyes blazing to full brightness when they were in his bedroom and she was wearing nothing but the sexy lingerie.

But then reality intruded and reminded her that fantasies like those would only set her up for heartbreak.

"I've been trying to come up with a way to break this spell for four years," she said quietly. "I've read hundreds of ancient grimoires, talked to dozens of witches and warlocks, and even tracked down a few other supernatural magic users. It always came down to the same answer. Marko's magic locked me in this torturous cycle of human and familiar, and it will have to be his magic that releases me."

Rachel and Khaki didn't bother asking if that was a possibility. The answer was obvious. Kat was trapped in this vicious cycle for the rest of her life—or until Marko caught her and she became his permanently mindless familiar.

"What are you going to do about Connor?" Khaki asked as she took the two pairs of jeans off the rack and draped them over her arm.

Kat would have protested, but Rachel and Khaki were already heading to the checkout counter. They were both so stubborn.

"What do you mean?" Kat asked when she caught up to them.

"You're already sleeping with him," Khaki said. "Does he realize your...condition...can't be cured?"

The woman behind the counter tallying up Kat's purchases tried to hide the fact that she was eavesdropping, but it was impossible to miss the way her eyes kept curiously darting to them.

Kat didn't say anything as Rachel put everything on her credit card. Knowing Rachel was paying for the stuff made Kat feel horrible, but there was nothing she could do about it. She hadn't owned a wallet, credit card, or driver's license for four years. It was like she didn't exist. Well, as a human, at least. Which was technically true for fiftysome weeks out of the year.

The cashier took her time folding the clothes and slipping them into shopping bags, probably hoping she'd hear a little more about the man Kat was sleeping with and her *condition*. But Kat didn't feel like sharing with a complete stranger, so she remained silent. Much to the cashier's obvious disappointment.

Once they were out of the store and heading toward the food court—because it had been at least two hours since Rachel and Khaki had eaten, and they were already hungry again—she finally decided to answer Khaki's question.

"Connor and I only slept together for the first time yesterday," she said, leaving out the part about making love several more times throughout the day and into the night, then again this morning. "And yes, he's fully aware that I don't have a lot of time left in my human form. That's kind of why we ended up in bed together. It's probably naive, but I'm trying to stay focused on the present and let the future take care of itself."

Neither of her friends said anything, keeping their thoughts to themselves as they reached the fast-food chicken restaurant. Rachel put in the order for three chicken sandwiches with waffle fries on the side. Kat was definitely going to miss fries when she went back to her cat form. Nobody would ever give her fries when she was four-legged and furry. They thought they weren't good for her. And ketchup? Forget about it. There'd been times over the past four years that she'd actually dreamed about lapping up a bowl of ketchup. That told her how much she'd missed it.

"You really like Connor, don't you?" Rachel asked when they sat at a booth in the far corner of the food court.

Kat dunked a fry in ketchup and nibbled on it thoughtfully. "Would you think I'm weird if I admit I fell in love with Connor the moment I met him back when I was a cat? He smelled so good and looked so damn sexy in all that tactical gear. And when he started scratching behind my ears, I knew he was a keeper."

Her friends laughed.

"Hard to go wrong with a man who knows how to scratch that special itch," Khaki said, pausing to take a bite of her sandwich. "How's he at giving belly rubs? That's the true test of a good man."

"Absolutely divine," Kat admitted. "He could probably be a licensed massage therapist if he wanted. Not that I'd let him touch another person's belly, of course. Or anywhere else for that matter."

"Of course not," Rachel murmured with a smile.

As Kat ate, she caught Rachel and Khaki glancing covertly at each other, making it impossible to miss the fact there was something they wanted to talk about.

"Go ahead and say whatever you're thinking," she said with a sigh. "I can tell there's something on your minds."

"Do you think Connor could be your soul mate?" Khaki asked. "I know you heard us talking enough on the subject over the past nine months to recognize the signs. Is there any chance at all that Connor is *The One* for you?"

That question probably should have provoked some kind of denial on her part. There'd been times after she'd heard the endless conversations around the Pack about what it felt like to find your soul mate when she wondered if it was even possible for a cat to develop that kind of bond with a werewolf.

There had also been times when she'd tried to convince herself that the connection she felt with Connor was nothing more than an addiction to his belly rubs. Or maybe she simply appreciated how he'd go out of his way to serve her perfectly prepared beef or seafood every night. In the end though, long before she'd transitioned back into her human form, she'd come to accept none of that was true.

"I have no doubt that we're soul mates," she admitted softly. "I think I've known for months. Unfortunately, I'm not sure it matters."

"What do you mean by that?" Rachel demanded. "How can it not matter? If you two are soul mates and meant to be together, isn't that the most important thing ever?"

Kat dunked another fry in ketchup but didn't eat it right away. "Okay, yes, it matters, all right? But even if Connor and I accept that we're soul mates, what's going to happen in a week when I turn into a cat again and stay that way for the next eleven months? Connor may be able to go through that once or twice, but is he going to be okay with that for the rest of our lives? How is that even fair to him?

Constantly forcing him to put his life on hold for most of the year while I pad around his apartment shedding on the carpet would be a cruel torture. Do I have the right to put him through that kind of pain? Do I want to put myself through that?"

"But—" Khaki started, before Kat held up her hand.

"And there's something else to consider," she added. "Marko. That man is an evil, vindictive jackass who is seriously powerful. You weren't there, Khaki, but I'm sure Rachel told you what it was like fighting those witches and warlocks at that farmhouse and how they went through your pack mates like a hot knife through butter. But as scary as that might sound, Marko makes the rest of his coven look like a class of preschoolers. He's that much more powerful than the rest. And if he gets his hands on me, he'll become even stronger. So strong that no one in the world could stop him."

"But—" Khaki began, only to have Kat cut her off again.

"By now Marko knows I'm in Dallas in human form. I have no idea what he's doing here, but if he thinks he can finish the familiar binding spell, he won't hesitate to do it. And if that means tearing his way through Connor and every other member of your pack, he won't think twice about it. In fact, if he discovers Connor and I are together, it's almost a guarantee he'll go out of his way to hurt him to get back at me for getting in the way of his plans."

Rachel frowned. "You make it sound like you've already decided to give up and leave Dallas before we even try to stop this jerk. Before you even consider if there might be a future with Connor."

Kat let out a heavy sigh. "The thought has crossed my mind. Keeping Marko from getting any stronger than he is already might be the best I can do when it comes to helping everyone. There's a chance if I run, he'll come after me and give up whatever crazy scheme he has going with those kids. That helps everyone—the kids, Connor, you and Khaki, the whole pack. It may be the only way I can protect everyone I care about."

Khaki reached out to take Kat's hand and hold on tight. "You can't just run away, not without talking to Connor about it first. If you two are soul mates and you leave, it will rip him apart. You can't do that to him."

Kat knew that Khaki was right, but she couldn't imagine having that kind of conversation with him, especially not when she'd already fallen in love with him. The fact that she loved him only firmed her resolve. She refused to let the man she loved get hurt.

"I can't make any promises," she said. "Except to say that I'll talk to him before I do anything drastic."

CHAPTER 14

KAT WAS MAKING DINNER WHEN SHE HEARD Connor let himself into the apartment. It was sloppy joes and a tossed salad, and nearly everything had come out of a bag or a can, but at least she'd browned the ground beef by herself. After everything he'd done for her, she wanted to do something special for him.

"Mmm. Something smells good," Connor said.

She glanced over her shoulder to see him standing near the peninsula that separated the kitchen from the living room, his gaze fastened on her butt. She was wearing a tee and the yoga pants she'd gotten at the mall, and she had to admit that seeing him looking at her like that made the hassle of shopping worth it.

"It's only some sloppy joes," Kat said, laughing as she attempted to focus on her cooking and not the naughty thoughts Connor's scrutiny had provoked. "It smells good but not *that* good."

"Who said I was talking about the food?" Connor murmured, his low, rumbling voice having an even greater effect on her than his gaze. "You know, you didn't have to make dinner," he said. "We could have ordered takeout."

Slipping up behind her, he tried to sneak a finger

into the beef mixture in the frying pan. She playfully slapped his hand away before he could get near the food. "One, you haven't washed yet, and two, I wanted to do something nice to repay you for everything you've done for me. Not just over the past couple days, but also when I was a cat. I tend to remember using your pants leg as a scratching post quite a few times."

He reached out to brush her hair over her shoulder with a smile. "Don't ever think like you have to repay me for anything. And feel free to use me as your scratching post anytime you like."

His words conjured up images of how she'd scratched him yesterday and last night, while in the throes of lovemaking, when she'd given into that irresistible urge to mark him and claim him for herself. The scratches she'd made hadn't seemed to bother him at all, mostly because they'd healed up and disappeared within minutes.

"Why don't you go get cleaned up while I finish cooking?" she said, nudging him with her hip. "And hurry up about it. Dinner will be ready in a few minutes, and I know you're hungry."

"I'm always hungry," Connor quipped in a sexy growl as he headed for his bedroom, making Kat wonder if he was talking about food or sex. Considering he was a werewolf, it was probably both.

Kat heard the shower turn on while she was busy toasting up the burger buns and getting the rest of the salad put together. The distraction served to cool her down a bit, and her thoughts strayed to the conversation she'd had with Rachel and Khaki earlier. The one where she'd talked about walking away from Connor to keep him and the rest of the Pack safe. At the time, that had sounded so easy. But now that she was with him, she realized it would be much more difficult than she'd thought. And talking to him about it first would be damn near impossible.

She had everything ready and on the small table in the kitchen by the time Connor came out of the shower. He was wearing shorts and a T-shirt again. And yeah, they still looked good on him.

"How was your shopping excursion with Rachel and Khaki?" he asked, slipping into the chair opposite her and picking up his glass of iced tea. "Get everything you need?"

"More than I needed actually," she admitted. She told him how she'd tried to get Rachel and Khaki to understand that she didn't need so many clothes. "Since...well...I won't be wearing them for much longer."

That announcement sucked the fun right out of the room, and while Kat knew it needed to be said, that didn't mean she enjoyed saying it. She hated seeing the light of happiness dim so drastically in Connor's eyes.

An uncomfortable silence filled the kitchen as

they started eating. Kat realized there'd never been one uncomfortable moment between them before, not even after she'd chased his dates out of the house by hissing at them and shredding the clothes they wore with her nails. But it was awkward now because she'd reminded him that she'd be a cat again in a few days.

She played with her salad, considering whether she should drop the other shoe and bring up the idea of leaving Dallas before Marko could catch up to her. But as she opened her mouth, Connor spoke, the words rushed and his voice uncharacteristically nervous. Which was another first.

"I was talking to Gage today. He mentioned your situation to a supernatural expert that we lean on now and then. Her name's Davina and she's a witch. She's already looking into what Marko might be up to, and I thought maybe she could help you, too."

"Help me?" she echoed, her fork halfway to her mouth, not sure where this was going. "Help how?"

He looked down at his plate. "Well, I was hoping you could talk to her and, maybe between the two of you, come up with some way to beat this familiar spell so you don't have to turn back into a cat. Not that I don't like you as a cat. It's just…you know?"

"Yeah. I get it," she said softly, putting her fork back in her bowl and playing with her salad again. "And if it means anything, I would definitely prefer to be human instead of a cat."

Connor lifted his gaze to hers, his expression hopeful. "So you'll talk to her?"

"Definitely. I'll call her later," she said. "But it's unlikely that Davina will be able to come up with some magical answer to this thing. Unfortunately, magic doesn't work that way."

"I don't understand," he said, looking so confused and lost that her heart spasmed in her chest. "If magic did this to you, can't magic fix it?"

"In theory, yes, magic could fix it," she said, wishing it were that easy. "But in reality, with the binding spell Marko put on me, there are only two people in the world who'd be able to break it— him or me. He's obviously not going to do it, and with the majority of my magical gift inaccessible, it doesn't seem like I'll ever be able to do it, either."

Connor frowned. "Maybe I don't understand how magic works, but what's so special about this binding spell Marko used on you? Why can't someone like Davina be the one to fix it? And how can you say your magic is inaccessible, especially after the way you stopped that wall of fire Tatum Graves tried to kill me with? It was amazing."

Kat ate a few bites of salad, chewing slowly as she tried to come up with the best way to explain it.

"To understand what Marko did to me and how I stopped that wall of fire, you first need to realize that witches and warlocks don't create or possess magic," she said, using the same words her grandma had said to her so long ago. "When I say Marko is stronger than I am—stronger than anyone—it's not because he's carrying around this huge stash of magic in his back pocket that he can whip out and throw around whenever he wants. It's because he's more naturally gifted at channeling magic. Does that make sense?"

Connor took a big bite of his sloppy joe, chewing thoughtfully When he was done, he shook his head. "Nope, not even a little."

"Okay, let's back up," she said, nibbling on her own sloppy joe. "Remember what I said in Addy's room about magic being all around us and in every living thing? That's the magic that witches and warlocks normally use to do their spells, charms, hexes, and curses. There's natural magic in me, too, but that's not the magic that any sane witch would want to use. You can, but it's never a good idea to drain your own core because it can kill you. That's why I was so exhausted after the fight at the farmhouse. I was so tired from everything that has happened to me over the past few days that I had no choice but to use some of my own magic to fight Marko's people. Especially when it came to stopping Tatum and his fire."

"You could have died from that?" Connor asked, eyes wide in alarm.

She smiled. "Relax. I'm smart enough to know when to stop. I was able to pull back before I got too weak. But back to what I was saying about using the living magic that's all around us. That's what a magic user does. They simply tap into the magic around them. We draw it in, refocus it for our own purposes, and then send it back out. The only difference between someone as powerful as Marko and me is how much of the living magic we can take in and then send back out. How much we can channel. Get it now?"

"I think so," he said slowly. "But I still don't understand what any of this has to do with the binding spell Marko used on you or why your magic is inaccessible."

Tears formed at the corners of her eyes as Connor's question forced her to replay the memories of what had happened to her and her coven, and she quickly looked down at her plate before he could see.

"The ritual Marko used on my coven sisters ripped the gift from their cores and their ability to channel magic and gave it to me," she explained softly. "He was going to make me into this super conduit for magic, which would allow me to channel more of it than any human has ever been capable of, then bind me to him as a feline familiar. He would then be able to access that power through me, while I'd be trapped and bound to him forever."

"But he wasn't able to finish the ritual, right?" Connor said, looking concerned and worried all over again. "You got away before he could finish the binding part of the spell."

She nodded. "Yeah. I was able to get away before he finished the binding part of the ritual. The spell he used to hold me down to the altar was made for a human. When he turned me into a cat, the spell loosened long enough for me to slip out a paw and smudge the ritual circle. Everything unraveled after that. I used the distraction to slip out of the circle and run."

"But?" he asked slowly, apparently picking up on the fact that there was more to the story than she was letting on.

She let out a sigh. "But while Marko wasn't able to bind me to him as a familiar, he was able to block a good portion of my channeling gift. He'd done that early in the ritual, afraid that I'd somehow find a way to channel magic from inside the circle and screw everything up. Truthfully, I think he was terrified that once he'd sacrificed my coven sisters and given their channeling gifts to me, I'd be able to turn all that power on him. So he controlled the amount of magic I could channel to little more than a trickle. And since I broke free and ran before the ritual was over, he never had a chance to reopen the channel."

"But the things I've seen you do..." Connor said, still plainly confused.

"I've learned to be extremely efficient with the

limited amount of magic I can access so I'm not help-less, but don't mistake that for anything more than it is—me doing the best I can with a bad situation. I can only tap into a fraction of the power I could before the ritual and none of the power that should be mine now due to the addition of my coven's gifts."

"So Davina won't be able to help then?" he asked.

The hopelessness in that question almost made her lie to him simply to make him smile again. But she knew that would be wrong and would only bring him more pain later.

"I'll talk to her," Kat promised, reaching over to take his hand. "But I don't expect much to come out of it. If there were a way to break the binding or help me access more of my gift, I think I would have found it over the years. But who knows? Maybe I'll get lucky, and she will be able to help me."

That part seemed to offer at least some consola-tion to Connor, which is why she'd said it in the first place, and soon both of them went back to eating, the tone lighter now, especially as he continued to praise her cooking skills. That made her smile.

After they finished dinner and loaded the dish-washer, she thought they might sit on the couch for a while and watch some TV, but instead Connor took her hands in his and turned her to face him.

"I'm not sure if it was the shopping or maybe you're still worn out from the fight at the farmhouse, but you should get more rest," he said, his eyes full of concern again. "I'm down with turning in early if you are?"

Kat nodded. She'd never pass up a chance to cuddle in the bed with Connor. For one quick moment, she considered wearing the ridiculous lingerie her friends had insisted she buy, but then she chickened out and went with a tee and a pair of panties instead.

She barely got the blanket on the bed turned down before Connor came in from the bathroom.

Once in bed, Connor pulled her back against his chest, wrapping his arm protectively around her. She wiggled back against him, smiling to herself as she felt him harden against her butt. Knowing he wouldn't start anything because he was too concerned about her getting some sleep, she took the lead. Skimming her panties down over her hips, she reached back to caress his hard-on.

Connor took over from there, sliding his hand under her T-shirt to tease her nipples for a little while before running that same hand down her stomach to rub her clit. She was already wet and ready but sure wasn't going to complain as he teased her some more.

He paused long enough to grab another condom from the nightstand, somehow able to put the thing on with one hand. If she weren't so interested in what was coming next, she might have asked where he'd picked up that particular talent, but right then, she couldn't find the energy to care.

Connor moved up behind her again, his chest pressing against her back as he teased her with his cock, sliding in just a little and then withdrawing.

"How many times have I told you not to tease me?" she asked, groaning in frustration.

He chuckled but took pity on her, one hand squeezing her hip in a tight grip as he slid in deep. She'd never made love in this position but quickly decided it was the most beautiful and erotic thing she'd ever experienced. He gently glided in and out, touching her in the most delicious places, while his warm hand wandered all over the place. Her thighs, her stomach, her breasts, up into her hair. When his fingertips slipped down between her legs to tweak her clit in that mesmerizing rhythm, she thought she could stay like this forever. Then he started nuzzling her neck with that clever mouth of his, and she was sure there could never be anything more perfect than this in the world.

They took their time making love—oh so much time—and when they finally climaxed together, Kat imagined this must be what heaven was like.

Even if there was a voice whispering in the back of her head that she shouldn't get used to it, for the time being she chose to ignore that warning, taking this one moment of happiness and holding on to it as hard as she could.

CHAPTER 15

WHEN CONNOR HEARD THE SOFT KNOCK AT THE door, he was tempted to ignore it. The tapping was too timid to be anyone from the Pack, and if he left the stove now, the omelets he was making for breakfast would almost certainly burn. When the knock came again, he leaned out a little way from the stove, trying to put some distance between him and all those scrumptious peppers and onions sizzling in the frying pan so he could get a sniff of whoever was out there. But before he could, Kat was walking across the living room, heading for the door.

"I got it," she called over her shoulder even as Connor had an urge to tell her to check the peephole before opening it. Like she was a kid.

The sound of popping grease forced him to turn his attention back to the eggs, making him miss the door opening. He heard Kat's welcoming voice, then a murmured response so low and timid that even his werewolf ears couldn't clearly make it out. But as he picked up the visitor's scent, he decided he recognized it from somewhere. It was right on the tip of his tongue.

Or the tip of his nose maybe.

He quickly finished the omelet in the pan, flipped it over without making too much of a mess, then added it to the plate warming in the oven along with the first one he'd made. He walked into the living room and almost fell over when he saw his sister standing there with an amused and somewhat bewildered expression on her face. A little shorter than Kat, with long, wavy blond hair, she was wearing distressed jeans and a graphic print tee.

"Jenna?" he said in surprise. "What are you doing here?"

His heart clenched in his chest as his sister winced and took half a step back, the almost happy look she had on her face while talking to Kat instantly disappearing to be replaced with hurt. Wanting to make up for the slight, even if unintended, Connor stepped forward and swept his sister up in a big hug, hoping she'd accept that he was happy to see her, even if he'd been caught a bit off guard.

"Sorry. That came out all wrong," he apologized, picking her up off the floor a little as he hugged her. "You know I'm thrilled to see you, right? It's been a while."

Jenna whacked his shoulder until he put her down, but when he did, it was to see her smiling again. That was something at least. He liked to see Jenna smile—she didn't do it often.

"Yeah, it has been a while," she complained.

"But whose fault is that? You never come to visit me anymore."

He opened his mouth to apologize again because Jenna was absolutely correct. The truth was that he'd been avoiding a trip out to California to see her for a long time now. But before he got the words out, he caught sight of Kat standing there.

"Oh, I guess I should make introductions," he murmured, a comment that earned him a clear and obvious nonverbal *no duh* from Kat.

"You probably already figured it out, but this is Jenna, my sister."

Connor flourished his hands toward Jenna as he spoke, making claw gestures behind her back and then shaking his head so that Kat would realize his sister had no idea he was a werewolf. Kat seemed to figure it out quickly enough but continued to look his way expectantly. It took a second for him to realize she was waiting for him to finish the introductions. Unfortunately, he was somewhat confused when it came to introducing the woman he'd been sleeping with for the past couple days. What if he said the wrong thing and ended up offending her?

"Jenna, this is Kat," he started confidently, forcing himself to finish strong as he looked over at Kat. "My girlfriend. We've been seeing each other for a while."

Connor wasn't sure who looked more stunned, Kat or his sister. Both were staring at him wide-eyed.

Crap, had he just messed up by calling Kat his girl-friend? But it felt like she was, regardless of the weird place they were in right now.

"Glad you've finally accepted what everyone else already knew," a voice said from outside the still-open door. Connor turned to see Trevor standing there, a big grin on his face. "It took you long enough."

Kat's mouth curved into a teasing smile. "I think we'll all agree that he's always been a little slow picking up on things. Look how long it took him to see the real me."

Connor would have complained about that slam, but then he realized Jenna was still standing there looking kind of shell-shocked.

"You're in a relationship, and you never even mentioned her?" his sister demanded.

"In his defense," Trevor said before Connor could answer, turning to Jenna with a charming expression that immediately put Connor's hackles up, "I'll be the first to admit that their relationship is a little complicated. By the way, I'm Trevor McCall. I don't think we've met."

Alarm bells immediately started ringing as Connor realized his teammate—his *pack mate*—was flirting with his sister. His fangs and claws threatened to come out when Jenna extended her hand and slowly shook Trevor's, a smile crossing her face as she introduced herself. What the hell did Trevor think he was doing? He had to know Jenna was off-limits—to everyone!

"You're a lot prettier than Connor," Trevor pointed out, all suave and smooth. "Are you sure you're related to him?"

Jenna giggled. She frigging *giggled*. And blushed. His sister had no business blushing for anyone, especially not one of his teammates.

"So, Jenna," Connor cut in, glaring at his pack mate. "You never did say what you're doing in Dallas. Did work bring you out here?"

Connor doubted that. Jenna was a special-effects artist out in LA. The company she worked for did a lot of stuff in the movie industry, but unless someone was coming to Dallas to film a zombie apocalypse movie or something, there was no chance that was the answer.

"Why does there have to be a reason?" his sister asked, sounding a little defensive. "Can't it be as simple as a girl missing her brother and wanting to spend some time with him?"

"Yeah, of course," Connor answered, stepping forward to hug her again, even though he didn't buy a single word of what she said. There was something else going on, only he wasn't sure what it was. Knowing his sister, she wouldn't tell him until she was ready.

Before he could say anything else, Trevor's phone started making noise, his ringtone a car engine revving. The sound was irritating as crap, in Connor's opinion.

"McCall," Trevor said, putting the phone to his ear.

With his werewolf hearing, Connor could have eavesdropped on the conversation easily if he wanted to, but Jenna was regarding him with a curious expression that changed his mind.

"So how did you and Kat meet?" she asked. "And why haven't you mentioned her when we talked on the phone?"

"We actually ran into each other at one of his crime scenes," Kat said, throwing a smile Connor's way. "He looked so sexy in all that tactical gear that I couldn't help but follow him home like a little lost kitten. And once I'd sunk my claws in, he couldn't shake me. Not that he tried very hard. He's a sucker for a cute kitty."

He knew Kat was taunting him, her smile broadening as his sister started getting all emotional and dewy about how romantic their meeting had been.

As Trevor hung up and came over to join them, Connor couldn't miss the way his buddy's gaze tracked toward Jenna or the way that both of them smiled at each other. Now that crap was gonna have to stop—ASAP!

"I know now probably isn't a good time for this, but that was Rachel," Trevor said, turning his attention to Connor. "There's been another kidnapping, this time in full daylight, with witnesses. We need to get over there."

Connor hated to leave Jenna when she'd only just gotten there, but on the upside, at least it would get her away from Trevor. His pack mate was displaying way too much interest in his sister.

"Jenna, I'm sorry, but we have to take off," he said. "We're working a case involving some missing kids."

"Kids?" His sister waved her hand. "Oh my gosh! Don't apologize. Go do your job. I'll hang out here with Kat and convince her to spill all your embarrassing secrets."

That provoked an uncomfortable silence before Connor realized it would be up to him to say something. "Actually, Kat needs to come with us on this one. She's been consulting on this case. But you're welcome to hang out here. I just put some omelets in the oven to stay warm, along with bacon."

She smiled. "Well, I happen to remember how good your omelets are, so I certainly don't mind eating them."

"Okay, great," Connor murmured, getting that out of the way at least. "I honestly am sorry for having to bail on you. I have no idea how long this is going to take, so if you want, I can come by whatever hotel you're staying at later."

Jenna got that hurt look on her face again, making Connor wonder what the hell he'd done now. "I was hoping to stay here with you. But if that's too much trouble, I suppose I could find a hotel nearby."

"Definitely not," Kat said, giving Connor a pointed look. "We'd never want you stay in a hotel. You can even take the bed, and we'll use the couch."

His sister's lips curved. "No way am I chasing you guys out of your bed. I'm cool with the couch."

"You could always stay at my place," Trevor suggested. "I have a guest room with a real bed instead of an uncomfortable couch."

"No!" Connor damn near snarled. "She's my sister. She'll stay here with Kat and me."

Trevor ignored him, still looking at Jenna. "I can give you my number in case you change your mind."

She nodded eagerly. "Sure."

Connor bit back a growl as he watched Trevor add his number to his sister's contacts. He and his pack mates might get into scuffles with each other on an almost daily basis, but the thought of seriously hurting any of them had never entered his mind until now.

Before anyone could say anything else that bordered on stupid, Connor motioned for the door. "I'm really sorry to rush this, but we need to go. Kat and I will be back as soon as we can." He gave his teammate a scowl. "Trevor will be busy doing something else, I'm sure."

Connor shoved his pack mate toward the door before Trevor could reply, then stepped back so

Kat could walk out ahead of him. His sister was still telling them to be careful when he closed the door, forcing a sigh from his throat. Something told him that his confusing and complicated life had just taken a turn for the worse.

CHAPTER 16

"WHAT THE HELL WAS ALL THAT ABOUT?" CONNOR demanded the moment the three of them were seated in his truck and headed toward the address Trevor had provided. Kat had seen this coming from a mile away, so she carefully bit her tongue to hold in the laugh threatening to slip out. "Macking on my sister like that, dude? And don't even try to act like you didn't already know that Jenna is off-limits."

"Seriously?" Trevor snorted from the back seat. "Off-limits to who...me?"

"To everyone!" Connor snarled.

Beside him, Kat could tell he was fighting the urge to turn around and rip his teammate's face off. When his claws actually came out, she reached over and rested one of her much smaller hands on his as he gripped the steering wheel so hard, it creaked. She made soft soothing sounds that thankfully seemed to help.

"Connor, relax. It's okay," she said softly. "No one's going to hurt Jenna, especially not Trevor."

"Hurt her?" Trevor said in a shocked voice. "What are you talking about? You don't think I'd actually do anything to hurt your sister, do you? What kind of guy do you think I am?"

Connor didn't respond right away, seemingly content to let Kat's soothing touch calm him a little more. She could practically see the thoughts spinning through his head.

"It's not you," Connor finally said, glancing at Trevor in the rearview mirror. "It's Jenna. You already know what happened to my older sister and what happened to Jenna after Hannah disappeared. I worry that whatever she saw that night has damaged her beyond repair, and I don't think it will help having you mess with her head."

"I'm not messing with her head," Trevor growled. "She's the sister of one of my pack mates. One of my friends. I was being nice to her."

"And if, in her fragile state of mind, Jenna perceives your *being nice* as something more than that? Are you prepared to go further if that's what she thinks she wants? What she needs? Would you leave the Pack and move to LA, the only world she knows and feels comfortable in, if she decided after a few days that she was in love with you? What if you said no and it crushed her? My sister has already dealt with a tremendous amount of loss. She simply can't take anymore."

"I think you're underestimating your sister," Trevor said softly. "The fact that she survived what happened when she was a kid makes me believe she's a lot stronger than you give her credit for."

"Maybe," Connor agreed. "But I lost Hannah ten

years ago, and for all intents and purposes, I lost my parents the same night. As far as I'm concerned, Jenna is the only family I have left, and I can't lose her. You can say I'm being overprotective, but I won't let anyone hurt her. No one."

Connor and Trevor both fell silent after that, and Kat feared she'd just seen the end of their friendship. The two of them might belong to the same pack, but Connor had essentially come out and said Trevor wasn't good enough for his sister. She knew Connor was simply trying to protect Jenna, but words like that had a way of sticking with people for a long time.

When the silence started to get uncomfortable, Kat decided that if she didn't want it to continue, it was going to be up to her to say something.

"Connor and I talked to Davina DeMirci last night, and she said she'll use her contacts at STAT to do a deep dive into each of the kids that Marko kidnapped," Kat said, glancing over her shoulder at Trevor. "Hopefully she can find a connection between them that the rest of us have so far missed."

"We probably should have thought to ask them before now," Trevor said. "STAT has more resources than the DPD ever will, especially if the connection we're looking for is supernatural in nature."

Kat glanced at Connor, hoping he might have something to add to the conversation, but he kept his eyes fixed on the road, acting like he hadn't heard a word that had been said.

"She's also looking closer at the murder in San Antonio," Kat added when it was obvious that her first attempt at building a bridge between Connor and Trevor had failed. "Davina is certain that what happened down there is connected to what we're dealing with here in Dallas. Either as a dry run to what Marko plans to do this time, or maybe some kind of ritual to collect and store magical energy."

"Collect and store magical energy?" Trevor asked, mirroring the same question Connor had asked when he heard the phrase last night. "That sounds ominous. What does it mean?"

"You missed out on one of my earlier lessons on magic," Kat said, remembering that Trevor hadn't been in Addy's room when she talked about this. "Bottom line, magic exists in every living thing, but especially in people. Davina reminded me that there are some rituals—nasty, dark, ugly rituals—that will let a witch or warlock tear that magic out of a person and either use it or store it, at least temporarily. Few witches or warlocks would ever consider trying it because trying to control raw power like that is dangerous as hell, but Marko definitely has the ego to attempt it."

Trevor let out a breath. "That sounds horrifying. What the hell could Marko be planning to do with all this raw power?"

"That's the million-dollar question," Connor said, finally joining the conversation. "We talked about it for over an hour with Davina and still didn't come up with anything concrete."

Kat was glad to see that Connor was willing to talk to Trevor again, and the three of them spent the next few minutes of the drive going through different what-if scenarios concerning what Marko might be up to. But after a while, it became clear they were all simply making crap up. The truth was, all they really knew for sure about Marko was that he was a psychopath. The idea that they could even guess what someone like him was planning was ludicrous.

When they'd reached the address Trevor had given them, there were loads of police cars, ambulances, fire trucks, and media vans parked along the street in front of the apartment building. The exterior walls on one of the upper floors had been ripped away, exposing the rooms beyond. Smoke still slowly rolled out of several places, and broken glass, bricks, and concrete rubble littered the street and sidewalk. It looked like the scene of a terrorist attack.

"What the hell happened here?" Connor asked as he tried to find a place to park, eventually turning around and pulling up on the curb about a quarter mile from the damaged building.

"According to what Rachel told me when she called, Franklin Gutierrez went into his daughter's bedroom on the sixth floor this morning to tell her breakfast was ready, only to find Anabella trying to climb out the window," Trevor said as they got out of the truck. "When he tried to pull her back in, she fought, much harder than a petite fifteen-year-old should have been able to do."

"How did we go from a girl fighting her father to the building getting blown up?" Kat asked as they approached the crime scene and got waved through. But before anyone could answer, she stopped in her tracks when they reached the debris along the front of the apartment.

"What's wrong?" Connor asked.

She didn't answer right away, instead closing her eyes to take in the chaotic flows of the magic all around the building. When she opened them again, it was to find Connor and Trevor looking at her expectantly.

"A tremendous amount of magical energy was released out here," she murmured softly so no one else would hear. "There were at least six of them down here waiting, and when the girl didn't come out the window like they wanted her to, they pulled half the building apart to bring her out themselves."

"Damn," Connor whispered, looking up at the inspection crews and firefighters crawling through several of the apartments above them. "What the hell was so special about this one girl that they were willing to do this in broad daylight?"

Kat didn't have an answer to that question as they slipped inside the building and made their way up to one of the stairwells, weaving their way around all the firefighters and paramedics still helping people out of the building.

The Gutierrez apartment looked like a bomb had gone off in it, with walls caved in or missing and whole sections of the floor and ceiling gone. Detective Sandoval was in the kitchen talking to the chief of police, Shanette Leclair. If an apartment complex that looked like it had been blown to hell wasn't a sure enough sign that the situation was bad, then having Chief Leclair there sure was. Kat didn't miss the way the dark-haired woman took note of their presence, especially the curious glance she threw in Kat's direction, followed by the blatant way she purposely turned her attention back to the detective, like she'd never seen them.

After a moment, Rachel and Hale came over along with Detective Sandoval, joining them in the middle of what remained of the living room.

"We got a statement out of the father, but I think it's safe to say that no one is going to follow up on it," Sandoval said, shaking his head. "He seems to be dealing with a severe concussion, though a few of the paramedics think it's PTSD from seeing his daughter fall."

"Humor us," Connor said, crossing his arms over his chest, "with his version of the story."

"Mr. Gutierrez said he had to wrap his arms around his daughter to keep her away from the window, but that she fought him like she was possessed. He practically had to tackle her to the floor keep her from jumping. That's when the story went off the rails."

"Meaning?" Trevor prompted.

Detective Sandoval hesitated, looking from Trevor to the rest of them in turn, like he was afraid to even say the next part out loud for fear of them telling him he was crazy.

"Because that's when the walls of the apartment were ripped away, and a tall, slim man wearing a long, black cloak floated inside the room, threw Mr. Gutierrez aside with a flick of his finger, and then took Annabella away with him."

Sandoval paused again, as if he expected them to start laughing.

They didn't.

"Did Mr. Gutierrez happen to mention what this man looked like?" Kat asked, though she was sure she already knew.

The detective eyed Kat, likely wondering who she was and why she was there in the first place. The man glanced at Connor, then Trevor and Rachel, but when none of them said anything, he must have decided he could answer.

Sandoval glanced at his little flip notebook before answering. "Six three or six four, maybe a hundred and ninety pounds. Pale skin and long, straight, black hair tied back with a piece of leather. Dark eyes."

Kat had been expecting this answer, and yet she still felt her stomach clench. "It's him," she whispered. "Marko."

Connor and his pack mates didn't seem surprised by her announcement. Kat knew she shouldn't have been shocked, either. When she'd seen those witches and warlocks at the farmhouse, especially Tatum Graves, it was clear Marko was involved in all of this. But even knowing all that, there'd been a part of her hoping she was wrong. That maybe Tatum had struck out on his own. That would have still been bad, but not nearly as terrifying as facing Marko again.

"Gutierrez wasn't making that stuff up, was he?" Detective Sandoval asked softly, looking around the destroyed apartment as if seeing it for the first time. "This guy he saw really floated up here and kidnapped that girl?"

Kat expected Trevor to answer, since he seemed to have the best relationship with the detective from the Missing Persons Unit. If not Trevor, then Connor, for sure. When neither of them said anything, Kat decided it was up to her instead.

"No," she said simply. "He wasn't making it up."

Detective Sandoval didn't seem to know what to say to that. He looked at Connor and his SWAT teammates like he was praying one of them would come out and say this was all a joke.

"Can you guys do anything about someone like that?" he finally asked when no one spoke up to spare him the discomfort of knowing the truth.

"We're going to try," Connor promised quietly.

The detective nodded, then walked back over to talk to the chief. Kat doubted the man would say anything to her about what they'd told him. Everyone would consider him as mad as the missing girl's father.

"Not wanting to seem too pessimistic here, but *can* we actually do something about someone like Marko?" Hale asked. "I mean, the man can apparently fly. And we didn't exactly fare too well against the ones who stayed on the ground."

Connor shrugged. "I guess we'll find out. Because one way or the other, I think we're going to be running into him sooner rather than later."

Kat wandered into the rubble that used to be Anabella's bedroom, making it seem like she wanted to search for clues. In reality, she didn't want them to see her face. Because they'd almost certainly see that she didn't think they had a snowball's chance in hell of standing up against Marko.

CHAPTER 17

"I COULDN'T HELP BUT NOTICE HOW SHAKEN YOU were when you realized the man Sandoval was describing was Marko," Connor said as they climbed the steps up to his apartment after spending hours at the latest crime scene with absolutely nothing to show for it. "You want to talk about it?"

When Kat didn't answer right away, Connor found his thoughts turning back to the chaos they'd left behind at the apartment building. While the official story the department was putting out suggested Anabella had gone missing when the walls of the apartment had collapsed due to some undefined structural defect, Connor knew that wasn't going to hold up for long. He only hoped they'd have Anabella and the other teens back safe and sound before then.

"I guess it caught me a little off guard," Kat finally said as she moved ahead of him on the stairs. "It's one thing knowing his coven is in town and another to realize that Marko is here and taking a personal interest in kidnapping these poor kids. He's not usually one to get his hands dirty doing grunt work. He usually likes to show up for the endgame when all the blood is being spilled. The fact that he was at the apartment building and went up to grab Anabella himself tells me that whatever he has planned is huge and extremely important to him."

Wonderful.

"If it weren't for all these kidnappings, I'd think Marko was in town to finish what he started with me," she added. "But it doesn't seem that way now. With all these kids involved, it definitely feels like this is something else."

When they got to his door, Connor reached for the knob, but Kat put her hand on his arm, stopping him. He looked at her curiously. "What's wrong?"

"Nothing," she said softly. "I just wanted to ask you about something before we go inside."

"What is it?" he asked.

Clearly, it had to be something she didn't want to say in front of his sister, which worried him a bit. What if Kat decided that moving out of the apartment might be best for the duration of Jenna's visit? He could see her suggesting that as a way of helping him and his sister get closer. But Kat only had a few more days left in human form, and he didn't want to waste the time they had.

Kat took a deep breath, like she was planning to tell him something he didn't want to hear. "What you told your sister, about me being your girlfriend. Did you mean that, or was it merely a convenient way of explaining why I'm staying at your place?"

And there it was.

"Yeah, I meant it," he said softly, stepping a little closer to her. "Though I know springing it on you in front of her like that was a crap thing to do. It's just…when I started making the introductions, that was the word that popped into my head. From there, I went with my instincts."

She seemed to consider that for a moment. "So what does that mean for us going forward, knowing that I'm going to be turning back into a cat soon?"

It hurt like hell to hear Kat say those words with such complete certainty, but there was no denying it was the reality she was facing. The reality *they* were facing.

"I don't know," he said honestly. "But I promise that no matter what happens, I won't walk away. I won't abandon you."

Connor realized that wasn't exactly a grand proclamation of undying love, and he couldn't help but notice that Kat hadn't offered any promises of her own in return. But at least the tension visibly eased from her back and shoulders. At this point, it seemed that was the best he could hope for.

Giving her a gentle kiss on the lips, he turned and opened the door. Jenna was in the kitchen, a bottle of disinfectant and a cleaning rag in her hands. As she danced around the kitchen to some song she was humming to, he realized his sister seemed more relaxed than he'd ever seen her. It was a good look on her, but unfortunately not one he'd seen in a long time.

As he closed the door behind him and Kat, he caught sight of a weekender over by the wall near the couch, along with one of those purses that was really more like a small backpack. His sister had obviously brought her stuff up from her rental car, and Connor had to admit to being kind of shocked by how little she'd brought with her. Then again, that was sort of his sister's MO. She liked to maintain a small logistical footprint. That way, she could bail on any situation at a moment's notice.

Jenna jumped a little when she finally saw them, and just like that, the tension was back in her shoulders, the slight smile that had been playing across her lips as she hummed disappearing, and her expression closing off until it was almost blank. The sudden change was jarring, and it was hard to put into words how much it hurt when Connor realized she was happier when he wasn't around. Then again, maybe it was because she had to be someone else around him. Someone she no longer was.

"You two are so quiet, I didn't hear you come in," she said, tossing the cleaning supplies back in the cabinet under the sink, then coming into the living room, a fake smile finding its way onto her face. "Hope you don't mind that I cleaned up a little. I thought I'd keep myself occupied until you came home. I didn't know if you'd have a chance to eat, so I got takeout for dinner. It's in the oven staying warm."

Jenna was putting on a good face, and it hurt even more to see her trying so hard to hide the fact that being in the same room with him obviously made her uncomfortable. It had been like this right after Hannah had gone missing and she'd realized that no one believed anything she had to say. In those early years, she'd been closed off around everyone. He thought she'd gotten past all of that, but now he realized she'd gotten better at hiding it.

"You didn't have to buy dinner for us, but thank you," Kat said, stepping forward to give Jenna a quick hug, which his sister seemed to accept far more readily than Connor would have thought. In his experience, his sister didn't like strangers touching her. Actually, he'd been the only person she'd ever hugged without a fuss.

The table in the kitchen wasn't big enough for the three of them, so they brought plates and all the takeout containers to the coffee table in the living room. Connor felt guilty about his sister paying for all that food. He'd have to remember to pay her back.

"I've learned from Connor's visits out to LA to always order extra," Jenna said, glancing at Kat as she helped herself to some beef and broccoli. "My brother never ate like this when he lived in Los Angeles, but now he eats like a horse. I don't know how he can still stay so fit. I'm jealous."

As he grabbed some sweet and sour chicken, fried rice, and two egg rolls, he realized that the restaurant forgot to give them any sauce. Luckily, he had a wicker basket filled with packets of soy and duck sauce, hot mustard, and chili paste, not to mention condiments from about twenty other local restaurants. Jenna must have been amused because she cracked up at the sight of it.

"Having a basket full of condiments and sauces in your cabinets might be a sign that you order takeout way too often," she said, reaching in for a pack of soy sauce.

"Says the woman who ordered takeout," Connor pointed out, grabbing a few packs of his own.

"Only because I couldn't find any real food in the cabinets. I would have been out of luck if it weren't for all the takeout menus you have tacked to the wall beside your phone," his sister said with a smile that seemed almost genuine. "You two seriously need to go shopping for some real food, especially now that Kat is spending more time at the apartment."

The coy way his sister said it had Connor glancing at her out the corner of his eye to see Jenna making a face at him.

"Bro, I know you said you've been seeing each other for a while, but it doesn't take a genius to figure out that she's started staying here since her toiletries are in the bathroom." His sister's smile was a little more mischievous now. "Plus, she offered to give up your room and volunteered both of you to sleep on the couch, remember?"

He grunted and went back to eating.

"So what happened today with the kid who got kidnapped?" Jenna asked a few minutes later. "Were you able to find who did it?"

Connor shook his head with a sigh. He shouldn't be talking about this stuff with Jenna at all, but after what happened to Hannah, he knew she had a special place in her heart for missing kids, so he knew he had to tell her something that would relieve the worry.

"I can't get into the details of the case," he said. "But unfortunately, no, we haven't found the kid yet. Or any of the kids who have been kidnapped over the past few days. Thanks to Kat, though, at least we have a lead on who took them. We're hoping that gets us somewhere soon."

He thought that answer would put an end to the questions, but it turned out he was wrong. The moment he'd mentioned Kat helping, his sister's face lit up.

"That's right," his sister said, looking at Kat eagerly. "Connor mentioned you're a consultant. Are you a profiler or something?"

"No, nothing like that," Kat started, smiling a little as she threw a glance Connor's way. "The people who kidnapped the kids are part of a group that I had a bad experience with a few years ago. I was lucky enough to get away from them, and now I'm trying to help Connor find the kids before they have to go through anything bad, too."

Jenna's eyes widened, and Connor knew from experience that his soul mate was about to be on the receiving end of about a hundred completely unfiltered questions that would sooner or later verge into subjects he definitely didn't want to get into with his sister.

"Enough about us and the case we're working," Connor said, knowing he had to distract his sister before she got going. "You haven't told us a single thing about what you've been up to out in LA. How's work going?"

It was usually difficult to pull Jenna off a topic of conversation once she sank her teeth into it, but thankfully, there was one thing she was always willing to talk about—her job. It wouldn't be a stretch of the imagination to say that her love of the special-effects industry was her life. Connor didn't understand her fascination with the world of make-believe, and he knew his parents blamed that fascination with monsters on the stories she'd told about Hannah. Sometimes, Connor worried Jenna was disappearing further into a fantasy world of her own making more and more every day. But in the end, the stuff made Jenna happy. He tried to tell himself that was the only thing that mattered.

His sister's face lit up all over again as she told them about the makeup and special effects she'd been doing over the past few years for the fancy company where she worked. Connor listened and nodded his head at the appropriate moments, but Kat mostly asked questions and guided the conversation. She was exceptionally good at getting his sister to open up, and within minutes, the two of them were deep in conversation about the TV shows and movies Jenna had been working on. Connor was shocked to realize he recognized many of them. Some part of him always assumed Jenna worked on those obscure sci-fi shows involving flying sharks and face-sucking aliens, but now, he realized her job was much more than he'd ever expected.

"The rapid growth of the various streaming services has really opened up new demand for special-effects talents," Jenna said excitedly. "My company is hiring people left and right and still has to turn down major contract work every week. I've made more in commissions and overtime in the past year than in the three previous years combined. My salary has been bumped up half a dozen times in that same period because my boss is worried someone's going to poach me."

Connor wasn't sure why he felt the need to interrupt, but he was going to do it anyway. "If work is going so well with all the overtime and everything,

I'm a little surprised you found time to slip away and come all the way to Dallas to visit me."

Jenna stared at him like a deer caught in headlights. She opened her mouth to say something, then closed it again.

"There was a lull in work, and I decided to do something spontaneous," she finally said, breaking eye contact with him and looking away. "So I jumped on a plane and here I am."

Some of his pack mates could read people well enough to know when they were lying. Unfortunately, Connor didn't possess that particular ability. But in Jenna's case, he didn't need to. His sister was the worst liar he'd ever seen.

"Jenna, I know there's something else going on you're not telling me," he said. "The fact that you're scared to even talk about it means it's serious. I can promise you that delaying won't make it any easier. Why don't you just tell me what it is so we can at least discuss it?"

His sister's shoulders sagged and for a moment, he thought she was about to cry. But then she took a deep breath, determination seeming to surround her.

"I saw her," Jenna finally said, her voice so low that both he and Kat had to lean forward to hear it. "Three days ago."

From the corner of his eye, Connor saw Kat glance at him, clearly confused. He wished there was something he could say that would help, but he was as lost as she was.

"Who did you see?" he asked his sister when nothing else seemed forthcoming.

"Hannah," his sister said, voice a little stronger now. "I saw her three days ago, in an unhoused camp near Skid Row. I was out late at night and saw her darting through the shadows. I called out to her, and she turned to look at me. I could see in her eyes that she recognized me, but then she turned and ran away."

Connor set his plate on the coffee table with a sigh. "Oh, Jenna."

This was so much worse than he'd ever imagined. It wasn't simply that Jenna thought she'd seen their dead sister. It was with the fact that she'd obviously been wandering around some of the worse parts of LA in the middle of the night looking for her in the first place.

"It was her," Jenna practically shouted, hands clenched tightly around the plate on her lap. "I chased her for three blocks, but when I finally got close, she turned down an alley and disappeared down into a manhole in the ground."

Crap, this was getting worse by the second. Connor knew there was no one to blame but himself. He should never have left Jenna alone in Los Angeles by herself, with no one to be there for her but the awful nightmares that wouldn't let her heal. This was all his fault.

"Jenna," he said softly. "I'm sure you think the woman you saw was Hannah, but it's been a decade since she went missing. It's unlikely you'd be able to recognize her, even if it had been her."

"It was her, dammit!" his sister shouted, fists clenching in anger, her heart thumping like wild as tears ran down her face. "I think I'd know my own sister, no matter how long she's been missing!"

Connor wanted to tell her she was wrong, that Hannah wasn't simply missing. She was *dead*. "So that's it? That's why you came all the way to Dallas? So you could try and convince me that you saw Hannah?"

His sister wiped the tears from her face with a furious hand. "No. I didn't come to tell you that. I came to bring you home with me so you can help me find her."

Shit.

"I'm not going back to LA with you," he said quietly.

"Why not?" she demanded. "I told you I saw her. I can't believe you're going to sit here and act like it means nothing."

"It means exactly nothing!" he growled back, hating that he was shouting at his sister but unable to stop himself. "You didn't see Hannah because she's dead. And you're crazy if you think any different."

Jenna froze, all the color draining from her face.

Connor caught movement out the corner of his eye, and he saw Kat sit up straighter, like she knew something had just gone very wrong.

Fresh tears spilled down his sister's face. A split second later, she was slamming her plate on the coffee table. She was off the couch like a shot, grabbing her weekender and purse and heading for the door.

"Jenna, stop!" he called out, jumping to his feet and hurrying after her.

He finally realized what had set her off. The one word his sister had heard too many times. *Crazy.* He hadn't meant it that way, but it didn't really matter at this point.

She jerked away from him and ripped open the door without saying a word.

"Jenna, don't go," he begged.

But it was too late. The damage was done. And all Connor could do was watch helplessly as she ran out of the apartment and kept going.

He started to chase after her, but then Kat was at his side, her hand on his arm. "If you follow her, she'll only run faster. You have to let her go for now."

Connor knew Kat was right, but that didn't make it any easier.

CHAPTER 18

THE COMPOUND WAS QUIETER THAN IT NOR-
mally was for a workday as she and Connor slipped
through the gate, locking it again behind them. It
reminded Kat of those times when she was a feline
and she and Connor would come here on the weekends to run the obstacle course together or rappel
down one of the training buildings. It had always
been fun and relaxing. But as much as Kat would
have preferred it, today they weren't here to run
around the obstacle course or slide down the sides
of buildings. No, this morning they were getting
together with Trevor, Hale, and Rachel to have a
videoconference with Davina because she'd found
some information on Marko.

As they reached the admin building, Connor
took his phone out of his pocket and glanced at the
screen, then put it away without saying a word.

"Nothing from Jenna yet?" she asked as he held
open the door for her, even though she already
knew the answer.

Connor shook his head but didn't say anything.
He'd been unusually quiet since his sister had run
out of the apartment the previous day. The conversation between the two of them had been a horrible

scene to watch. Like a slow-motion train wreck. As soon as Jenna mentioned seeing Hannah, Kat knew there was no way in hell the evening was going to end well. It had simply been a matter of how big the explosion would be.

The answer to that would be *nuclear*.

When Connor had called his sister crazy, it had been like watching a video of one of those old buildings implode. Jenna's eyes had first filled with pain, then tears, and finally anger. Five seconds later, she'd left. Kat knew nothing good would come of chasing after her, which was why she'd convinced Connor not to. Going after her would only have pushed the anguished woman farther away—maybe forever.

"I don't even know where she slept last night," Connor said, stopping to look at Kat as he closed the door behind them. "I mean, did she get a hotel or drive straight to the airport and leave? Hell, what if she spent the night in her rental car to save money?"

"I'm pretty sure we can rule out that last one," Kat said.

In some ways, Jenna would never be anything but Connor's baby sister in his eyes. In his mind, she was still the same little girl she'd been when Hannah had gone missing. Too scared and too damaged to function on her own. That clearly wasn't who Jenna was now, but Kat doubted Connor would ever realize that.

"Jenna said she had plenty of money from all those overtime hours, so I think it's safe to say she's not living in her rental car."

He nodded. "I guess you're right. Do you think she went back to LA then?"

His voice was barely above a whisper, and the pain in those words made her heart ache. Connor was fully aware of what he'd done and how badly he'd screwed up. He also knew there might be no way to come back from it.

"I don't know," she said softly, reaching out to take his hand and give it a squeeze. "Hopefully, she just went someplace to cool off and will reach out to you later, so you'll be able to fix this."

Connor gazed down at the floor, broad shoulders slumping. There was so much baggage between him and his sister that it almost seemed insurmountable.

"I never meant to yell at her," he said. "I only wanted her to have a normal life. I thought if she could accept that Hannah was gone, she could get on with her life and we could go back to being the family we used to be. But Jenna would never let it go, which only made me feel more like a complete jerk for letting go so fast myself. The truth is, she's a much better sister to Hannah than I could ever be a brother. That's hard to deal with."

Kat wrapped her arms around him. Doubt, guilt, and self-recrimination were all emotional burdens she knew a lot about. She'd been carrying them around with her ever since her coven had been killed right in front of her. She'd lived under the constant crushing weight of wondering what she could have done differently, the knowledge that she'd played a big part in all their deaths, and the pain of trying to move on but feeling like it was wrong to do so. Connor was going through something similar and had convinced himself that he couldn't get past it, not while Jenna was still trapped in the past.

Kat wished there were something she could say, some sage advice she could offer that would help Connor get through this a little easier. But if there were any magical words floating out there in the void, she sure as hell didn't know them.

"Are you two planning to join us?" a voice asked.

Kat looked up to see Gage leaning out of the doorway to the bullpen, his expression curious. Connor started a bit, as if he'd been taken by surprise, which shouldn't have been possible considering he had all kinds of werewolf senses. But she supposed he'd been too lost in his own head.

"Sorry," he mumbled, tugging Kat gently toward the bullpen. "Just dealing with something personal that came up."

Gage regarded them worriedly, his gaze swinging back and forth between them. "Do you two need to skip the call with Davina so you can focus on whatever it is? We'll make do if we have to."

Connor shook his head. "No, it's okay. We're taking care of it."

Gage didn't seem to believe a word of that, if his expression was any indication, but he gave them a nod and headed back into the bullpen.

As they followed Gage across the bullpen and into his office, Rachel, Trevor, and Hale eyed them with the same curiosity as their pack leader. Kat knew their hearing was exceptional enough for all of them to have easily heard everything, but she was used to them tuning out other people's conversation as a way of maintaining privacy. Hopefully, that meant they hadn't heard her and Connor talking about Jenna running away.

"There you are! I was starting to get worried," Davina said.

Kat turned a couple times before realizing that the woman's voice was coming from Gage's computer. The monitor and attached camera had been turned to face the middle of his rather large office. She did a double take. They were seriously going to have a videoconference about witches and warlocks and sacrifices.

The woman with shoulder-length blue hair on the screen was studying them thoughtfully, her face showing the same concern that Gage had earlier.

"Sorry. We didn't mean to worry you, Davina," Kat said, taking one of the chairs they'd rolled away from the conference table and placed in front of the screen. "We just had to deal with some personal stuff."

"Ah." Davina's mouth curved. "I completely understand. My daughter is going through some drama right about now. She's trying to convince me that she's in love with our gorgeous bartender, no matter how many times I tell her it can't work between them."

"Why can't it work?" Trevor asked. "I met Lydia when I was out there in LA to help clean out that vampire nest. She seems like she has a good head on her shoulders."

"She does," Davina agreed. "But the bartender in question happens to be a skin walker. He's very attractive at the moment, but how is Lydia going to handle it when she comes to work one day and the new love of her life is wearing the body of a sixty-two-year-old grandmother? They say that love conquers all, but in this case, I don't think that's true."

Kat had about a hundred questions—most revolving around skin walkers, which she knew almost nothing about—but Gage chose that moment to interrupt.

"As interested as I am in this conversation, I'd rather hear what you found out about Marko," he said, grabbing a chair with everyone else.

Davina nodded, the amusement on her face immediately fading. "To start with, I can confirm he's by far the most cold-blooded person any of us have probably ever dealt with."

"You won't have to work hard to convince me of that," Kat said. "I watched him murder the other members of my coven without a trace of remorse."

Davina let out a shudder. "I began looking closer at that murder Zane and Alyssa were sent down to San Antonio to investigate. I don't know if you know this, but the murder victim was a teenager, too. I'm guessing it's no coincidence that the four kidnapping victims in Dallas are also teenagers."

Beside Kat, Connor muttered a curse.

"It gets worse," Davina said. "That poor kid in San Antonio isn't the only one Marko murdered."

Kat's stomach dropped like a rock. She probably shouldn't have been surprised Marko had killed others. She already knew how vicious he was. But it was still hard to imagine anyone targeting kids like that.

"Why haven't we ever heard about any of these murders?" Connor asked.

"Because they occurred over an eight-month period, scattered throughout the entire southern portion of the country, with most of them happening in very rural areas," Davina said.

A few seconds later, a map of the southern part of the United States popped up on the monitor, showing all of Texas, as far east as Louisiana, and northward up to Oklahoma. As Kat watched, red dots appeared on the map in seemingly random fashion.

"I'd like to say that's why STAT didn't pick up on them, but the truth is, Marko found a way to obscure what he was doing and keep anyone from noticing the crimes outside the small area where they occurred," Davina said. "It was pure chance that someone in San Antonio contacted STAT directly, or we probably would never have stumbled on any of this at all."

Kat could practically hear the alarm bells ringing as Connor and his pack mates abruptly realized how dangerous Marko and his coven could be.

"I tracked the first ritual murder to a small town in west Texas called Gail," Davina continued. "The body was found in a shallow grave in late February, but the autopsy and forensic evidence was able to pinpoint the time of death to the twenty-first of December—winter solstice for those of us who care about that kind of thing."

The picture of the victim was small when it popped up on the screen, but Kat could still tell that it was a boy of maybe sixteen or seventeen. It was soul crushing to imagine someone murdering the poor kid.

"Next was a girl from Kingfisher, Oklahoma," Davina said, another red dot highlighting for a moment on the map along with another picture. "She was kidnapped and killed on the twentieth of March—the spring equinox."

Davina didn't even pause this time as another

dot was highlighted on the map and another picture appeared off to the side. "This one was in Northpoint, Arkansas, this time, killed on the first of May—Beltane."

Kat groaned to herself, picking up on the trend. Beltane, or the May Day festival, was celebrated by a lot of different cultures around the world, but it was especially important to witches and warlocks. To them, it was a celebration of the coming together of male and female energies to create new life. Taken by themselves, the dates of each murder could have been a coincidence, but when Davina threw in the winter solstice and spring equinox, it was obvious that Marko was working his way down the list of every important day on the calendar.

"The fourth body was found outside DeRidder, Louisiana, on the twenty-first of June—the summer solstice," Davina continued. "And then, most recently, there was the one down in San Antonio. The medical examiner puts the victim's death as the first of August—Lammas, the first grain harvest of the season."

Kat continued to stare at the map on the screen with the pictures of so many kids and the dots that represented the location of their makeshift graves.

"Davina, is it my imagination, or does the positioning of those dots seem a little too perfect for chance?" she asked.

"You noticed that, too, huh?" Davina leaned

forward to tap something on her keyboard. A second later, red lines appeared on the screen, connecting the dots until they formed a pentagram. With Dallas dead center in the middle.

"I assume that the figure we're looking at has some special significance for witches and warlocks?" Connor asked.

Davina nodded. "Pentagrams are an important symbol for us. The five points of the star represent earth, water, air, fire, and the spirit to our followers. The circle that's typically shown around the outside of the pentagram represents protection and the ever-changing, everlasting circle of life, nature, eternity, and infinity. I doubt Marko cares about any of that, though. When a witch uses pentagrams, one point of the star is always facing up—that's critical to us. You'll notice Marko planned out his murders so there are two points facing upward, and he's made no attempt at a protective circle. By using the inverted pentagram and murdering those kids on our most special days, he's spitting on everything we believe, twisting it to suit his own purposes."

"What kind of purpose?" Hale asked. "Any idea what he's trying to accomplish with all these killings?"

Kat could only shake her head at the way these werewolves thought. Most normal people would be freaking out and yelling that this was all insane. But the Pack had been dealing with the odd and supernatural for so long, they didn't even bat an eye at what Davina was telling them.

"After doing a little digging in my library, I'm almost certain that by conducting these ritual sacrifices at these specific pentagram locations, Marko is creating nexus and terminus points. The only reason a mage would do something like this is in order to create their own ley lines."

"That's not possible," Kat said immediately, disturbed at the very thought. "Ley lines simply exist. You can't make them!"

"It would seem that Marko and his coven feel differently," Davina said, the map they'd been looking at for the last several minutes disappearing to be replaced by the other witch's very concerned expression. "There's no other explanation for what he's done. Marko has figured out how to create and harness ley lines."

Trevor frowned. "What the hell are ley lines, and what does it mean to us if Marko is able to harness them?"

"Ley lines are ancient pathways that exist along the earth's surface," Kat said, remembering all the books her grandmother had made her read on the subject. "They're found around all the old magical sites—Stonehenge, the Pyramids of Giza, and Machu Picchu—but they're also found along any path that humans or animals trod in large numbers, like the Oregon Trail. There are even ley lines in places like New York and Chicago, where people walk to work day after day for years on end."

"Okay. But I still don't see the relevance," Connor said, sounding slightly exasperated. "Why would Marko want to make something like that for himself?"

"Because ley lines carry a huge amount of magical energy," Davina said. "A near-unlimited amount of power that would be constantly recharged by the presence of any life near those lines. With the familiar curse he put on Kat, Marko was trying to use her and her coven's inherent gifts for channeling magic to access the naturally existing power around her. More than he could ever channel on his own. But if my understanding of what he's trying to do with this pentagram is correct, Marko won't simply be harnessing the power around him. He'll be able to tap into the magic of every living creature anywhere inside the lines."

"Crap," Kat whispered, feeling a shiver run up her spine. "He'll become the most powerful magic user who's ever lived. He'll be unstoppable."

"If he's figured out a way to regulate the huge amount of raw power that exists within those lines, yes," Davina murmured. "Otherwise, he'll turn himself into a burned-out husk."

Connor, Gage, and the other werewolves spent an inordinate amount of time trying to pin down exactly what she and Davina meant by *the most powerful magic user who's ever lived.* They seemed obsessed with having Davina describe all the different ways Marko would be able to use that power against them while Kat silently focused instead on how all of this could have happened. If Marko had succeeded in making her his familiar, would he have even bothered to attempt this pentagram thing with the ley lines? Would those poor kids still be alive? Was this all happening because she'd escaped? Would she ultimately be responsible for even more deaths?

"I think I've come up with a way to find out who Marko's fifth and final kidnapping victim is going to be," Davina announced suddenly, the words yanking Kat out of her reverie and turning everyone's attention back to the most important matter facing them. "Hopefully in time to stop them from grabbing the kid."

"How can you be so sure there's going to *be* another victim?" Gage asked. "How do you know Marko doesn't already have enough kids?"

"Because the ley lines are in the shape of a five-pointed star and create a five-sided pentagon shape around Dallas," she said simply. "They're going to need one sacrifice from each of those locations. The symmetry is impossible to ignore. On top of that, there are the birthdays of the missing kids."

Connor leaned back in his chair and folded his arms. "You mean they weren't random?"

"No," she said. "They were each born at noon on

those holidays I mentioned earlier. Addy Lloyd on the winter solstice, Ben Sullivan on the spring equinox, Cheyenne Owens on Beltane, and Anabella Gutierrez on the summer solstice."

"Marko needs one more victim," Kat said, realizing what Davina was getting at. "Someone born at noon on the first of August—Lammas. All we have to do is find them before Marko does, and it will disrupt the entire ritual he's spent all this time preparing for."

"Is that something STAT can do?" Connor asked eagerly. "That would require access to birth certificates, maybe even medical records."

Davina nodded. "STAT analysts are already working on it."

"That's good," Rachel murmured. "Also more than a little disturbing. But right now, I'll take whatever we can get. The problem is that Marko and his crew have been grabbing up these kids at a rate of one every two or three days. That means they could be heading after this fifth kid as early as tonight. That doesn't give us much time to find the kid first and lay a trap for them."

That was an understatement, but Kat had to put her faith in Connor and his teammates. She'd seen what the Pack could do when they were desperate to help people. They'd find this last kid in time. They had to. And if they were lucky, they'd get Marko at the same time. Though Kat wasn't sure what they would do when they ran up against him face-to-face. Tatum had been more than they could handle, but maybe if they had the entire Pack together, with her limited magic, they might stand a chance. If Marko didn't have too many members of his coven with him.

"While I agree that it would be best if we could stop Marko and his coven before they kidnap their fifth victim, we have to remember that the true goal is stopping them before they hurt the kids, which I assume will happen when they conduct this ritual to fire up these ley lines," Gage said, his tone indicating he was already thinking of a backup plan. "So, bottom line, we have a little more time than Rachel implied."

"Actually," Davina said, looking grim. "We probably don't have as much time as you might think. If Marko sticks with his trend of following the calendar, he'll likely conduct the ritual during the autumn equinox, which is the twenty-second of this month."

"Why do you think he'll do it on this particular date and not sometime later?" Connor asked.

"Autumn equinox, which we call Mabon or the harvest home, comes during the final harvest of the year. It marks the time when the beauty and bounty of summer gives way to the first desolation of winter, and the darkness begins to overtake the light. I can't think of a better time for Marko to try and pull off the ritual to create these ley lines."

Kat silently agreed with Davina's assessment. If she had to guess, she'd say Marko had built his entire timeline for this scheme around the autumnal equinox. But if Davina was right about everything going down on the next equinox, that meant they had only a couple days to not only find this fifth kid but also figure out exactly where Marko would be holding this ritual and then come up with a way to stop him—once and for all.

She gave Connor and his pack all the credit in the world, but bringing all this together in such a short amount of time was still a big ask.

———

After the bomb Davina had dropped on them, there wasn't much left to say. Normally, Connor and his pack mates would sit down with Gage and try to come up with a plan on how they were going to deal with Marko, but if one thing was certain, it was that planning alone wasn't going to see them through the coming confrontation. Considering how badly they'd gotten their asses kicked in their first run-in with Marko's coven, they were going to need more than a little luck on their side for the fight looming on the horizon with the man.

Even though he was concerned about that—and what failing to stop Marko might mean for Kat—after they were done talking to Davina, Connor's thoughts turned back to his sister and how he might find her. Assuming, of course, that she hadn't already left town, which was a serious possibility, especially considering how badly he'd screwed up by saying what he had.

Connor cursed silently. What the hell had he been thinking, using that word around her?

He had his parents to thank for making Jenna hate the word when she'd overheard them call her crazy during the arguments that always followed his sister's first few sessions with her therapist. No teenager should ever hear a parent use that word to describe them, but Jenna had, and it changed everything.

And then Connor had used it, too, at the worst possible time—in the worst possible way. His sister had been reaching out for help, desperate enough to fly halfway across the country on a whim, and he'd thrown that awful word right in her face. He wondered if she'd answer her phone if he tried her number. Considering he'd called her twenty times already and gotten nothing, the possibility seemed slight.

Maybe he should call in a favor with a few TSA agents he knew at the airport to find out whether she'd already left Dallas. If she hadn't, he'd drive around to all the hotels and motels near his apartment and see if she'd checked into one of those. It would take forever and would also torpedo his original plans of spending the entire day chilling with Kat, but what else could he do?

"Kat, could you stay a minute?" Davina's voice intruded on his thoughts, making him realize the woman hadn't disconnected from the call. "There's something else I want to talk to you about."

Everyone else had already moved into the bull-pen, but Gage turned back at Davina's words. "Take all the time you need. We'll be over in the training room if you need us."

Davina glanced at Connor, then looked at Kat. "I thought maybe we could talk in private?"

"It's okay. Anything you have to say to me, you can say in front of Connor," Kat said without a moment's hesitation.

He breathed a sigh of relief. His gut told him Davina had something serious to say, and he was hoping it had something to do with breaking the binding spell Marko had put on Kat. He'd prefer to be in on that conversation.

Davina glanced at him again, then nodded before turning her attention to Kat. "I think you should seriously consider leaving Dallas."

Connor was pretty sure his jaw hit the floor. Because of all the things he'd been prepared for Davina to say, this definitely wasn't one of them. Beside him, Kat looked as stunned as he was.

"Are you saying Kat is in danger if she stays in Dallas?" he asked.

The expression on Davina's face seemed to suggest she thought Connor was an idiot. "Did you miss the part where Marko turned her into a cat for the express purpose of enslaving her as his familiar? Of course she's in danger. But in this particular case, it's not only Kat I'm worried about."

"What do you mean?" Kat asked.

"Remember what I said about Marko needing some way to regulate the raw power that exists within the ley lines?" Davina asked. "Well, I didn't want to talk about this in front of the others, but I'm almost certain he already has a way to regulate the power in those lines—you. Worse, I think he's had you in mind from the very beginning. In fact, it's probably the reason he attacked your particular coven in the first place. And how you were able to get away from him."

Connor tried to work his way through all of that but ultimately decided he simply didn't have the background in magic to understand any of this.

"That's not possible," Kat finally stammered, her voice filled with confusion. "I got out of that protective circle Marko put me in on my own. I got away on my own."

"Did you?" Davina asked softly. "You think a warlock as powerful as Marko, who wiped out your entire coven and subdued you and bound your body into a cat's form without breaking a sweat, botched a simple binding spell so badly that you were able to slip out a paw and smudge the protection circle?"

"But…" Kat said, looking so helpless, it hurt. "Why would he do something like this?"

Davina shook her head. "I'm not sure why he let you get away. Maybe because he had something bigger planned for you right from the start."

"Like using Kat to access the ley lines?" Connor asked. He'd never felt so completely out of his depth in his life. Even with all the supernatural creatures the Pack had dealt with over the past year or so, he still felt unprepared for this magical stuff. He yearned for a situation he could punch or claw his way out of. "Are you're saying Marko was planning the murders all across the southwest and the kidnappings in Dallas more than four years ago?"

"That's exactly what I'm saying," Davina told them. "Though I doubt he knew then that it would all come down to Dallas, I think he let you slip away so you had time to recover from the familiar spell he used on you, then he kept an eye on you until you found a reason to stop moving, so he could put the final phase of his plan into action."

Kat paled, and Connor slipped a comforting arm around her. If he knew her—and he did—she was probably blaming herself for those five murdered kids right now, thinking that if she'd never stopped moving, Marko would have never had an opportunity to kill them.

That was all crap, of course. If Kat hadn't found

him, she would never have stayed in Dallas. So if anyone was to blame, it was him.

"But how did Marko even know I had stopped running once I reached Dallas?" Kat asked, still looking lost and devastated.

"Marko took some of your blood to perform the familiar curse, didn't he?" When Kat nodded, Davina continued. "If he had enough, he could have set up a nearly permanent Find Me charm on you and then sat back and waited. It's probably no coincidence that the murder of that boy in Gail, Texas, was about a month after you and Connor met. Marko would have waited a while, making sure you were going to stay put, and then he started building the ley lines around you and Dallas."

"And if Kat leaves Dallas?" Connor asked. "Then what? Marko won't be able to complete his mad scheme. He'll have to what, start over somewhere else?"

Connor's tone was a little harsher than maybe he'd intended, but the idea of Marko slipping away to kill other kids, simply because they'd failed to confront him and end this now, didn't sit right with him.

"That's exactly what I'm saying," Davina answered. "And yes, I know how bad that sounds. But you need to realize that if Marko gets his hands on Kat and finishes whatever ritual he has in mind, it's very unlikely that the Pack will be able to handle him. Hell, if these lines make him as powerful as I think they will, we could throw both the Pack and every agent STAT has at its disposal at the man and still lose. The best we might be able to hope for is to simply keep him from getting that strong. It would be a win for us. The only one we might get."

Connor couldn't even consider that they might be so outmatched in this fight. That had never happened before, and it wasn't going to happen now.

"You seriously think our only chance is depriving him of the opportunity to get to Kat?" he demanded. "There has to be another option. I refuse to believe that there isn't."

Unfortunately, according to Kat and Davina, Marko had no weaknesses.

"I mean, I guess you could always take him out from long distance," Davina said. "Kat mentioned that you're sniper qualified. I'm sure you could do it."

Connor wanted to think she was kidding, but something told him she wasn't. "You think he's really going to let me get a clear shot at him like that?"

"Probably not." Davina was silent for a moment, then sighed. "Connor, could you give us a moment?"

He hated leaving Kat, but when he glanced her way, she nodded. "Go ahead. I'm okay."

After giving her hand a squeeze, he got up and slipped out of Gage's office, closing the door behind him. He wandered across the bullpen area to the far side, doing his best not to eavesdrop on the conversation Kat and Davina were having, but he couldn't completely shut it out.

"You're stronger than you realize," Davina was saying. "You'd have to be, to survive what Marko has planned for you with the ley lines. If you decide not to run, then you need to figure out how to access whatever gifts Marko's familiar ritual provided you with. If you can't, you and Connor won't make it through the coming fight."

Connor couldn't listen to any more. He appreciated bluntness as much as anyone, but the stuff Davina was saying was unbelievably harsh. When Kat came out a few minutes later, it was obvious she was as upset by what the woman had said as he was.

"Everything okay?" he asked.

Kat nodded. "Yeah. Let's go home."

CHAPTER 19

"Maybe I should leave Dallas," Kat murmured as she rested her head against Connor's chest, listening to his heart slowly come down from the rapid drumbeat it had been only moments before.

Connor didn't say anything, his left hand busy making little circles on her upper back. His touch was so warm and soothing, she never wanted him to stop. She wondered if he'd even heard her since she didn't doubt that his mind was a million miles away.

After leaving the SWAT compound, they'd come straight home to regroup. Connor had spent some time trying to reach Jenna at her cell number, and when that hadn't worked, he'd called a friend at DFW International who'd been able to confirm that his sister hadn't flown out of that airport or Love Field at any point in the past twenty-four hours. While that was good news for the most part, it still left Connor wondering where the hell she'd ended up. They'd tried to call a few of the local hotels, but that had been a waste of time. Not only were there too many hotels in this town, but few of the ones they talked to seemed unwilling to tell them whether Jenna had checked in, even when Connor had tried to pull the cop card. Driving around and trying to ask in person wouldn't accomplish much more than the calls had.

So, after hours of frustration, Connor had given up and accepted he'd hear back from his sister only when she was damn well ready to talk to him. Kat only hoped it was before she left to return to California.

Not wanting him to dwell too much on either his sister's fate or what Davina had said earlier, Kat had led him into the bedroom, deciding that a distraction was in order. Not that she was only doing it for his benefit. With the short amount of time she had left in her human form, she was determined to enjoy every second she had with Connor.

Their lovemaking had been intense, urgent, and bordering on desperate. Connor had held her tight, his fingers laced with hers the whole time, as if afraid he was going to lose her any second. Kat supposed, from his perspective, that was exactly what was going to happen. She had reveled in the moment but ached at the same time.

Now, as they cooled down from their hours of lovemaking, Kat knew they could no longer avoid this conversation. Davina had told them so many disturbing things that morning, it was difficult to figure out which concern to address first, but the idea that it might be best for her to leave town was the elephant in the room that couldn't be ignored anymore.

"If you leave, there won't be any way for us to break the curse Marko put on you," Connor said, his deep voice jarring her out of the post-sex daze she'd settled into. "You'll turn back into a cat soon and stay that way for almost another year."

"That's all true," Kat agreed, not lifting her head from Connor's chest. "And while I'd much rather be a human than a cat, at least being a cat again is no worse than the life I've been living for the past four years. It's not much of one, but at least I'm free. On the other hand, if I stay and Marko gets his hands on me, then I'll likely be a cat for the rest of my life with no free will of my own. And if Davina is right about him wanting to use me to access the ley lines, then it will be even worse. I'll be his weapon, forced to watch as he destroys you and everyone I care about."

Connor sat up so quickly that Kat practically fell off the bed. But then he tugged her close again.

"We're not going to let any of that happen," he said firmly. "We're going to come up with a plan to beat this a-hole. I'm not sure how yet, but we will. No matter what, though, I'm not letting Marko get near you. And if we think it might happen, then you'll leave and I'll go with you."

Kat had a hard time resisting the urge to lean forward and kiss him. He was so damn amazing, it almost hurt. But that didn't keep her from shaking her head. "I appreciate the gesture, but you can't leave your pack. I know how important they are to you. And what are we going to do if we run? Wander the country in your truck, while you work odd jobs to pay for my fresh tilapia fillets?"

"If we have to, yes," he said firmly. "And I'll do it gladly. This is a promise. If you leave, I won't let you go alone."

"But—" she started, only for him to cut her off.

"Kat, please," he said softly, gently cupping her face with his hand. "I know that you must have heard my pack mates and I talking about what it's like when a werewolf meets *The One* for them, right? I think we both know that's what's going on between us. You're my soul mate, there's no doubt of that. Which means there's no way I'm letting you go alone. I'm not losing you. I love my pack mates like brothers and sisters, but if it comes down to you or them, I'll choose you. Every time."

Tears welled in her eyes. It made her feel stupid good to hear Connor say he was willing to give up everything to be with her and that they were soul mates. She'd already believed that they were, but it still felt amazing hearing him say it out loud.

Kat leaned forward and kissed him long and slow, trying to express everything she felt right then without saying a word. Part of her wanted to pull back, look him deep in the eyes, and tell him how much she loved him, but she was still too scared to say those words, worried it would mess something up when it was going so perfectly.

They were still kissing when Connor's stomach rumbled, making both of them laugh.

"You should get something to eat," Kat said, breaking the kiss to smile at him. "It *has* been four whole hours since you munched your way through that entire bag of Oreo cookies while we were looking for Jenna. I know you're probably starving, especially considering all the energy we just burned off."

He chuckled and climbed off the bed. "You want to come with me to the kitchen? I can fix us both a snack."

Kat shook her head as she dropped back down to the plump pillows and snuggled into their warmth, giving a lazy stretch and arching her back like the cat she was so used to being. It was impossible to miss the way his eyes raked across her naked breasts, stoking fires that hours of lovemaking hadn't done anything to extinguish.

"I think I'll stay here and hang out in these nice cozy blankets for a little longer."

Given the smoldering gaze he tossed her way, she thought he might skip the food and climb back on top of her. But then he bent down to give her a tender kiss.

"I'll make us some peanut butter crackers. Those are fast, and we can eat them in bed."

Kat was tempted to make a joke about leaving crumbs on the sheets but didn't have a chance to get the words out before Connor slipped out of the room, his naked butt looking incredibly sexy as he moved away.

She lay back on the bed, stretching and wiggling around a little more until she found the perfect warm spot, tugging the sheets up to ward off the chill from the air conditioner. She listened as Connor moved around the kitchen, the clatter of metal on metal as he dug a knife out of the drawer, the thud of cabinet doors as he pulled out the peanut butter and crackers. From the amount of rustling he was making, she got the idea she could look forward to a lot of peanut butter crackers. Knowing him, he'd probably use a whole sleeve of crackers. And that would only be for himself.

Kat smiled at the thought, burrowing even deeper into the sheets and pillows, relishing the way Connor's scent enveloped her as she lay there. Falling back into her drowsy, post-lovemaking haze, Kat found her thoughts turning to what was going to happen between her and Connor.

She loved him, even if she hadn't told him yet. And it seemed that he loved her as well, since he was ready to walk away from his pack and everything else in his life for her. But could she truly ask him to do that?

Kat didn't have to think about that for very long. It was one of the few things she'd learned from her mother. If you love someone—really love them—then you never want to see them in pain. And that's what leaving his pack would mean for Connor—pain.

But if she left on her own and tried to lure Marko and his coven away, that would only end up hurting Connor, too. They were soul mates. She'd never heard any of the werewolves in the Pack talk about what it would mean to lose their soul mate, but Kat didn't imagine it would be anything good. So how could she leave him even if it was for his own good?

Okay, so she'd stay. But even if they somehow managed to survive the coming confrontation with Marko, how would that be any better? She couldn't come up with a single scenario that didn't involve her being trapped in a cat's body for the majority of each year. How was that going to be any easier on Connor? He'd be forced to basically put his life on hold when she was a cat, living for those few days when they could really be together. That seemed like a completely different kind of torture and more pain for the man she loved.

Kat didn't realize until that moment that there were tears sliding down her face as she lay there agonizing over what she was supposed to do. Was there any way this could ever end well for both of them?

She was still thinking about that a few minutes later when she heard Connor's phone ringing out in the kitchen. She couldn't hear what he was saying when he answered—it would have been nice to have a werewolf's enhanced hearing right then—but whatever it was, she got the feeling it was serious. Connor's voice took on a decidedly business tone whenever he was talking about something work related. Especially if it was dangerous.

Connor came into the bedroom a few moments later, still naked but without any peanut butter crackers. That's when she knew she'd been right. Kat couldn't stop the nervous tremor from slipping into her stomach, worried that everything was about to go completely wrong.

"That was Gage," Connor said, heading straight to the dresser on the far side of the room and pulling out a DPD uniform T-shirt. "Davina called and said she found three possibilities as far as the teens Marko might go after next. All of them were born on the first of August at noon, and they live in the Dallas area. Since we don't know which one is the right kid, Gage is sending out the whole Pack to bring in all three of them and put them in protective custody. Trevor, Hale, and Rachel are meeting me at the address for one of the kids."

"Meeting *us*," she said firmly, climbing out of bed and padding over to the bags from her shopping spree that she hadn't unpacked yet. Connor had offered some space in his closet, but she hadn't been able to commit to that yet. It would have felt like she was tempting fate or something.

Connor looked ready to argue, but she arched

a brow in his direction as she pulled on a pair of panties and a bra. He gave up the fight at that point, though Kat wasn't sure if it was the glare on her part or the view of her dragging the black bikini briefs up her thighs.

"Okay, but if Marko or his crew shows up, I want you to promise me that you'll bail, okay?" he said, yanking the dark blue T-shirt over his head.

Kat turned to reach back into a bag for a fresh tee and a pair of jeans so he wouldn't see her face. "Definitely. No worries about that."

She supposed she should have felt badly about lying, but she didn't. Because there was no way she was going to let Connor and his pack mates face Marko by themselves.

CHAPTER 20

"The boy's name is Demarcus Jones," Trevor said the moment Connor stepped out of the truck, following him around to the passenger side as he helped Kat out. Not that she actually needed help, of course, but he liked making the gesture anyway.

Rachel and Hale were standing a little farther away, their eyes focused on a ranch-style home toward the far end of the cul-de-sac.

"He's sixteen years old and just came home from school about an hour ago," Hale said, never taking his eyes off the home.

"How many other people are in the house?" Connor asked, taking in a middle-aged couple casually walking along the sidewalk across the street, the older woman sitting on a porch swing one house over, and three teens playing basketball farther down the street, close to Demarcus Jones's house.

"Parents and a younger sister," Rachel said. "How the hell are we going to do this without creating a scene?"

"I think I can handle that," Kat murmured.

Connor watched as his soul mate—he still couldn't believe they actually had that discussion so calmly—took several small strides along the residential street, head moving side to side like she was looking for something. He was about to ask what she was doing when she suddenly leaned over and began to sweep up some dirt with her hands. When she had a pile about the size of a thimble, she scooped it up into one hand and began to mumble something softly as she turned and came back to where they stood.

It sounded like she was speaking Latin, but Connor wasn't sure. He had enough time to catch Rachel and his other pack mates regarding her in confusion as the dirt in her hands began to give off that familiar dim green glow. A moment later, Kat spun in a circle, blowing the dirt out of her raised palm. He was more than a little surprised when the entire pile of dirt and dust flew from her hand and simply disappeared into the air.

A few seconds later, Connor saw the couple who'd been walking along the sidewalk suddenly stop and reach up to rub at their eyes, like they'd suddenly become dry and itchy. At the exact same time, the three teens with the basketball did the same thing, and then the lady on the porch swing. Connor opened his mouth to ask Kat what she'd done, but before he could, the couple went back to walking, the old woman opened the book on her lap and started reading, and the teens began tossing the ball back and forth. Not a single one of them seemed to have the least bit of interest in Kat or him and his pack mates.

"Okay. We're clear," Kat murmured, turning to walk casually down the street toward the Joneses' residence. It was impossible to miss the fact that the people who'd noticed them moments ago didn't so much as look her way even though she was walking right down the center of the road.

"What did you do?" Connor asked as he and his teammates hurried to catch up to Kat.

"It's called the Look Away charm," Kat said. "We could dance down the street with a marching band behind us now and no one would notice a thing. Well, Demarcus and his family would be able to see us, but no one else within about a quarter mile."

Connor slowed his strides at that announcement, thinking about how handy something like that would have been all those times when a member of the Pack had to wolf out in public for one reason or another. It would have been cool to have all the witnesses look the other way with nothing more than a finger wiggle and a whispered *Nothing to see here...move along.*

They approached the Joneses' house slowly and carefully, his pack mates scanning the neighborhood as they went.

"What exactly are we going to say to these people?" Rachel asked when they got to the front door. "It's not like we can tell them there's a warlock out there looking to kidnap their son because he was born at noon on the first of August." When no one said anything, she added, "Or can we?"

Connor shrugged and reached out to ring the doorbell. They were just going to have to wing it. It was what they usually did anyway.

Before he could push the button, the front door swung open. The next thing Connor knew, he was flying backward all the way across the front lawn, wondering what the hell had happened before he landed with a thud that rattled his teeth and slammed the air right out of his lungs.

Pain radiated through his body as he fought to clear his head, still attempting to figure out how he'd ended up lying in the street in front of the house. Then the sounds of shouting and screaming broke through the fog that filled his head, and he jerked himself up into a sitting position, ignoring the crunch of bones moving around inside him in ways that had never been intended.

Gaze still a little blurry, Connor took in the scene in front of him in shock. The front of the house was in complete shambles, with the entire entryway and most of the living room exposed where the door and the walls around it had been blown away. He caught movement out of the corner of his eye: the same three kids playing basketball less than a hundred feet away as if nothing had happened. He guessed it was Kat's Look Away spell, but it still seemed surreal as hell.

Turning, Connor caught sight of Rachel, Trevor, and Hale climbing to their feet at different points around the lawn. Obviously, they'd been thrown there by the same blast that had tossed him out into the street. Their uniforms were as torn and tattered as his. Panicking, he looked around, desperate to find Kat, terrified she was lying somewhere horribly injured right now. Werewolves could absorb a lot of damage, but she couldn't.

Then he saw her, kneeling in a flower bed to the left of the driveway. From what he could see, Kat seemed physically okay, looking less abused and tattered than him and his teammates. Then he noticed her hands held defensively in front of her, that greenish glow emanating from her fingertips. Maybe she had protected herself with magic?

Protected herself from what?

Before his muddled mind could follow that line of thinking, a swirl of movement inside the smoke-filled remains of the Joneses' home caught his attention. A second later, four figures began to emerge, the cowls of their black cloaks covering their heads. It was impossible to see their faces, but he was definitely picking up two distinctly masculine scents and two equally distinctive feminine scents.

The man bringing up the rear was huge and impossible to miss as anyone other than Tatum Graves. He was carrying a burden over one shoulder, and it wasn't a leap to assume it was the kid they were here to save.

Connor had been so focused on Tatum that he'd missed the other three moving down the front steps of the home, heading straight for Kat. Their intent to harm her seemed clear, even from where Connor was still sitting on the ground.

Surging to his feet, he partially shifted, the muscles of his legs, shoulders, and arms twisting and thickening, claws and fangs elongating even as he closed the distance between him and his soul mate. A remote part of his mind attempted to point out that he was carrying a gun for a reason, but his ingrained werewolf instincts demanded that he protect Kat using his natural weapons. Any attempt to use logic to reason with his inner wolf was impossible.

When he reached the flower bed where Kat knelt, Connor leaned down without slowing and scooped up one of the stone pavers edging the bed. Without hesitation, he stood and hurled it at the man only a few feet away from his mate. He expected the paver to knock the guy the hell out, but it was deflected away with little more than a twitch and a soft word. It gave Connor the distraction he needed, though, and in the next heartbeat, he leaped over Kat and slammed into the man who'd been mere seconds away from attacking her.

The grunt of pain told Connor that the guy had

definitely felt the impact of their collision. Connor tore into the heavy cloak he found under his hands, but the thick fabric seemed to resist his attack, like it was the strongest bulletproof vest ever, yet after a few seconds, it began to shred nonetheless. He was a little shocked at his willingness to physically rip into someone like this, but knowing the man would have tried to take Kat from him made him keep going.

As his claws penetrated the last layer of fabric, finally coming into contact with the skin beneath and drawing blood, Connor felt a punch in the chest that cracked bone and threw him violently through the air. He slammed into what was left of the front of the Joneses' house, dropping to the stone front steps with another bone-jarring thud. He shoved himself up, ignoring the pain in his arm. It was when he looked up to get his bearings that he realized the front lawn of the quaint home had turned into a damn combat zone.

Hale and Rachel were fighting Tatum, who was still carrying the sixteen-year-old Demarcus Jones around as if he were nothing more than a rag doll. Trevor was dealing with two female magic users—or at least trying to—but was getting pushed steadily back across the lawn as one invisible blow after another rained down on him, regardless of the gun in his hand.

But concerns for his pack mates faded the moment

Connor looked back at Kat and saw her facing the same man he'd been grappling with mere seconds ago. The one who'd blasted him twenty feet through the air. Kat was out of the flower bed now, kneeling in the grass in front of it. She was hunched lower than before, her glowing green hands still raised to protect her against whatever her attacker was trying to do.

At some point in his struggle with Connor, the warlock's cowl had gotten pushed back, revealing a pale face, dark eyes, and straight, dark hair tied back with a piece of leather. Connor's stomach clenched. The man he was looking at had to be Marko. And the asshole was within inches of his soul mate, reaching toward her even now.

Connor grabbed one of the large pieces of the stone set into the edge of the porch steps, heaving on it with a low growl. The moment the twenty-pound piece of rock came loose in his hand, he turned and slung it as hard as he could toward Marko's back with an angry snarl.

The chunk of ragged stone flew across the intervening space between him and Marko in the blink of an eye. Connor knew for a fact that he'd thrown the crude weapon with enough force to kill the man, but that didn't stop him from dropping a hand down to his thigh holster and pulling his gun, aiming at Marko's head even as he fought to get his claw-tipped finger through the trigger guard of the weapon.

The stone he'd thrown came to a sudden halt bare millimeters from Marko's back, and the warlock snapped his head around to glare at him with an expression so cold and evil that it sent a tingle of electricity down Connor's spine. Hell, if looks could kill.

Preferring for the warlock to keep his attention on him and not Kat, Connor took a step forward, pulling the trigger over and over, sending one bullet after another at the man.

Marko's dark eyes burned with anger, and Connor watched in disbelief as the bullets began to burst into flame before disappearing into thin air. At the same time, the large chunk of rock that was still hovering in the air suddenly started moving again, coming straight back at Connor even faster than it had on the way out.

Connor ducked, snarling as the damn rock nearly took his head off. The sound the stone made as it tore through the home behind him confirmed that he'd be dead now if he hadn't moved. It seemed Marko was just as deadly as Kat had made him out to be.

He risked a glance in Kat's direction, catching her eye.

"Run!" he shouted. "Get the hell out of here and don't stop!"

He didn't wait to see if Kat did what he asked, instead turning back to face Marko. He prayed she left now that Marko was here, like she'd promised she would.

Connor emptied the rest of his magazine in the guy's direction, dropped it, then quickly reloaded, and started firing again, all while moving steadily closer. The .40-caliber rounds from Connor's gun never reached the dark-haired magic user, but at least they kept him occupied. They also apparently irritated him, if the twisted grimace on his face was any indication. It wasn't the best outcome, but at this point, he'd take a distraction if it gave Kat a chance to get away free and clear.

When Marko lifted a hand in his direction, Connor knew he was screwed. The only question now was whether the warlock would simply blast him through the nearest wall, as he'd tried to do before, or do something much worse. He had a feeling there was no end to the horrendous things a man like Marko could do to him.

Fortunately, he never got to find out how vicious Marko could be because Kat popped up behind the man and shouted something in that language she was always using that Connor didn't recognize. Suddenly, the tall warlock was completely enveloped in a fireball of white-hot flames. Instead of screaming in pain and batting the fire engulfing his clothes, Marko simply stood there, slowly turning to face Kat. Even though Connor couldn't see the man's face, he could still sense the anger roiling off him. It was even more intense than the flames surrounding him.

A part of Connor wanted to scream and shout at Kat for not running when she had the chance, but there simply wasn't time for that, especially with the way Marko was fixated on Kat. It was like he was planning something next-level bad expressly for her.

Connor loaded up his last magazine and charged toward Marko, praying the warlock would be distracted enough by the flames to allow at least one round to get through. Because one round was all it would take. Connor would make sure of that.

One of his pack mates must have had the same idea because suddenly, gunfire was coming at Marko from a completely different direction. Connor glanced over to see Rachel moving their way, her handgun pointed straight at Marko. Rachel had apparently left Hale to deal with Tatum, clearly thinking their best hope was to take down Marko first. Connor couldn't argue with his pack mate's logic. Hell, if they took out Marko, maybe the others would simply give up—or at least leave without Demarcus.

For a moment it seemed like the plan would work, as at least some of their bullets appeared to get through the warlock's defenses, ripping through the heavy material of the man's cloak. But then something punched Connor in the chest, and he flew through the air—again. He lost his grip on his weapon as he suddenly became unsure which way was up and which was down—until he slammed into a wall and dropped once more to the front porch of the house.

Connor allowed himself half a second to grumble about how being thrown around like this was starting to get old. Then he pushed himself upright, frantically looking for Kat—and his weapon. He found her kneeling once more on the front lawn, except now the grass around her was scorched black. She looked more exhausted than he'd ever seen her. If Marko attacked her now, he'd take her down for sure.

But he didn't attack.

Glancing around, Connor realized that the four witches and warlocks they'd been fighting were gone, disappearing without a trace. His three pack mates were all okay, even if they looked like they'd had their asses handed to them. From the scowls on their faces, it was obvious Marko had gotten away with Demarcus Jones. The whole reason they'd come here was to keep that poor kid from getting kidnapped, and they'd failed. Hell, it hadn't even been close.

While Trevor and Rachel went to check on the teenager's family, Connor moved toward Kat, his strides slow and painful. He felt every broken bone and fragment of wood and stone piercing his skin.

Pushing aside the discomfort, he took in the scene around him. The Joneses' place was torn apart, pieces still falling to the ground even as small fires smoldered here, there, and everywhere. The front yard looked like it had been bombed, craters large enough to hide a small car dotting the landscape. Even the air smelled scorched, as if someone had transported them all to the middle of a battlefield.

And yet the three teens at the end of the cul-de-sac had never once stopped playing their game of basketball, laughing and joking as they took turns making shots. As for the woman across the street in her porch swing, she never even glanced their way.

It had been surreal before.

Now it was simply creepy.

Connor dropped beside Kat on one knee, heart seizing in his chest as he realized how wiped out she looked. It was as if all the energy she'd replenished since that battle at the farmhouse was completely sapped. And as devastated as he felt for failing Demarcus and losing the fight with Marko, he knew Kat felt worse. She'd had to face Marko again and lost badly. That had to be traumatizing.

"You okay?" he asked, gently taking her in his arms and searching her body for injuries.

She had more than a bit of black dirt smudged across her face and clothes, and her hair looked and smelled slightly singed, but other than that, his soul mate seemed okay.

"Yeah," she murmured, finally allowing Connor's chest to loosen. "Creating fire and holding it for that long took a lot out of me, that's all. I'll be fine. I just need to get my wind back."

"They took the kid," Hale said, even as they heard terrified voices inside the Joneses' residence calling out for Demarcus. "Is there any way you can do that tracking thing you did before, so we can find them again?"

Kat shook her head. "Even if we could find some of his blood—and if Marko weren't obscuring their trail—I simply don't have enough energy to attempt it right now. Even if I did, I don't think we should walk back into the middle of that fight after how badly this one went until we come up with a way to stop Marko."

Connor couldn't disagree. In a battle between the Pack and Marko, they were going to come out on the losing end every time. At least until they found a way to change the odds.

CHAPTER 21

"As far as when Marko is going to perform this ritual, do you have anything more precise than the autumnal equinox?" Rachel asked, looking at Kat from one of the other tables that filled the SWAT compound's training room. "That's sort of a broad time frame."

Even though they'd been going over these kinds of questions since well before dawn, Connor and the rest of the Pack still turned to look her way like they thought Kat had all the answers. She only wished she did. Because right now, she could feel the pressure of the moment weighing on her shoulders, making it hard to breathe. Even Tuffie, who was sitting on the floor in front of Kat with her head resting on one of Kat's knees, seemed to be eyeing her as if waiting for the answer on how to save the world.

Sighing, she reached out to pet Tuffie, at the same time leaning to the left a little to rest her shoulder against Connor's. That gave her enough strength to admit she had very few answers.

"Marko will almost certainly start the ritual at sundown tonight," Kat said, her fingers caressing Tuffie's head. "When the sun drops down below the horizon, at around eight o'clock, that's the true beginning of the equinox, when darkness overtakes the light. He'll be able finish the entire thing in thirty minutes or less."

Kat suspected everyone already knew that since Gage had told them about Davina's theories. But from the expressions on their faces, it was clear they'd been hoping they'd have more time. She couldn't blame them. Realizing they had fewer than twelve hours to figure this all out or lose those kids was tough on all of them.

"Okay. So we know when Marko will act," Cooper murmured, not even bothering to look up from the cell phone he'd been focused on for the entirety of the meeting. "Any clue about where this crap is going down or how we're going to stop it if we get there in time, especially considering how easily they dealt with the five of you last night?"

Beside her, Connor frowned. They might have gotten their butts kicked, but that didn't mean they wanted to be reminded of that fact, especially by one of his pack mates. Kat was about to defend Connor and the others, but then she realized Cooper had zoned out completely, totally focused on whatever was on his phone.

"Earth to Cooper," Connor said, apparently noticing how distracted Cooper was, too. "If you want, we can try and get a message to Marko and see if he's willing to put off his plans to take over this part of Texas until you aren't so preoccupied."

Cooper stared at his phone for another moment before giving himself a shake. "What? Oh...sorry." He glanced around with a slightly glassy-eyed look. "I was paying attention. For the most part. It's just that Everly is dealing with contractions right now, and I'm a little worried about her."

Kat looked around at everyone else, wondering if she'd heard right. Given the alarmed expression on their faces, it seemed that she had.

"If your wife has started going into labor, what are you still doing here?" she asked.

Cooper shrugged. "According to her, she's been dealing with these contractions off and on for days now. Her water hasn't broken, and she doesn't want me hovering around until she needs me. According to her, I make her nervous when I hover."

Kat was about to suggest that he should go home and be with his wife, regardless of what Everly said, but he spoke before she could.

"So any idea about where this ritual is going down and how we'll stop it?"

"As far as where, I'm hoping Gage will be able to help with that," Kat said. "He's been in his office on the phone with Davina for more than an hour talking about it. As for your other question on how to deal with him and his coven once we find them, I'm sorry to say, I've got nothing."

Most of the Pack let out a collective groan of disappointment, while Connor, Rachel, Hale, and Trevor simply looked resigned to the fact. She suspected that was because they were already well aware of exactly how screwed they all were when it came to dealing with magic.

"Hale mentioned that you can do a magical tracking spell." Cooper glanced down at his phone again then up at her. "Can't you do something like that to find Demarcus Jones?"

Kat was kind of amazed at how fast the details of her abilities had made the circuit through the Pack. People liked to think that women gossiped a lot, but in reality, there wasn't any group of women that could hold a candle to a pack of werewolves. They loved to talk.

"Normally if I had a sample of Demarcus's blood or anything else containing his magical essence, I could do a Find Me charm," she said, feeling like she'd already explained this a hundred times already. "Not only has Marko magically obscured the boy's track, but he's also purged the Joneses' home of any trace of him. There isn't anything left behind that I could use to follow Demarcus. For right now at least, there's simply no way to find him. Or any of the other missing kids, for that matter."

Her answer obviously disappointed everyone, but there wasn't anything else she could tell them.

She'd spent half the night trying—and failing—to get a bead on any of the missing kids, but it was no good. Marko had covered his tracks too well.

As the room filled with the hum of general conversation, she realized most of the werewolves were rehashing the events of last night's doomed battle at the Joneses' home. She supposed she could understand why they were still talking about it. It had been a catastrophe of epic proportions.

One moment, she, Connor, and the other three werewolves had been standing in the middle of the yard, trying to comprehend the magnitude of their defeat, and the next her Look Away spell had faded, and everything had turned to complete chaos.

The kids who'd been playing basketball had understandably lost their minds. They'd been hanging out tossing a ball around, and just like that, a blown-up, postapocalyptic war zone had made an appearance. But the shouts those three boys cut loose with had been nothing compared to the scream the older woman on the porch swing had let out. Kat's ears were still ringing a little bit.

The police and fire department had arrived quickly, neither group really sure what had happened. Connor had gotten everyone pointed in the right direction soon enough, the firefighters dealing with the parts of the house still burning while the uniformed officers talked to the Jones family about their missing son—the one they seemed to have no pictures of, thanks to Marko scrubbing the scene of anything related to Demarcus.

Detective Sandoval had also shown up, along with a woman Kat was quickly becoming very familiar with—Chief Leclair. Kat had slipped away to hide out in Connor's truck, having no desire for people to ask her questions that she couldn't answer.

Connor had later told her that the official story from the fire department was that the explosion had been caused by a gas leak and that Demarcus Jones was currently being listed as missing, probably running away in terror from the blast and fire that had ripped apart his family's home. Sandoval hadn't been fooled, though. The detective from Missing Persons seemed to realize he had another strange disappearance on his hands.

When Chief Leclair had wanted to know how her SWAT officers had ended up all bloody and scorched, Connor had spun a story about being in the area and seeing the flames, then running into the burning home to look for survivors. Connor made sure the story lacked a lot of details so it would be harder to catch them in the lies. The chief had apparently bought the fabrication without too many questions. Still, by the time everything was done, it had been midnight before Kat, Connor, and the others were allowed to leave. Kat had spent most of that time sleeping in the back seat of Connor's truck, wrapped up in one of his uniform tops, having nightmares about Marko finally getting his hands on her.

The murmur of conversation stilled when Gage walked into the room and made a beeline toward the computer in the corner.

"I just got off the phone with Davina," he said, not looking away from the monitor as he booted up the overhead projector. "She's come up with something that might tell us where the ritual will be held. Or at least get us close. She believes Marko will want to conduct the ritual from a place that will allow him to control every aspect of these new ley lines. She said it's the epicenter of the convergence."

Kat knew where this was going before Gage said another word, and all she could wonder was why she hadn't figured it out before now.

"He's going to find a place near the center of the pentagram," she said. "The closer to the exact center, the better."

"That's what Davina said, too," Gage replied, pulling up the map Davina had shown them a couple days ago, the one with the red lines connecting the five points of the inverted pentagram. As they watched, he used a graphics program to start laying lines across the middle of the pentagram. "This isn't going to be the most precise method, but I'm hoping that the point where all these lines intersect will be close to the place Marko plans to use for the ritual."

It didn't take long to figure out that the crossing lines were leading them toward a section of northwestern Dallas, above Las Colinas but below Valley Ranch. Kat waited impatiently as Gage continued to work, until the crisscrossed lines came to rest over a part of the map covered with mostly green and blue.

"That's the Sam Houston Trail Park," Hale announced. "I go there on the weekends sometimes to jog or bike. There are a lot of trails, a dozen ponds, and a few places where the interstate crosses overhead, but not much in the way of buildings."

"Would Marko be able to use a place like the one Hale's describing for his ritual?" Connor asked. "Doesn't he need some kind of building?"

"A building, an open field, a graveyard," Kat said with a shrug. "Marko can do the ritual anywhere, as long as it's large enough to carve out a protective circle. He'll probably want a place that's relatively quiet and mostly private. Even with Obscuring and Look Away charms, he still can't take the chance that someone may see or hear something."

"Well, the park definitely fits the bill for those requirements," Hale murmured, getting up and moving closer to the map on the projector screen. "There are over twenty miles of trails and paths in there, with little secluded spots big enough for that circle all over the place. This time of the year, the park closes at around five, so the place will be completely deserted by the time the sun goes down at about seven."

"Anyone notice that this park is barely two miles away from the farmhouse where we fought with Tatum and the other members of Marko's coven?" Trevor said, walking over to the screen and pointing at the location near the North Lake. "We should have realized there was a reason they were keeping those kids out there in the middle of nowhere."

"How could we have known?" Rachel said. "And at this point, I don't think it matters anyway. All that matters is finding those kids before the ritual starts. At least now we know where they're going to be."

Hale crossed his arms over his chest. "It still doesn't help us a lot. Like I said, with twenty miles of trails and paths, the place isn't exactly tiny. If Marko's Look Away charm is as good as Kat's, we could walk right past those kids and never realize it."

"I think it might be worthwhile to have a look around the park while it's still open to the public," Gage suggested. "I'm hoping that if we get a peek at the place before Marko arrives, maybe we'll see something that will tip us off to where he plans to set up."

Kat couldn't argue with his logic, even if she doubted they'd get that lucky. Of course, Connor wasn't thrilled when Gage refused to let him, Trevor, Rachel, and Hale go with them. "If Marko's people are in the park, we can't take a chance that they'll recognize any of you from your previous encounters."

She could tell that Connor and his pack mates wanted to argue, but at the same time, they had to know Gage was right. Still, none of them looked happy as the room cleared out, Gage and everyone else leaving them behind.

"I can't just sit here and do nothing," Connor said after the training room had been silent for a good five minutes. "Maybe we could drive around the neighborhoods near the park and see what we can find? Marko was obviously keeping Addy, Ben, and Cheyenne in that farmhouse because it was close to where they were going to do the ritual. It stands to reason he still has them somewhere nearby."

That made sense to Kat, and she joined the rest of them around the map, scouting out different places around the park they thought might have potential as a hiding place for five teenagers and a coven of witches and warlocks. They came up with a long list of possibilities, and Kat was excited about getting out there to start looking when Connor and his pack mates suddenly turned and looked toward the door of the training room.

"Someone's at the gate," Connor said.

For one terrified moment, Kat thought Marko had come after them, ready to finish them off before he even started the ritual. But before she had a chance to go into complete freak-out mode, it dawned on her that Connor and his teammates didn't seem to be too concerned with whoever was out there.

Kat followed Connor and his pack mate out of the training building, relaxing when she saw that it was Detective Sandoval and a half dozen other cops she assumed were people from his Missing Persons Unit.

"I'm probably going to regret this, but we're here to help with whatever you're about to do to find those kids," Sandoval said. "Even if it's likely to get us all killed."

Connor regarded the men and women with Sandoval before looking at the detective. "We appreciate the offer from all of you, but none of you have a clue what you're getting yourselves into by volunteering to help."

Detective Sandoval snorted. "If we did, I doubt we'd be here. But there are five kids missing, and every cop instinct I have is telling me that if we don't do something soon, no one is ever going to see them again. Why don't you tell us what we're up against so we can help get them back?"

Each of the cops with Sandoval nodded at that, their faces full of determination.

Connor glanced at his pack mates, who nodded as well.

"We can use all the help we can get," Rachel murmured.

Connor hesitated for a moment, then finally unlocked the gate and opened it, motioning Detective Sandoval and the other cops in.

"If we're going to do this, you might as well come into the training building and have a seat," Connor said. "After you hear what we have to tell you, you're going to need it."

When they were all back inside and Detective Sandoval and the others were sitting down, Connor and his pack mates took turns telling them everything. Well, everything except the part about Kat living most of the past four years of her life as a cat and that she was on top of Marko's most-wanted list. They also left out the whole werewolf thing. But other than that, Connor and his teammates were surprisingly honest.

There were a lot of stunned looks and mutters of disbelief when they were finished.

"You can't be serious, right?" Sandoval said. "Magic?"

Connor didn't even blink. Instead, he glanced at Kat. "Are you up to giving them a demonstration?"

Kat blinked, a little surprised by the request. But one look at Sandoval and his fellow detectives and she knew that a demonstration of what she could do was the only way they'd believe magic existed.

Nodding at Connor, she stepped forward. Since she was still a little tired from yesterday, she decided to do something small. Holding out her hand, palm up, she made a circle with the index finger of her other hand above it, creating a perfectly formed globe of light. Detective Sandoval and the others stared at her like they couldn't believe what they were seeing. Before anyone could say anything, she wiggled the fingers of her free hand, turning the sphere into a tiny flame, letting it flicker for a moment before extinguishing it with a *poof*.

"Believe in magic now?" Connor asked.

Sandoval let out a slow breath, regarding Kat in amazement before turning his attention to Connor. "Okay, let me see if I've got this right. You think Marko and his coven will be somewhere inside the Sam Houston Trail Park a little while before sundown, preparing to murder those poor kids as part of some scheme to make himself more powerful. Gage and the rest of your team are heading to the park right now hoping to find where Marko plans to conduct his ritual while the rest of you are going to wander around the neighborhoods near the park on the off chance you stumble on where they're holding the kids. Did I miss anything?"

"Nope," Connor said. "That pretty much sums it up. We could use your help searching those neighborhoods, if you're willing. The fact that Marko and his coven won't recognize you would definitely be a big advantage."

Sandoval and his fellow detectives immediately agreed, moving closer to the map still being displayed on the projector screen, pointing, and taking notes on how best to split up to cover the large area.

"Where are you thinking of starting?" Kat asked Connor as she stood beside him in front of the map. "Maybe somewhere close to the farmhouse and go from there?"

Connor nodded, then took her hand and led her into the hallway. Tuffie followed, standing beside them and tilting her head, gazing up at them curiously.

"I was thinking that maybe you should head back to the apartment for a while so you can get some rest before tonight," Connor said softly.

When she opened her mouth to say she didn't need to rest, he gently put a finger to her lips.

"You need to recharge, or you won't be of any use tonight when everything goes down," he pointed out. "Take my truck and go home. Get something to eat, then crawl into bed and sleep for a few hours. Do it for me if for no other reason."

The idea of trying to sleep without Connor's arms wrapped around her was a frightening concept, but she had to admit he was right. She'd gotten some rest last night, but not enough. If she was going to trade spells with Marko in a few hours, she needed to reenergize some.

But still…

"This isn't some kind of trick, is it?" Kat asked,

having visions of waiting and waiting at the apartment as sunset came and went, without Connor ever showing. She knew that even with his truck, she'd never find the park. She was horrible with maps and even worse with navigating around big cities. "You're not planning to leave me behind for my own good, are you?"

When he gave her a sheepish look, she knew that the thought to leave her behind had at least crossed Connor's mind.

"The only reason I would ever consider something like that is because I love you and I can't stand the idea of you getting hurt." He sighed. "But because I love you, I'd never take away your choice to decide something like that."

Kat stood there, stunned. They were soul mates, so obviously she'd known there were intense feelings between them. And yeah, she was ready to admit—to herself at least—that she was in love with Connor. But hearing him say the words out loud stole the air right out of her lungs. She wanted to tell him that she loved him in return, but she simply couldn't get her mouth to work.

Connor's eyes widened, and he immediately started to stammer. "Crap. I'm sorry. I should never have dropped that on you out of the blue like that. It's how I feel, but I don't want to make you think you have to say anything in return. I didn't mean to put you under any pressure."

She went up on her toes and kissed him until he stopped talking. Only then did she pull back and smile at him. "There's no pressure, silly. I love you, too. I have for an embarrassingly long time—like back when I was a cat. But thank you for saying it. It's exactly what I needed to hear right now."

He opened his mouth to say something, but she silenced him with another kiss while Tuffie sat there with a big doggy grin on her face.

CHAPTER 22

KAT TOOK HER TIME MAKING A TURKEY AND cheese sandwich before turning to the fridge to pour herself a glass of milk. She considered adding some chips but decided against it as she gently set the plate and glass on the table and took a seat. Truthfully, she knew she had to eat something, but that didn't mean she was excited about it. Eating alone sucked.

As she nibbled on her sandwich, she found herself thinking about what it meant to have someone who loved her now, especially since she'd given up on finding love a long time ago.

When she was younger, she had all the usual dreams of romance and happily ever afters. But then she started studying magic with her grandma and devoted nearly every waking hour to becoming the best witch she possibly could. There'd been no time for boys, dates, or anything silly like that. Even when she'd gotten older and hung out with guys now and then, there'd never been any time or desire for a relationship. She'd slept with guys, of course, but nothing real.

Then Marko had shown up, and she'd been too busy trying to survive as a cat to worry about guys, even during those short periods of time when she'd been human. She'd given up on the entire idea of ever finding another person to spend her life with. She hadn't realized it until recently that in those few blessed days she'd been granted to be human, she'd avoided contact with other people, afraid to get close to anyone. She'd stayed focused on finding a place to sleep, getting something to eat, thinking about where she should run to next when she went back to being a cat and, of course, finding a way to break the spell. She'd told herself it was safer that way, that she could worry about love in the future when she could be human full-time again. It seemed smart, protecting herself like that.

But now everything had changed. Now she had someone she was in love with and who loved her back. While she was thrilled, she was also terrified. She'd never had anyone to love before, which meant she'd also never had anyone to lose, especially since she'd made sure her family was safe with that spell.

She couldn't do that with Connor. Because he was a werewolf, he was a threat to Marko and his plans. But because he was her soul mate and the man that she was in love with, he was so much more than a mere threat. He was leverage that Marko wouldn't hesitate to use. If he had Connor, there was nothing he couldn't make her do.

She sat there stuck in a loop, wondering again if

it really would be better if she left Dallas. At least then, there'd be no way Marko could use her against Connor and the other members of the Pack that had become her family. With her out of town, Marko's plans for the ley lines would be useless. He'd almost assuredly leave without bothering Connor and the Pack at all. But could she honestly leave Connor?

The sound of a ringing phone echoed in the apartment, making Kat jump. It took a good five seconds of ear-splitting noise to realize it was coming from the landline mounted on the wall over by the takeout menus. She hesitated, not sure if she should answer Connor's phone, but then she realized it might be him calling.

That thought had her up and out of her seat, snatching the receiver off its cradle so fast, she almost dropped it.

"Hello?"

"Hi, Kat. It's Davina. I didn't wake you up, did I? Connor mentioned that you might already be in bed sleeping."

Kat leaned back against the counter. "No. Not at all. I was just having something to eat. What's up?"

"Well, this might be out of left field, but after getting off the phone with Gage earlier, I spent a few hours brainstorming the rituals I think Marko might be planning to use. It's a long shot, but I think I might have come up with something that could help you."

Kat pushed away from the counter, her pulse quickening, but before she could say anything, Davina continued.

"Have you thought any more on what I said about leaving Dallas?"

Her mouth curved into a wry smile. "Actually, that's exactly what I was thinking about not ten seconds ago. I don't want to be the reason Marko becomes even stronger than he already is, and I don't want to be the reason Connor or anyone else in the Pack is hurt. But at the same time, leaving makes me feel like I'm deserting Connor when he needs me the most. Even if it's for his own good, I can't do that to him."

"Good," Davina said. In the background, Kat heard what sounded like heavy books being shoved around on the woman's desk. "I was hoping you'd say that. Because I may have come up with a way you can beat Marko. Unfortunately, the only way my plan will work is if he captures you first."

"Wait. What?" Kat froze. They must have a bad connection because she'd obviously misunderstood that last part. "You're joking, right? I thought the idea was to keep me out of Marko's hands so he can't gain control of the ley lines?"

On the other end of the line, Davina let out a sigh. "Unfortunately, that will only delay Marko for a while. If he can't get you, he'll eventually go find another coven, sacrifice as many of its members as necessary, and create another familiar just like you. Now that he knows it works, he can accelerate the process and be ready to conduct the ley-line ritual again by Samhain. He could decide to keep the five teenagers he's already kidnapped or kill them and grab more later."

Kat felt positively ill at that thought of any of those scenarios. She didn't want the horrible events she'd been through to happen to another witch or warlock, she couldn't let Addy, Ben, and those other kids remain in captivity, and she refused to even consider the possibility of them being killed and other kids being kidnapped in their place.

"Okay, so running away isn't an option even if I wanted to," Kat said. "And staying out of Marko's hands obviously isn't much better. So what's this plan of yours where he captures me?"

The mere thought of willingly allowing Marko to get his hands on her made her blood run cold, but if that's what it would take to stop him, then she'd do it.

"It came to me as I was reading through the various binding and power-channeling rituals," Davina said casually, as if this were the most normal conversation in the world. "That's when I realized every one of the rituals I could find had one thing in common. In order for Marko to tie himself to you—which he'll need to do to be able to control the ley lines—he'll have to be inside the protective circle with you during it. That's when he'll be at his most vulnerable."

"Vulnerable to what?" Kat asked.

She wasn't sure she liked where this was going. Actually, she was *sure* she didn't like it.

"Vulnerable to you," Davina said matter-of-factly. "At some point during the ritual, Marko will have to allow you to access the gifts your coven gave you four years ago. Allowing you to access them is the only way you could possibly survive being connected to the ley lines."

Kat winced. "That's not exactly a comforting thought."

She didn't want anything to do with the gifts her coven members—her friends—had died to give her.

"It should be," Davina responded. "Because for a short period of time, probably right before the ritual ends, you'll be the one in control of all the power in the lines. During that same moment, Marko will be essentially defenseless. If you're able to attack him at that point, he won't stand a chance. With that much power at your disposal, you can vaporize him."

Kat waited for Davina to say more—specifically the details on how she was going to do what the other witch was suggesting. But as the silence stretched out, it became clear that none of those details would be forthcoming. At least not without some prompting on her part.

"Okay," she said, deciding she'd play the game.

"There are a few areas of the plan that seem a little vague, so I have some questions."

"Sure," Davina said almost cheerfully. "Go for it."

Kat leaned her hip against the counter. "You said that at some period during the ritual, I should make my move and attack. How will I know when to do that? It's not like I can keep asking if we're there yet. Will there be some kind of sign?"

"The crescendo of all rituals of this type is the sacrifice," Davina said, her voice turning serious now. "The teens will be positioned outside the protective circle, and their sacrifice will initiate the final step of the ritual that will trap you as Marko's familiar forever. He'll be most vulnerable then, which means that's when you'll need to make your move."

Kat's heart started to pound faster, as memories of the last time she'd seen these kinds of sacrifices, when Marko had brutally killed her coven members, came to mind. She took a deep breath and shoved those thoughts aside. Nothing but panic lay in that direction, and it wouldn't do her any good.

"Okay, so when the blade comes out, that will be my signal to act," she said. "But what do I do? You said I'll need to use the gifts my coven gave me to somehow take control of the power coming through the ley lines and turn it against Marko, but I'm not sure how to even do that."

"Unfortunately, neither do I," Davina admitted.

"But you're smart and you're powerful. I know that when the time is right, you'll know what to do."

Kat resisted the urge to scream. She needed Davina to give her more than meaningless platitudes. She needed real answers on what she was supposed to do. Without that, getting anywhere close to Marko would be flat-out suicidal.

She took another breath, forcing herself to calm down. "If I somehow happen to figure out how to do this and find a way to deal with Marko, what happens to the familiar bond? Will Marko's death break the spell, or will I end up being a cat for the rest of my life?"

"I wish I could tell you definitively that it will break it, but I'm not sure," Davina said with a sigh. "Most spells are tied to the person who sets them, so Marko's death should end it. But he's wicked smart. I'm almost sure he powered the spell with your own magic. That's why you're so exhausted after turning back into a human. It's draining you at the same time it's transforming your body. If that's the case, there's a chance that killing him will have no effect on the spell."

Kat closed her eyes to let that sink in, then opened them again. "So even if I survive this, I won't know one way or another until midnight tonight, which is when I would normally go through the change?"

"Sorry…but yeah. You won't know for sure until midnight."

She spent some more time talking to Davina about how she needed to center herself and focus on her core, feeling the magic and letting it work through her. It all probably would have fit nicely onto a fortune cookie paper or maybe on a T-shirt, but Kat wasn't sure it was going to help her at all.

When the doorbell rang a little while later, interrupting them, it was a relief, even if she didn't have a clue who it might be. She appreciated everything Davina had done for her, but right now, talking about it was only making her more freaked out.

"I have to go. There's someone at the door," she said. "I'll call you later to let you know how it all turns out. Unless it goes badly, of course, in which case, you won't hear from me at all. If that happens, it might be a good idea to go somewhere Marko can't find you. If he succeeds here, something tells me that he'll be heading your way next."

Davina wished her luck, told her once again to trust her magic, then hung up. The doorbell rang again, and Kat hurried across the living room to answer it. She quickly checked the peephole, surprised to see Jenna standing there, looking nervous as hell. Probably at the prospect of facing her brother again. Kat could understand that.

Kat unlocked the door and opened it, ready to give Connor's sister a big hug and a promise that it was going to be all right. But then a big man dressed in a black cloak appeared out of nowhere and stepped in front of her, his equally huge hands clamping around Kat's neck with enough force to make breathing impossible.

That's when Kat realized why Connor's sister had looked so terrified and how incredibly screwed she was right then.

CHAPTER 23

"She's still not answering the phone," Connor said.

He pressed a little harder on the gas pedal, weaving the SWAT SUV in and out of late-day commuter traffic.

"Calm down," Rachel murmured from the back seat. "You talked her into going home to get some rest, so she's probably sleeping. Or she's in the shower getting ready for tonight. Either way, you need to relax. There's nothing wrong. And slow down some, before you get us in an accident, and it takes even longer to get to your place."

Connor glanced at Hale in the passenger seat, who nodded in agreement, before forcing himself to let up on the accelerator a bit, dropping his speed even as his inner wolf chafed at the delay. No matter how reasonable Rachel's explanation was, he couldn't shake the sensation that something was wrong. There was a tiny part of him worried that Kat had decided to leave town without telling him in a foolish ploy to keep him and the Pack safe.

As Connor continued to fight an ongoing battle with his inner wolf, he listened with half an ear while Rachel and Trevor discussed what the Pack had found when they'd searched the Sam Houston Trail Park that afternoon. Their pack mates had wandered around the trails for hours until they realized there was a section of the park on the map they couldn't seem to reach on the ground. Every time they walked in that direction, something distracted them and nudged them in a different direction.

According to Gage, it was only after half the Pack had walked purposely toward a wall of vines and thickets that seemed like they were too thick to ever make it through that they'd found the location for the ritual. A section of trees had been cleared from an area along the banks of the river, giving Marko and his coven a circular space of a hundred feet across to work with. There was already a large protective ring inscribed in the earth with a pentagram placed inside it. Once Gage confirmed they had the right place, they'd all pulled back, marking a few trees outside the area so they'd be able to find the place again in the dark.

"It's kind of terrifying how these witches and warlocks can hide something like that in plain sight," Hale murmured with a shake of his head. "It's even scarier to think what would happen if one of these covens turned their attention to crime."

"How do we know they haven't?" Connor questioned. "With their ability to hide stuff and distract people, they could rob a bank vault and walk right out the front doors with the bags of money over their shoulders and no one would even notice."

That comment seemed to have a sobering effect on everyone, and silence reigned in the truck for the next mile or so.

"At least we have Kat on our side to help us deal with the magic stuff," Trevor finally said as Connor turned onto the road that led to his place. "It's going to be an uphill battle no matter what, but without her, we wouldn't stand a chance of dealing with Marko and his crew."

Talking about Kat got him worried all over again, and the tires on the truck squawked as Connor pulled into the parking lot of his apartment building way too fast. Hale's head almost bounced off the dash as Connor slid into the empty space beside his truck and slammed on the brakes.

"Will you calm down?" Hale growled as he glared over at him. "Your truck is right there, so Kat obviously didn't go anywhere."

Connor knew he should have been relieved, but for some reason, he was still worried. That concern had him out of the SUV in a flash and running for the front door of his building. Hale and the others followed at a slower pace.

When he picked up his sister's scent on the stairs, Connor finally started relaxing, slowing his strides as he planned exactly how he'd apologize to her for being a jackass. They wouldn't have much time to talk before he needed to leave for the park, but he definitely had a few things he wanted to tell his sister. The first being that he loved her, no matter what.

He got a whiff of a few other scents that seemed familiar when he noticed the door of his apartment standing wide-open. Cursing, he sprinted down the hall, sliding to a stop as he entered the living room.

"Kat!" he shouted, eyes darting back and forth around the space. "Where are you? Jenna, are you here?"

Before the words were out of his mouth, Connor knew the answer. His nose confirmed there was no one there. Trevor, Hale, and Rachel raced inside, spreading out through his tiny apartment to search it, though he wasn't sure why they bothered. It was obvious the place was empty.

"Connor!" Trevor called out. "In the kitchen."

He ran that way to see his teammate standing beside the small table, looking down at the glass of milk and the plate with a half-eaten sandwich.

"The glass is warm," Trevor said. "It's been sitting here for a while."

Heart thudding, Connor turned and hurried into the outer hallway. Closing his eyes, he slowly inhaled the scents he'd picked up before.

"Jenna was here, but she never went inside," he murmured, more to himself than his pack mates, who had moved out of the apartment to join him. "There are also at least three other scents that I recognize. I don't know from where, though."

He opened his eyes to see Trevor and Rachel sniffing around while he and Hale stood waiting to see if they could shed more light on things.

A moment later, Trevor's eyes widened. "It's the big warlock we fought in front of Demarcus Jones's home the other day—Tatum Graves. I'm almost sure the other scents belong to a witch and warlock we faced out at the farmhouse."

"Marko has Kat," Connor growled even as his inner wolf let out a howl of its own. "He must have had someone watching the apartment all along, waiting for the right moment to grab her. I'm assuming Jenna was just in the wrong place at the wrong time."

He couldn't believe he was speaking so calmly, especially since his inner wolf was on the verge of completely losing it. His soul mate was in the hands of the most dangerous man in this part of the country. A man who intended to use her for a horrible ritual that would take away her freedom forever. Take her away from *him*. Not to mention the fact Marko also seemed to have his sister now, too. Would he keep Jenna alive until the ritual or kill her before?

"We're going to get both of them back," Trevor promised as Connor led the way to the stairs. "We need to call Gage because this drastically changes our plan. Without having Kat with us, we're going to have to go in there blind. It'll just be our Pack against a whole coven of magic users."

Kat desperately tried to convince herself that she was in Connor's big, comfortable bed, sleeping in after another late night of lovemaking. But then she felt something hard digging painfully into her back, followed immediately by a surprisingly cold breeze blowing across her face. That's when she realized she wasn't in Connor's apartment. And she definitely wasn't in bed.

She forced her eyes open, wincing at the sense of disorientation that came over her when she saw the tree branches waving above her head. The sky overhead was growing dim, telling Kat that twilight was approaching fast. That meant it had been hours since Tatum had kidnapped her and Jenna from Connor's apartment.

The ritual would be starting soon.

If it hadn't already.

Kat tried to move, not only to get a look around, but also to get that stabbing pain out of her back. But moving proved nearly impossible. When she felt the tingling tension course through her, she realized she was being held in a binding spell. One that was much stronger than the one Marko had used on her four years ago. Luckily, she was still able to turn her head to the left and right a little bit. It wasn't much, but she could make out at least part of the scene around her.

She was in a forest, that much was obvious. It was fairly dark under the trees, but the guttering lights of several nearby torches allowed her to see that she was in a small clearing with pine trees all around her. She could hear a soft gurgling sound to her right, so there was probably a stream over there.

That's when she realized she was in Sam Houston Trail Park. At least, she hoped that's where she was, since that's where Connor and the Pack would be coming to stop the ritual. She simply had to hold out until they arrived.

She had a momentary spike of fear. What if Marko and his coven were expecting the Pack to show up? Considering Tatum had come to the apartment, that almost guaranteed the coven had been watching Kat and Connor and were aware of the connection between them. Did Marko know they were soul mates? And that Connor would do anything for her?

Around her, the soft murmur of chanting began to fill the air, almost blocking out the soothing sounds of the nearby stream. Kat couldn't see anyone, but she had no doubt it was Marko's coven starting to collect power for the ritual. She knew she was right when, a split second later, the fine hairs on her arms began to stand on end. It reminded her of the tingle of static electricity she sometimes got when she took clothes out of the dryer.

Trying to be as subtle as possible, Kat turned

her head to the left as far as it would go and saw two of the kidnapped teens lying on the ground in that direction, outside the protection circle. A tilt to the right revealed the other three kids. For a moment, she wondered where Jenna was. Had Marko killed her?

Pushing that horrible thought from her mind, she focused on the kids again, only to realize that none of them were moving. What if they were already dead? What if the ritual was only seconds away from being completed and it was too late for her to stop it?

She was on the verge of losing it when she caught movement from the corner of her eye. She turned her head again to see that the teenager on the ground closest to her was indeed breathing. She could tell by the slight rise and fall of the boy's chest.

Kat let out a sigh of relief. Hopefully that meant they were all merely caught in a binding spell like she was.

She looked around again, trying to find Jenna, craning her head around as much as she could in every direction. But Connor's sister was nowhere to be seen. That scared the hell out of her. Had Marko and his people already gotten rid of her?

Not wanting to even think what that would do to Connor, she resolutely pushed the possibility aside and reached out for the magic she felt pulsing all around her, hoping she could use it to break free of the invisible cords encasing her body. But it was no use. While she could sense the power of life flooding the clearing, she couldn't grasp it. Every time she reached for the magic, it slipped away.

Damn, it was frustrating.

"So, you're finally awake," a deep voice said from somewhere behind her, out of her line of sight. "And right on time, too. We were about to start the ritual without you."

Kat tipped her head back as far as the binding would allow it to go, catching sight of Marko standing there in his black cloak, his face covered with a light sheen of sweat despite how cool it was tonight. He'd obviously been working a lot of magic already, setting up all the binding spells and starting the process of energizing the protective circle. Seeing him again in person brought back all the horrible memories of him killing her coven. Her heart started beating faster and it was suddenly hard to breathe. This was the man who'd taken everything from her, and now, he intended to take even more.

"And before you waste your time trying to use magic to free yourself, don't," Marko added. "Even though the circle isn't completely closed yet, I've already cut you off from the flow of magic. You're as helpless against me as any hapless mortal."

"You're an evil a-hole, you know that?" she said, locking eyes with him—as hard at that was to do when she was staring at him upside down like this. It was impossible to put into words how much she hated him. "You can't possibly think you'll get away with this."

Marko chuckled and moved around to Kat's right, stepping carefully over the circle his coven had dug into the soft earth. The circle started to glow soft green as it was slowly filled with magic. It wasn't enough to keep him from moving back and forth across it yet, but it soon would be.

"I could argue that the term *evil* is merely a matter of perspective." Crouching beside her, he reached out to run his hand over her hair. Kat couldn't stop herself from jerking away. Not that she could move all that much. That only earned her a snort of derision. "But in this case, I won't bother. You have something I want, and I'm going to take it. If that meets the definition of evil to you, I'm fine with that. Mostly because in a very short period of time, you won't even have an opinion on the matter anymore."

She opened her mouth to respond, but Marko pressed a finger to her lips before she could say anything. "And as far as getting away with this, of course I will. Who's going to stop me—you? Or maybe you think your werewolf boyfriend and his pack of mutts will do it?"

Kat had to fight to contain the gasp of fear that threatened to slip out. She knew Marko was aware of her relationship with Connor but knowing that and hearing him say the words out loud were two completely different things. It only emphasized how much danger Connor and his pack mates were in.

"By the way," Marko said, as if an errant thought had just occurred to him. "What's with you and these mutts? Don't tell me you purposely tracked down a pack of werewolves and threw yourself at one of them because you thought it would provide you some kind of protection? Honestly, I never thought that much of you to begin with, but I would have thought you'd look for help from a better source. I mean, you ran back and forth across the country for more than three years only to decide to settle down with a werewolf pack, of all things. You would have been better to go underground and find yourself a clan of ghouls. They might have eaten you, but at least I never would have found you."

Kat ignored what he said, refusing to rise to the bait. Besides, she had some questions of her own. Even if Marko didn't give her anything useful in the way of answers, it might drag out the start of the ritual so Connor and his pack mates could find them. Even now, members of the coven moved around the clearing, taking the blankets off the kids, and positioning them at specific points around the circle. They were getting closer.

Would Connor get here in time? Did she

want him to, especially since Marko was clearly ready for him?

"Did you let me escape that protective circle four years ago?" she demanded.

Marko regarded her for so long, she thought he wouldn't answer. Then he snorted again and shook his head as if the question was stupid. "You have no idea how close you were to dying at that moment, do you?"

She glared at him. "What do you mean?"

"You're a powerful witch," he said. "That's why I chose you. But absorbing the channeling gift of all twelve members of your coven was more than your body could handle, even in the familiar form I trapped you in. You were seconds away from being turned into a burned-out husk. That was why I allowed you to smudge the circle. I let you run so your body could slowly get used to its new abilities, knowing I could track you anywhere you ran. Truthfully, I expected it to only take a few weeks at the most. It shocked the hell out of me when it took your body four years to adjust. It wasn't until you got here to Dallas and stopped running that everything evened out. While it took longer than I expected, it was worth it in the end."

It didn't surprise Kat that her body had only started to strengthen after she'd found Connor. It was because he was her soul mate. She wondered for a moment if Marko knew anything about that bond and how it helped her recover her magic. Probably not. The warlock would never be able to imagine a power greater than the magic he lusted after. Something told her that if he knew, there was nothing in the world that would have kept him from crowing about it.

Marko turned to murmur something to one of the members of his coven that Kat couldn't quite make out, but it almost certainly had to do with the ritual.

Things were moving too fast.

She needed to slow them down.

"What did you do with Jenna?" Kat asked.

Marko turned back to give her a frown. "Who?"

"The woman Tatum brought to Connor's apartment to trick me into opening the door," she snapped.

For a moment, it seemed like Marko didn't have a clue who she was talking about, but then he smirked, and Kat knew she definitely wasn't going to like whatever he had to say.

"Oh, her. Don't worry about her," he said. "She's fine. But that's only because I thought it might be good to have someone around after the ritual so I can test out how well it worked."

"What the hell does that mean?" she demanded.

What if Marko knew exactly who Jenna was and intended to use that against Connor? But before he could answer, Tatum came over and leaned down to whisper something in his ear. Whatever it was, it made Marko grin.

"While I would love to stand here and answer all your questions, it's almost time to start the ritual," he said as he straightened to his full height. "The last remnants of summer's light are fading, bringing on the desolation of darkness and winter. Besides, we both know the only reason you're asking all these questions is because you think that will give your werewolf boyfriend time to show up and save you."

Kat wanted to deny it, if only to try and drag the argument out a little longer. But then the sound of chanting grew louder, and she looked around to see all twelve members of Marko's coven standing outside the circle, their faces intent as they focused on their leader. The tingling she'd felt all over her body seconds before grew steadily stronger until she swore there were electrical currents running across the surface of her skin.

"For what it's worth, your werewolf and the rest of his pack are close by." Marko gazed down at her. "Unfortunately for you, they won't be able to find you. We've obscured this section of the park a dozen different ways. Even with whatever enhanced abilities they have, they could walk right past this clearing and never even know you're here, no matter how loud you scream. And trust me, you will scream before I'm done."

Kat told herself not to panic, that he was simply

trying to scare her. But then she remembered how painful Marko's spell had been the first time around, and her heart suddenly began to beat out of control. She struggled against the invisible bonds that held her again, even though she knew it would do no good. All she did was elicit a sardonic laugh from Marko.

"While that is fun to watch, we have to get started." He regarded her thoughtfully. "You might want to brace yourself. This is going to hurt like hell."

Marko turned his palms until they were facing her, then started speaking in barely comprehensible Latin. Burning hot fire immediately rushed through Kat, making it feel like her entire body was engulfed in flames.

And all she could do was scream.

CHAPTER 24

EVEN THOUGH THEY KNEW THE GENERAL LOCA-tion of the clearing where Marko was doing the ritual, it still took Connor and his team way too long to find the place. But now that they could see the thick wall of thickets ahead of them, along with the discreet trail markers Gage and the others had left earlier, he knew they were in the right part of the park.

Kat, Jenna, and the kids Marko had kidnapped were close.

And considering there was barely a glimmer of daylight left in the western sky, it wasn't an understatement to say they were definitely cutting it close, too.

"Connor, are you in position?" Gage's voice came over the earpiece he was wearing. "We've only got a few minutes before the sun drops completely below the horizon. We need to move."

"Roger that. We're on the south side of the clearing, two hundred yards from the edge of the objective," Connor told him, looking around at his pack mates and the half dozen cops Sandoval had brought with him. "We're ready to go on your mark."

"We're at two minutes and counting," Gage

confirmed. "And don't worry. You'll know when it's time."

Connor didn't doubt that for a second. The new plan they'd come up with on the way through the park was simple but functional. Gage and the majority of the Pack, including everyone who could handle a full werewolf shift, would hit the clearing from the north and the west, going in hard, fast, and loud. Once Marko and his coven were distracted by that full frontal assault, Connor, Rachel, Trevor, and Hale would slip in and grab Kat, Jenna, and the kids. Sandoval and his detectives from the Missing Persons Unit would wait outside the perimeter of the clearing, ready to take custody of the teens and run like hell to get them out of the park.

"You sure you don't want us to go in with you?" Sandoval asked softly, leaning in close as he eyed the section of vines and thickets ahead of them. "If those witches and warlocks are as nasty as you say, won't you need all the help you can get?"

"I appreciate the offer, Detective," Connor said. "But let us do our part, and you do yours. It's the only way we're all going to get out of this alive."

Sandoval seemed inclined to argue but then nodded, frowning as Connor and his SWAT teammates loaded their weapons and checked their tactical gear. "Did I hear one of your teammates say that warlock has your girlfriend and your sister now, too?"

Connor nodded grimly, waiting for the detective to say something about him being too close to the situation. But the rebuke never came. Instead, the other cop gave his shoulder a reassuring squeeze and murmured something about hoping Connor got them back safely.

Connor hoped the same thing.

A series of long, low howls echoed over the radio, making Sandoval and his people jump in alarm. A split second later, automatic gunfire ripped through the darkness.

Connor turned to signal his pack mates. "Time to go."

Giving Sandoval a nod, Connor turned and ran straight toward the heaviest section of thickets. He and his pack mates had to force their way through brush and vines that seemed to fight them every step of the way. When they finally broke through, it was like stepping into another world. The roar of the gunfire was louder in here, the darkness under the trees lit up by all the muzzle flashes and walls of roiling fires. His other pack mates, some partially shifted and others in their full wolf form, were darting everywhere across the clearing, clawing and biting at Marko's coven.

Even though they were outnumbered by the Pack, the witches and warlocks didn't seem concerned, and a few seconds later, Connor saw one of this teammates, all two hundred and fifty pounds of his shaggy wolf form, go flying into the darkness of the surrounding forest. There was a horrendous crash as the Pack's biggest werewolf smashed through several pine trees and kept right on going. Connor cursed. A werewolf could handle a lot of damage, but a crushed skull or a branch impaling one in the heart would be enough to finish them.

Praying his teammate would be okay, Connor turned his attention back to the center of the clearing.

A light-green glow filled the protective circle, and he could just make out Kat lying motionless on the ground, Marko standing over her.

Connor's heart constricted in his chest.

Was he too late?

But then he saw the warlock's lips move. Marko wouldn't be chanting right now if he'd already finished the ritual, right?

He strained to hear what Marko was saying but couldn't pick up anything. Even over all the growling and shooting, he should be able to hear what the man was saying.

It was the circle. It was trapping all sound inside it.

Connor quickly moved in that direction, intent on forcing his way through the circle to get to Kat. But he and his pack mates had barely taken more than a few steps before another disturbing sight caught their attention. Five members of Marko's coven were standing around the circle, each with a wicked-looking knife in their hands, one near each of the kids they'd kidnapped.

Kids who were in some kind of magical trance, if the vacant look in their eyes was anything to go by, and probably had no idea what was about to happen to them.

It wasn't that difficult to guess what they planned to do with those weapons.

And that they were going to do it right now.

Connor charged forward, heading toward Addy and the man reaching for her throat with his knife. Out of the corner of his eye, Connor saw Trevor and his other pack mates spreading out, knowing that every one of them would do anything necessary to save the other kids.

He was still ten feet from Addy and the man holding her, his gun trained on the bastard and ready to fire, when something slammed into him from the side. The impact was so sudden and violent, he thought for a second he'd been hit by a truck. He bounced and skidded across the clearing, slamming through two trees before thudding to a stop against a third.

Connor vaguely realized that his handgun had gone missing at some point during his tumble, but he didn't have time to look for it before invisible fingers wrapped around his throat and jerked him to his feet. Before he knew what was happening, he was dangling a yard above the ground, struggling to breathe.

He partially shifted, fangs and claws coming out as he tried to fight a threat he couldn't see. Then Tatum stepped in front of him, a broad smile on his face as he gazed up at Connor.

"Marko said you and your pack of mutts would show up," Tatum said, making sure to stand out of kicking range of Connor's boots. "I argued that you'd never be that stupid. Apparently, I was wrong. You werewolves really are that dumb."

Connor did his best to ignore the man's gloating, more concerned with breathing—and what was going on around them.

In the darkness behind Tatum, Connor could make out Rachel, Trevor, and Hale fighting to reach the five teens. They weren't getting any closer, but at least they were keeping the witches and warlocks busy. If not for that, those kids would probably already be dead.

As for the rest of Marko's coven, at least two of them were down and unmoving, but when Connor did a quick head count, he saw six of his teammates were missing.

Shit.

In the center of the protective circle, things were quickly going from bad to worse. Marko was kneeling at Kat's side now, the knife in his hand gleaming in the glow of the nearby fire. He twisted the blade this way and that as he spoke to her. Like he was taunting her. Something told Connor that the ritual was moving toward its conclusion. And if the knife in Marko's hand was any indication, that conclusion involved Kat's blood.

Connor refused to give in, struggling hard against the magical force slowly choking the life from him. All the while, Tatum continued to make snide comments about how werewolves were supposed to be such badasses.

"I guess that's merely another disappointing myth," the warlock said.

Realizing that Connor wasn't paying any attention to what he was saying, Tatum followed the direction of his gaze, to where Kat was lying in the center of the circle at Marko's mercy.

"Ah, that's right," Tatum murmured, turning back to Connor. "You and the witch have a thing for each other. I'm not even going to touch the whole *cats and dogs not getting along* thing because that would be too easy. But even I can imagine how hard it is for you to have to watch the ritual, knowing that when it's complete, the woman you love will be locked away in a cat's body forever, a slave to Marko and the rest of our coven."

Tatum was so busy gloating, he didn't realize he'd been wandering closer and closer until Connor kicked out with his booted foot and caught the warlock with a glancing blow to the head. It wasn't much of a strike, but it still opened a gash across Tatum's temple. More importantly, it was enough to break the spell. Connor immediately fell to the ground, finally able to suck in a grateful breath of air.

The warlock dropped to his knees, too, but he didn't stay there very long. With a curse, he shoved himself to his feet and charged at Connor, his face twisted with rage. The taunts and smiles were gone now as the warlock's hands came up with flame writhing from his palms, flowing outward in the blink of an eye.

Connor took another gulp of fresh air and launched himself at Tatum, meeting the warlock halfway. As they clashed, Connor led with a punch, claws extended to rip the man apart. The thick material of Tatum's cloak resisted for a moment, even as the flames in his hands flared up around both of them. Fire scorched Connor's arms, neck, and face, but he ignored it, focusing on forcing his claws into the warlock's gut.

He growled and dug deeper, tearing through the material and into the man's stomach. Tatum let out a cry of pain, and the flames around them surged before finally disappearing as the warlock collapsed.

Connor didn't wait for the man to hit the ground but instead took off running toward the protective circle and his mate. Out the corner of his eye, he saw Trevor and his other pack mates still struggling to reach the kids who were being held at knifepoint. None of the witches and warlocks seemed concerned there were werewolves all around them. Clearly, they didn't consider the Pack a threat.

He sprinted toward the simmering wall of glowing green light separating him from Kat and Marko, intending to tear his way through it by pure force and momentum. He braced himself, expecting some level of resistance going through the wall, kind of like the way he'd had to fight his way through those thickets earlier.

He was wrong.

When he slammed into the dome of light, it felt like running into a brick wall. Something in his shoulder crunched, and the next thing Connor knew, he was lying on the ground, his head ringing and vision blurred from the impact against something that was clearly nothing like a wall of thickets.

Even as he shook his head in an attempt to clear the cobwebs, Connor realized he was never going to get through that protective circle.

Not on his own.

A flash of movement caught his eye, and he looked over to see the witches and warlocks holding the teens hostage simultaneously lifting their knives for the killing blows.

At the same time, Marko reached for Kat's slender hand, the tip of his blade angling toward her palm.

Connor shoved himself upright already knowing it was too late. He and his pack mates weren't going to be able to reach Kat—or the teens—in time.

———

Davina had been right about one thing at least, Kat thought. Marko had joined her in the protective circle, standing right beside her as the magical energies flared to full life around them, locking them away from everyone and everything else in the clearing. She tried to convince herself that was a good thing, that it meant she'd have a chance to take down Marko at the moment Davina had promised he'd be most vulnerable.

Well, *promised* might be too strong of a word.

Perhaps *theorized* was better.

Or even *strongly hoped*?

Whatever the word might be, she had to believe Davina was right and that she'd be able to use the gifts Marko had ripped from the members of her coven and transferred to her four years ago. And that she'd be able to do it in time to control the power stored in the ley lines around Dallas and turn it against him before he took that control for himself and she never got it back.

But as Marko continued to chant the words of his ritual, the throbbing pain in her head and the fire burning under her skin got worse by the second, the thought that she could ever control any of this seemed like a joke. How was she supposed to consider regaining use of her magic when she could barely even think?

Kat wasn't sure how, but she knew the exact moment when Connor and the Pack arrived. Not only because growls and gunfire filtered through the protective circle, but because she could actually *feel* Connor nearby. As she caught sight of wolves on four legs flying through the air, she knew he and his pack mates would fight with everything they had to save her and the kids. Unfortunately, she didn't know if it would be enough.

She gritted her teeth and fought against the binding spell holding her, doing everything she could to catch even a glimpse of Connor. But while she didn't see him, she did see witches and warlocks savagely toss other members of the Pack out of the clearing as others went down under one spell or another. Werewolves were tough, but she wasn't sure how they were all going to survive this. The original plan had depended on her magic to help them, yet here she was, bound inside a protective circle, letting them down.

Then she saw the coven members drag Addy and the other teens to their feet, knives in their hands, and the part of her mind still aware remembered Davina's warning, that sacrificing them would mark the crescendo of the ritual.

She would need to make her move against Marko soon, but she still had no idea what to do. She was going to fail the kids like she'd failed Connor and his pack mates...like she'd failed the members of her own coven four years ago. And as it had back then, her failure would only lead to anguish and death. More friends and more people who'd trusted her to keep them safe. But this time, the man she loved—her soul mate—would pay the price, too.

Forcing her attention away from the pain ricocheting around her body, she reached out once more to try and get a grip on the magic surging around her like a tidal wave. But no matter how hard she tried, the magic that had always responded to her so easily fluttered away from her grasp.

She kept at it anyway, alternating between forcefully grabbing at the magic and passively letting it come to her on its own. Neither approach worked.

Kat felt tears fill her eyes and slide down her cheeks as the frustration became overwhelming.

"You're wasting your time," Marko said in a bored tone. She darted her eyes in the direction of his voice to see him kneeling near her right shoulder, regarding her as if she were nothing more than an irritating chore he had to get done before moving on to better things. "I've completely blocked your access to magic until the right time in the ritual. I can't have you messing up all the work I've accomplished over the past four years."

"Marko, you don't have to do this." She bit her lip to stifle a scream as searing pain enveloped her mind and body. "You're already powerful. You don't need to hurt those poor kids or Connor and his pack. You're already the most powerful warlock in the country. If you walk away now, no one will stop you."

"Walk away?" Marko let out a low, menacing laugh. "Why would I do that and waste all the time and effort I've put into this? Why would I be content to simply be the most powerful warlock in the country when I can be so much more?"

Crap, he sounded like a psychopath. Actually, Marko Kemp gave psychopaths a bad name. "What more could you possibly want? What could possibly be worth all this suffering and death?"

"Ultimate power, of course," he said, his tone suggesting she was stupid. "The only goal in the universe worth pursuing. Once you have that much power, everything else is yours for the taking. And once I have full access to the ley lines, I will have more power than anyone in the history of the world. I will be a god."

He wasn't merely a psychopath. He was a *delusional* psychopath.

And talking to him was a waste of time.

A flash of movement caught her eye, and she turned her head to the left in time to see Connor sprinting at the glowing green protective circle, his uniform a scorched mess, his arms showing deep cuts and burns. She opened her mouth to cry out a warning, but it was too late, and she could only watch helplessly as Connor slammed into the protective circle and bounced off like he'd hit a brick wall.

Beside her, Marko chuckled. "Werewolves are so predictably physical. But it doesn't matter. There's nothing he or anyone else can do to stop this now."

She turned back to tell him to go to hell, but he grabbed her hand and lifted the knife he held, ready to slice open her palm. Outside the circle, the witches and warlocks who held the teens captive stared at Marko, transfixed, waiting for a sign from their leader.

Damn it all. This was happening right now, and Kat still had no idea what she was supposed to do to find this hidden wellspring of magical abilities Davina seemed so sure she'd be able to tap into.

Kat was so focused on watching Marko's coven shove the kids to their knees right outside the circle that she didn't even feel the knife sliding across the palm of her hand. The blade bit in deep, and blood ran across her hand onto the ground. Marko immediately began chanting again, with more urgency this time.

The pain tearing through her was so extreme now that Kat was sure she'd pass out. She turned her head to look at Connor, watching him slash at the glowing walls of the protection circle with his claws, his face filled with terror and anguish. She wished she could tell him that what he was doing wouldn't work. But more than anything, she wished she could tell him one more time that she loved him.

Her eyes were still locked on Connor as Marko slit his own palm and pressed the open wound against her own hand. The contact was like touching a live electrical wire, and even within the constraints of the binding spell, her back arched so much that the only things touching the ground were her heels and the back of her head.

As she lay there spasming, sure it was over, Kat realized that something had drastically changed. While she would definitely still describe the sensations coursing through her as unbelievable agony, it took only moments to recognize that the source of that pain was completely different than it had been only seconds earlier.

It wasn't Marko stabbing into every cell in her body and making them explode.

It was magic.

Pure, raw, unlimited magic.

She was experiencing the power collected and stored within the ley lines.

Kat didn't think and pause to evaluate the risk she was taking. She simply reached out and buried her force of will into the middle of all that power.

Then she started praying she'd survive.

There was nothing but the pain, as she felt like

she was being sucked down into a whirlpool of burning oil that was thick, viscous, and white-hot. She couldn't imagine living through this situation for one more second. But then that second turned into two…and then four…and then ten. And she was still alive. At least, she thought she was. Then again, it was also possible that she was already dead, and the agony was so bad that it would keep haunting her into the afterlife.

Kat had no idea how much time passed. It felt like hours. But at some point, the sensation of being burned alive faded away to be replaced by the luxurious feeling of lying out on a sunny beach completely naked.

She was channeling the magic from the ley lines—all of it. The collective living magic of millions upon millions of people, animals, and plants. It was way more power than any human in the history of the world had ever attempted to harness without it killing them. And yet, she was still alive.

At least, she hoped so.

She opened her eyes, her gaze immediately going around the circle from one teen to the next as the witches and warlocks with the knives in their hands moved ever closer to completing the final step of the ritual.

"Prohibere," Kat whispered under her breath.

She doubted Marko would hear the single word over his chanting, which had only gotten more strident since he'd pressed his palm to hers. She had no idea if such a simple spell as the one she'd just invoked would find its way past the protective circle and actually keep Marko's coven from killing their captives. Normally, it wouldn't. Nothing was supposed to get in or out of a protective circle. That was kind of the point of the whole thing. But she was accessing the ley lines, which were outside the circle. So maybe this particular protection circle was unique. She prayed that was the case.

Kat damn near cheered when she realized that all five of the witches and warlocks holding the teens hostage had been frozen solid by her spell. A moment later, Connor's pack mates charged toward the kids and their captors, only to stop in their tracks, still held at arm's length by the residual magic coming off the circle.

Marko must have picked up on the disruption of his perfectly planned-out ritual right then because the chanting stopped, and his eyes snapped open. He frowned at his coven, the witches and warlocks still immobilized by her spell, before looking sharply at Kat. Rage and suspicion battled for dominance on his face before the latter won out.

"What did you do?" he demanded angrily.

He glanced down at their still joined hands, as if he thought that was the cause of the sudden hiccup in his mad scheme. Kat didn't say anything, but she couldn't control the smile that began to tip up the corners of her mouth.

Eyes wide, Marko tried to shake off her grip, his anger turning first to confusion, then all-out panic. She squeezed his hand more tightly, refusing to let go as she remembered Davina's words about her having all the control over the lines while Marko would essentially be defenseless.

"What's wrong?" she whispered, still holding on to the hand he was desperately trying to drag out of her grasp. "I thought you wanted all the power. That you wanted to be a god. Well, what are we waiting for? Let's see if the ley lines are everything you dreamed they'd be."

It was only then that Kat felt the familiar connection between her and Marko. She realized now that it had always been there. It was probably how he'd tracked her all over the country. Even now, she didn't need to reach for it to use it. It simply existed. And when she let herself sink once more into the whirlpool of endless energies welling up from the ley lines, it seemed almost comically easy to allow all that power to pass through her to Marko. All millions and millions of lives' worth of it.

It was, to say the least, a lot of power.

She felt the heat as all that magic came roaring through her, and she squeezed her eyes tightly closed. A split second later, Marko cried out in pain. She and the warlock were connected by more than merely the touch of their hands now. The sensation of all that magic coursing through her was intoxicating, but it was also terrifying. A part of her recognized that humans were never meant to access this much power. That's probably why it was almost easy to let the power slip through her fingers. And as her grasp on the magic began to fade, she wondered if it would be better if she never touched this overwhelming, almost intoxicating, level of power again. But could she turn her back on something so precious to her like that, even if she feared she might come to abuse it?

As she slowly floated down to lie on the ground again, she opened her eyes. While she didn't try to move, she instinctively knew she wasn't restrained by Marko's spell any longer. Realizing their hands were still clasped, she turned her head to look at the warlock, only to let out a squeal of disgust when she saw his hand was nothing more than a nasty carbon-crusted skeletal thing now. She let go and quickly looked away, not wanting to see if the rest of him was like that.

Thankfully, Connor appeared at her side at that moment, and she allowed the feel of his strong arms to distract her from thoughts of what she'd just done. She hugged him back tightly, not caring that his tactical vest was rough against her face. She'd stopped Marko from hurting him and every-one else she cared about.

Connor must have held her for nearly a full

minute before she finally figured out that the protective circle Marko had put up had collapsed. It
was only then that she noticed all the shooting and
growling and snarling and fighting had stopped.
Instead, moans and groans filled the air, the after-
math of the battle.

"Addy and the others?" she asked softly, pulling
back to try and get a look over his shoulder. "Are
they okay? What about Jenna?"

Even as she spoke, Kat caught sight of Trevor
carrying Jenna out of the clearing in his arms, walking past the other SWAT cops, all of whom seemed
pretty beat up, bleeding, and torn, but thankfully,
alive. Connor's sister looked confused, but she
seemed okay. And judging by the way she was
clinging to Trevor as he spirited her away to safety,
she adored being in his arms.

"Trevor promised he'd look after her," Connor
said, following her gaze. "Jenna is shaken up, but
fortunately doesn't remember a single thing after
getting grabbed outside our apartment and being
forced to ring the doorbell. I hate that she got
pulled into this, but at least I don't have to try and
explain about magic and werewolves. I don't think
my sister could handle that. She's fragile as it is."

Kat didn't think his assessment of his sister was
necessarily true but decided that right now wasn't
the time to make Connor understand that he
needed to stop coddling Jenna. That his sister was

much stronger than he seemed to want to give her credit for.

So instead of saying anything about it, Kat turned her attention to the other people moving around the clearing and saw Cooper take off running from the scene, pure panic on his face. She turned to ask Connor what that was about but forgot her question when she caught sight of Rachel kneeling on the ground, talking softly to Addy and Ben. Both kids seemed exhausted, shaken, and somewhat confused, but otherwise healthy. Hale, Sandoval, and another detective from Missing Persons were leading the other three teens out of the clearing. The rest of Sandoval's people were looking around the area in obvious amazement, taking in the unmoving figures of Marko's coven lying here and there. While the detectives clearly had a lot of questions about what happened, none of them said anything out loud.

Kat assumed that was probably for the best.

"Are any of the witches and warlocks still alive?" she asked. Considering none were moving, she didn't think so.

"Most of them, actually," Gage said, coming over to crouch beside them. "They were damn hard to deal with, but when you dropped Marko, the ones left standing went down, too. It was like they were connected to him somehow."

"They probably were," Kat murmured. It was a relief to know she hadn't killed them. "For all the power Marko already had, I wouldn't put it past him to have set up a siphoning charm to draw energy from his coven. When I did what I did to him, the blowback would have rippled through the connection. Luckily, they didn't end up like Marko."

Connor and Gage studied her intently for a moment, and she prayed they didn't ask her details about exactly what she'd done to Marko. She didn't want to relive the moment. Or take responsibility for it.

"While that explains a lot, it still leaves us with a problem," Gage said. "As in what the hell are we going to do with all of them? We can slap cuffs on them, but when they wake up, I doubt a prison cell will hold them or their magic for long. There'll be nothing to stop them from doing this same thing again, with or without Marko."

Kat thought about that for a moment, looking at all the possibilities, but could only come up with one solution. What she was considering was wrong on so many levels and went against everything she believed in as a witch. But what else could she do? If Marko's coven ended up in jail, they'd be out of it within hours. The only question would be how many lives they took with them.

"I might be able to do something about that," she finally said.

Connor's brow furrowed. "You can?"

She nodded. "There's a spell I can do that will bind

their magic permanently. Trying to do something like that, especially to so many witches and warlocks, would be impossible without the power from the ley lines, but with it, I should be able to pull it off. They'll still be able to feel the magic around them but not use it. It's the most horrible thing you can do to a witch or warlock, but at least it will give us a chance to figure out what we can do long-term. Maybe we'll get lucky, and STAT can find a way to help."

Connor and Gage exchanged grim looks.

"I'd never ask you to do this if there were any other way," Gage said.

Connor tenderly brushed her hair back from her face. "Are you sure you're up to this?"

When Kat nodded, Connor helped her to her feet, keeping an arm around her as she recited the words for the binding spell. The only thing that was more upsetting than the act itself was how easy it was. A short dip into the power of the ley lines along with a few murmured words of intent, and it was over. The spell would last for a few weeks. Hopefully, by then they'd have a long-term answer.

"Marko's coven won't be an issue now, but how are you guys going to explain all of this?" she asked Connor as she looked around the clearing. "Addy and Ben might not say anything because they know Rachel, but what about the other three kids?"

"Rachel will talk to them," Connor said. "She's good with kids. They'll go along with anything she suggests. And as far as explaining all of this? We'll say Marko and his followers were a bunch of kooks trying to sacrifice kids until Marko accidentally caught himself on fire. Trust me, people will believe it. Because the alternative is more than they're willing to think about."

Kat thought he was being a little too optimistic, but then again, the Pack had been dealing with this strange stuff for a while. Something told her they had it down pat by now. If they said people would believe the convenient lies, they were probably right.

Connor regarded her thoughtfully for a moment, his hazel eyes clouded with worry. "So with Marko gone, that means the familiar curse is broken, right? You won't need to worry about turning back into a cat anymore, will you?"

Kat's heart broke in half as a huge weight settled in the center of her chest and began to crush her. She wished she could give him the simple answer he was looking for, and for a moment she considered lying and telling him that it was all over. It would be horrible later if she was wrong, but right at this moment, it seemed an easy way to deal with the situation. But in the end, she couldn't do something like that to her soul mate.

"I don't know," she murmured. "Davina and I talked about it, and she said there's a chance Marko tied the spell to my magic instead of his. If he did, then the spell will still be there. We won't know for sure until midnight. If I'm going to turn back into a cat, it will be then."

Connor took a deep breath, like he was processing what she'd said. Then he glanced at his watch. "That gives us two hours to wait."

She nodded, swallowing hard. The wait was going to be horrendous. And while it was going to be difficult for her, she shuddered at the thought of how hard it was going to be on Connor if he had to watch her change back into a cat.

"Would you rather go somewhere else?" he asked gently, tipping her face up so he could gaze into her eyes. "I mean, instead of hanging around here?"

She gave him a small smile. "Yeah. Let's go to your place. If I only have two more hours in my human form, I don't want to waste it hanging around a crime scene."

Connor cupped her face in his hand. "Even if you turn back into a cat, I'll still love you the same. Well, maybe not exactly the same, because that would be weird. But I'll love you, and I'll never give up on us. You know that, right?"

Kat supposed she *had* known that, but it still felt unbelievably good to hear him say it out loud. She went up on her toes, pressing her lips to his. "Yeah, I know. Now, take me home and show me exactly how much you love me."

CHAPTER 25

KAT COLLAPSED FORWARD ONTO CONNOR'S chest, gasping for breath as her heart continued to pound out of control for several long, fabulous moments. She pressed her face against the powerful muscles under her, lulled to a near stupor by the strong, steady heartbeat of her soul mate. The one man who would stay with her forever.

Of their own accord, her eyes drifted to the clock on the nightstand, a cynical part of her mind noting that forever in this case might be actually defined as fourteen minutes. That's how long they had until the digital numbers on Connor's bedside clock flipped to midnight, and they learned what kind of future they would have.

They had come back to the apartment and immediately fallen into bed. There had been no talk, no quiet murmurs of their feelings or their fears. They'd simply let themselves exist in that moment and no other, taking comfort from each other's touch.

"What are you thinking?" Connor asked, his words rumbling up through his chest, vibrating into her own.

Kat almost lied and told him she wasn't thinking

about anything at all, that she was simply lying there enjoying the moment and the feel of his warm skin against hers. But considering that she might only have the gift of speech for a very short period of time, it felt horrible to even consider lying.

"I was thinking how ironic it is that I now have all this power," she said, turning her head so that her chin rested on his chest, her eyes meeting his. "Yet I can't use it to give us the one thing I want more than anything else in the world—to be able to stop that clock from changing and taking away everything we have."

Connor didn't say anything for a while, and Kat felt bad for ruining the mood.

"You may not have the power to stop time," he finally murmured, one of his hands coming up to trace warm fingers up and down her back. Even after the number of times they'd made love over the past hour and a half, it was stunning how much his touch could affect her. It was beautiful. "But now that you've leveled up, as far as with the power you have," he added, and she could hear the hopeful note in his voice, "are you sure there isn't some way you can break the spell Marko used on you? I know you said you'd tried for years, but maybe it will be different now that you're stronger."

She let out a heavy sigh. "Being stronger won't help in this situation. I wish it would, but it won't. I've spent the past four years doing everything I could to understand the familiar spell Marko put on me and locate where he buried it inside me, but I could never find it. I've never even come close. And being stronger isn't going to tell me where it is or how to undo it."

"But what if it does?" Connor pleaded. "You never know until you try. Maybe it will work this time."

Kat knew it was desperation talking, but seeing Connor looking at her the way he was, so scared and lost, she couldn't say no. So she rested her head on his chest again, then closed her eyes and tried to relax enough to feel the magic flowing through her.

Relaxing when there was a clock ticking on what was left of a normal life was rather difficult, but she forced herself to focus on her breathing as she slowly submerged herself in the magic that flowed all around her. As it had inside Marko's ritual circle, the magic was far more intense than it had ever been—hotter, almost abrasive. This time, Kat relaxed and let it happen.

Turning her attention inward, Kat tried to filter through the magic inside her, seeking out anything that seemed wrong or even different. Using magic to gently "see" inside herself versus using it to affect the world around her was difficult, to say the least. From experience, she knew there were few magic users who were comfortable with it, which was why she'd never found anyone who could help her.

Kat searched for what seemed like forever, not

even sure what she was looking for. And while she could certainly sense so much more of the power flowing through and around her, having access to it gave her no greater insight into her own body or what might be wrong with it. There was simply nothing she could find that screamed *here's why you're about to turn back into a cat!* In the end, she had no idea if the inability to find anything was because she couldn't see Marko's spell or because that spell had disappeared with his death. She hoped it was the latter, but she was too cynical from four years of this horrible life to think it was that simple.

Kat slowly opened her eyes, a glance at the clock revealing that she'd wasted far too many minutes on a fool's errand. Minutes she could never get back.

"Nothing?" Connor asked, the disappointment in his eyes making her think he knew the answer to the question before he'd even asked.

Kat shook her head, gaze slipping toward the clock on the nightstand again even as she knew she should stop torturing herself. Two minutes until everything changed.

"I can't lose you," Connor said brokenly, his arms wrapping around her, urging her higher up on his chest so her face was level with his. "Not after I've just now found you."

She dropped her mouth down to his, kissing him hard and trying to melt inside him. "You're never going to lose me," she whispered fervently against his lips, making that promise with everything she had. "No matter what happens, I will always be right here with you."

Connor buried his fingers in her hair, tipping his forehead up to touch hers. "Same. If I only get to be with you like this for a few days a year, I swear I'm going to love you more in those few days than anyone has ever loved in a lifetime. I promise you, Kat. I promise."

She knew crying wouldn't help, but as she laid there against him, her nose rubbing against his, the tears came anyway. "When I change back into a cat, it's kind of a mess," she murmured, tears falling freely now. "I should probably get off your chest. But I don't want to. I want you to hold me the entire time. No matter what."

"I will…always," he murmured, tightening his fingers in her hair and kissing her over and over until she was drunk on his taste. She refused to look at the clock anymore, wanting these precious few seconds left to last a lifetime.

Kat had no sense of how much time passed, but at some point, she realized Connor wasn't kissing her anymore. She opened tear-filled eyes to see him staring up at her, his gaze intense. She was about to ask what was wrong when he slowly turned his head to the side.

She followed his gaze, confused until she realized that the clock on the nightstand was displaying the number 12:01. Her breath caught, wondering if maybe the time was wrong. But then it flipped to 12:02 and still her body hadn't started that horribly painful twisting and spasming.

Kat held her breath for another whole minute, until she could finally accept that this was really happening. That it was finally over. Then she dropped her head down to Connor's big, strong chest and wept like a baby all over again.

She would have stayed there forever, content to simply lie there on top of him. But after a few more minutes, Connor picked her up in his arms and danced them around the bedroom like it was New Year's Eve. And if she noticed a few tears slide down his face, too, she didn't mention it. Instead, she kissed him and told him over and over that she loved him.

CHAPTER 26

"MAN, I LOVE THE SMELL OF BARBECUE IN THE morning," Connor said with a grin as he led Kat through the training building to the big open area behind it and all the people waiting for them.

Kat let out a small laugh. "You love the smell of barbecue at any time of the day. Or night, for that matter."

He chuckled. "Okay, you got me there."

She'd been to a lot of the famous SWAT team cookouts over the past nine months, but this was the first one she'd attended in human form. Being able to walk around the compound holding Connor's hand gave her a feeling that was impossible to put into words. It nearly brought tears to her eyes.

She had been doing that a lot since that night in his apartment when she realized she was going to get her life back. Even weeks later, she still felt like pinching herself sometimes, just to make sure this was all real. It was simply so perfect.

Kat took a deep breath, silently agreeing with Connor about the aromas. Whatever was cooking on the grills made her mouth water like crazy. She couldn't pick up all the individual scents like she had when she was a cat, but it still smelled absolutely delicious. She couldn't wait to sample everything, especially since now she'd be able to partake in all the different barbecue sauces without everyone complaining they were bad for her.

She glanced over to see Trevor manning the grills, five of the things all going at once, the fragrant smoke swirling around him as he deftly moved from one grill to the next, stirring and flipping as required. Beside him, Hale said something, but Trevor grinned and shook his head, replying something that looked along the lines of *nah, I got this*. Hale laughed, then turned to walk over to one of the many picnic tables, his steps noticeably slower than normal, courtesy of a warlock who'd broken his legs again. Kat had seen more werewolves in the Pack than she cared to remember damaged beyond belief since coming to Dallas, but none of them had ever been injured so badly that they'd still been limping days later. It made her realize once again how close she'd come to losing someone she cared for. Thankfully, all of them were okay.

Pushing that heartrending thought aside, Kat instead took in all the love and happiness filling the compound. There were probably forty people here today, some playing volleyball, others sitting at the tables, while several kids ran around with Tuffie and the other pets that belonged to various members of the Pack. Sandoval and the other detectives from Missing Persons who'd helped out that night were there, too, as well as Addy, Ben, the other rescued teens, and their families.

Sandoval and the other detectives from Missing Persons had stayed in close contact with all the rescued kids, stepping up to organize a fundraising effort to help the Gutierrez and Freeman families repair their homes. SWAT had thrown weight behind the project, along with STAT doing some stuff behind the scenes. With everyone working together, most of the damage had already been repaired and their homes should be completely done in another couple weeks.

She smiled as the teens laughed and joked with each other, having obviously bonded over their shared experience, even if they didn't remember most of it. The fact that they could laugh after what had happened to them was more than a little amazing, especially considering they'd only been rescued four days ago. But she supposed what they said about kids being resilient was true. Of course, it helped that the kids remembered very little about their time in captivity, and even less about the ritual in the forest. The only thing they remembered was Rachel telling them where they were and that they were safe, then being led out of the woods by Sandoval and the other detectives. While she hated Marko more than ever for what he did to those poor kids, she had to admit that their vague memories helped sell the cult story that Gage had come up with.

As she and Connor made their way around the compound, everyone they ran into gave her a warm hug as they welcomed her to the cookout and told her how glad they were that she was okay. It was a little odd being congratulated for still being human, but she understood and appreciated what they were trying to say. She was happy about it, too.

Addy and Ben ran past them, laughing and saying something about grabbing some burgers. They threw a quick wave in Connor's direction, barely giving Kat a second glance. They had no idea who she was or the role she'd played in their rescue. And she was more than fine with that. While she'd helped save their lives, that didn't mean she was part of the SWAT team. It was time to let Connor and the Pack worry about taking care of all the dangerous stuff out there in the world.

Although now that she was back to being human full-time and done saving the world, Kat supposed she'd have to come up with something else to keep her occupied—and help pay the bills. Connor had told her not to worry about money and that he'd be able to take care of both of them on his cop pay, but she wanted to contribute.

Before Marko had destroyed her life, she'd owned a shop in her hometown. It had been a rather eclectic place, selling holistic and metaphysical stuff, locally grown food, books on meditation and self-empowerment, even a few innocent charms and potions. It hadn't been a very big shop, and it hadn't made her a ton of money, but it had been all hers, and she'd loved it with all her heart. She wasn't sure if the same kind of stuff would sell as well here in Dallas, but she guessed she was going to find out.

"You're quiet," Connor whispered from beside her, glancing over at her with concern, having apparently picked up on the fact that she was lost in her own head. "Everything okay?"

She wasn't surprised he'd noticed her moment of introspection. He'd gotten pretty good at stuff like that. Perhaps it was the soul-mate bond they shared, but he always seemed to know when she was upset or worried about something.

"Just thinking about what to do for a job," she admitted. "I'm still not sure about that Little Shop of Magic idea I was telling you about. Besides the fact that I'm not sure if it'll work in Dallas, I don't know if it's where I want to put all my energies right now."

"Yeah. Opening a brand-new shop can be risky," Connor agreed, giving her a look that he probably thought was casual as he handed her a bottle of water he'd grabbed from one of the many coolers. "You know, since it seems like you've been getting more comfortable with this ley-line magic, maybe you could do something with that. So you can get better at controlling the power that comes off them while earning some money on the side, I mean."

"Uh-huh," Kat said, opening the bottle and taking a sip. "And did you have something specific in mind?"

It was obvious from the eager expression on his face that he did. She wondered if he realized how bad he was at being sneaky and whether she should tell him. Then again, maybe it was the connection the two of them had. Maybe it made it impossible for either of them to even think of hiding stuff from each other.

"Gage mentioned he might be able to get you a paid consultant position with the department," Connor said, as if the pack alpha had brought it up in the middle of a hostage negotiation or something. "We'd have to come up with a good cover story to explain your presence around the team and the department, of course." He flashed her a grin, then took a long drink of water from the bottle in his hand. "Since we obviously can't tell anyone you're a witch."

"Obviously," she agreed.

"And we'd have to use your skills sparingly so people wouldn't get suspicious," he continued. "But we're pretty good at that. I mean, we've been hiding the fact that we're werewolves forever."

She nodded. "Valid point."

Connor's eyes danced. "And think of all the awesome stuff you could do. You can help track down missing people, obscure the team with that Look Away spell, even stop bullets in midair. Those are all things that could really come in handy."

Kat couldn't believe it, yet she was not only considering the offer but liking it. A lot. Especially since she was a lot more comfortable with the leyline magic.

That night after the rescue—once it had become clear she wasn't going to turn back into a cat— she'd thought about what she'd done during the battle with Marko and admitted to Connor that she had concerns about accessing so much magic. She even wondered if she'd lost the ability to tap into all that power now that the ritual was over. But she hadn't, and as the days passed, being connected to the ley lines had become less scary and more comforting. That's when she'd come to the conclusion that maybe being one with the ley lines wouldn't be as bad as she'd thought.

"Hey," Connor said, taking her hand, concern on his handsome face. "If you're not comfortable using your magic anymore because of the influence of the ley lines, I completely understand. I'm not trying to force you into this. You know that, right?"

She smiled up at him. "I know that. And you're right, I am getting more relaxed using the magic from the ley lines. I think being a consultant would work. I definitely like the idea of helping protect people. I could also set aside some of the money I make if I ever do want to open that shop I told you about. And being able to work with you now and then would totally be a plus." She paused. Maybe she should slow down a little bit. She didn't have the job yet. "Do you honestly think Gage could talk the department into hiring me? Do they even hire consultants?"

Connor shrugged. "I have no idea, but if anyone can pull it off, it'd be Gage." He flashed her another grin. "So, what do you say? Should I give him the go-ahead to make it happen?"

Kat didn't even have to think about it. Going up on her toes, she kissed him. "Definitely. Let's do this!"

She opened her mouth to suggest talking to Gage about it right that second only to get distracted by a murmur of excitement ripple through the compound.

"I can't believe it. They actually showed up!" Connor chuckled. "And they brought Mini Cooper!"

Kat turned to see Cooper, his pretty wife, Everly, and their adorable lab mix, walking into the party, a tiny bundle held carefully in the former's arms. The sight of the big, strong alpha cradling his daughter like he was terrified he was going to drop her any second was about the cutest thing she'd ever seen.

Within seconds, everyone was up and hurrying

over to the newest addition to the Pack, rolling forward like an ocean wave. Kat couldn't help but laugh at the panicked expression that covered Cooper's face, as well as the way he protectively hugged the baby closer to his chest, like he was worried the Pack was going to knock them down. Thankfully, Everly was there to keep him in check or Cooper probably would have run off with the infant without letting anyone get a look at her.

Kat hadn't realized Cooper had been sprinting for the hospital that night after the battle with Marko and his coven in the park, when he'd taken off like a bat out of hell. It wasn't until the next morning that she and Connor learned that Everly had gone into labor just as the Pack had stormed the woods. Belle Renee Cooper had been born a little before sunrise. Gage and a few other members of the Pack had gotten a chance to see the little girl right away, but for the rest of them, this was the first time they were getting to meet the precious baby everyone in the Pack insisted on calling by the pet name Mini—as in *Mini Cooper*. Kat had to admit she was as excited as everyone else. She was a little surprised they could bring a baby out of the house so soon, though. She'd always thought babies had to stay inside for at least a few weeks. Or was it months?

It took a while for her and Connor to make it through the crowd around Cooper and Everly.

This was the first baby born to the Pack, so it was a very big deal. All Kat could say was that watching a SWAT team full of tall, muscular werewolves cooing and losing their minds over a tiny human had to be the sweetest—and most hilarious— thing ever. When she and Connor finally reached the front of the line and Cooper carefully placed the little girl in her arms, she suddenly understood what all the fuss was about.

"Oh, she's adorable!" Kat smiled down at the precious cherub in her arms with her beautiful green eyes and way more hair than she'd ever imagined a baby having. "I want one!"

Everyone within hearing distance—which meant every werewolf in the Pack—went completely still. At first, Kat wasn't sure why. It wasn't until she looked up from the baby in her arms and saw Connor gazing at her with a wide-eyed expression that she realized what she'd said.

"I didn't mean right away!" she said quickly in an attempt to clarify. "I was only saying that little Belle is so beautiful and amazing and that I'd like to have one of my own when the time is right."

Connor seemed to accept that, but then she caught the look on his face out of the corner of his eye—a look that had her thinking he was almost disappointed by her words. When she carefully placed Belle in his big arms, she felt even more sure that her soul mate was already coming up with a mental list of baby names. One sniff of little Belle and he seemed hooked. It made her wonder if babies were addicting. Or maybe Connor was more ready to start a family than even he knew.

Much sooner than Kat would have preferred, she and Connor had to hand over the tiny girl to the next person in line, barely remembering to congratulate the happy parents. But seriously, it wasn't their fault. Their daughter was as cute as a button.

Rachel and Khaki hurried up to them, dragging Kat and Connor over to the grills to grab some food before bringing them back to sit at their table. The cheeseburger, pulled pork, beans, and coleslaw were even more delicious than she remembered, and Kat said another silent prayer of thanks that she was human again. She was so focused on the conversation going on around her that she didn't realize Jenna had arrived at the compound until Connor waved, calling out for her to sit with them. His sister smiled and nodded then pointed toward the grills, motioning that she would join them after getting some food.

"I thought your sister was leaving today," Kat said.

Over by the grills, Connor's sister was smiling brightly at Trevor. As they talked, Jenna reached out to stir the chili simmering there while Trevor expertly flipped burgers. The whole thing looked so well-coordinated and effortless, it was like the two of them had done it dozens of times.

"She delayed her flight until later this evening,"

Connor said, eyeing his sister and Trevor with an expression that was somewhere between curious and suspicious. "Jenna said she wanted to be able to come to the cookout and spend a little more time with the two of us before she left."

Kat smiled at that. She and Jenna had become fast friends over the past few days. Connor's sister didn't remember much from the night of the ritual, but she definitely remembered the way Tatum had used her as bait to trick Kat into opening the door of Connor's apartment. Even though Kat had repeatedly told her that there was nothing she could have done differently, Jenna had still blamed herself. It took several long conversations over orders of takeout to get Jenna to understand that the confrontation with Marko had been a long time coming.

An unforeseen benefit of those long conversations was that Jenna and Connor had worked out their issues. Well…some of them, at least. The most important part was that Connor had apologized for using that horrible word in reference to his sister, while Jenna had admitted that maybe she hadn't actually seen Hannah that night in the dark alleys of Skid Row. Jenna had even agreed to stop looking for their sister and instead focus a little more on her own recovery.

Kat was so glad Connor and his sister were on speaking terms again. Connor had even broached the idea of the two of them heading out to California around Christmas to spend more time with his sister. Since she couldn't see her family now, being part of Connor's was extra special.

She was still thinking about how much she was looking forward to the trip when she glanced at Connor to find him openly scowling as he focused on something across the compound. She followed his gaze but didn't see anything in that direction to warrant that kind of irritated expression. Only Trevor working the grills and Jenna standing close by, laughing at something he'd said.

"What's wrong?" Kat asked softly, leaning close to whisper in his ear so none of the other members of the Pack would hear.

Connor shook his head but didn't say anything. His expression didn't change, though.

Kat leaned in and nudged him with her shoulder. "I know something's bothering you. So spill."

"Jenna said she was changing her flight so she could hang out with us some more, but it seems like she's more interested in spending time with Trevor than she is with us," he said with a slight growl.

Kat wanted to laugh but didn't. Doing that would only make the situation worse. Connor was being the prototypical big brother, thinking no one—including one of his own pack mates—was good enough for his little sister.

"What's the big deal?" she asked. "Jenna will be leaving in a few hours, so it's not like they're going to see each other again. Besides, even if they like each other, would that really be the end of the world?"

"Yes" was Connor's emphatic reply.

Kat snorted and went back to enjoying her juicy, perfectly cooked cheeseburger. She could tell from the looks on the faces of the other people at the table with them that everyone had heard their conversation and were as amused as she was, even if they hid it a little better. She was about to call out her soul mate on his childish behavior right there in front of his pack when cries of delight echoed around the compound.

She looked up to see Zane and Alyssa coming out of the admin building, Gage at their side. The couple was moving slowly, and there were still bandages on Alyssa's arms, but from the smiles on their faces, it was obvious they were thrilled to be out of the hospital and back with the Pack.

Thankfully, Zane and Alyssa's arrival had smacked Connor out of the grouchy mood he was in about what might or might not be going on between Jenna and Trevor, which was a good thing. Kat didn't want another argument between brother and sister.

Zane was in full-on alpha-protection mode, first finding Alyssa a seat at one of the tables and then getting her a plate of food. When Zane finally sat down beside his mate, Kat and Connor went over to give both of them hugs.

"We're both going to be off duty for another two

weeks, but the doctor says we'll be fine." Alyssa looked at Kat. "Now, tell me about this Marko guy. Gage said we have you to thank for taking him down—and for Zane and me being alive."

Kat did her best to downplay her part in the rescue in San Antonio and the ritual in the park, though it was pretty clear Zane and Alyssa didn't buy a word of it. Thankfully, neither of them pressed for more.

A few minutes later, Kat and Connor headed back to their own table, only to be intercepted by Gage. He had a grin on his face and a large manila envelope in his hands.

"I just got finished talking with our friends at STAT," Gage said, handing the envelope to her. "They wanted to let me know that they've found a safe place to keep those magic users we brought in. They're hoping in time they'll be able to rehabilitate them, so they won't have to spend the rest of their lives in a magic-dampening prison cell. They also wanted you to have this information. It actually didn't take as long to find them as I thought it would."

Kat stared down at the envelope for a moment, then looked back and forth between Gage and Connor. "Didn't take as long to find who?"

Connor grinned and motioned at the envelope. "Open it."

Even more curious now, Kat quickly lifted the

flap and reached inside, pulling out a handful of photos of her parents and the twins. She gazed down at the pictures in shock, tears coming to her eyes. It had been so long since she'd seen her family that all she could do was stand there speechless.

Beside her, Connor stuck his hand in the envelope to pull out a sheet of paper with an address and phone numbers, handing it to her. She studied it for a moment, then lifted her tear-filled gaze to look at him and Gage.

"Connor told me what you had to do to protect your family and gave me all the information he had on them, which wasn't much, other than what you told him," Gage said softly. "He asked if I could use my contacts at STAT to get a location on them. Turns out they didn't move all that far from Washington State. Right across the Idaho state line to Coeur d'Alene."

Kat turned her gaze on Connor, wondering when the heck he'd had time to fit this request into his busy schedule. Neither one of them had time to do much of anything since the night of the ritual.

"I called Gage that night as soon as we found out that you weren't going to turn back into a cat," he said softly. "I didn't want to mention it until we had something. I didn't want to get your hopes up, you know?"

All Kat could do was stare. How had she gotten lucky enough to stumble across this man? Yeah, being turned into a cat for the better part of four years had sucked, but if the payoff was being with Connor, she was fine with that.

"Your leave form has already been approved," Gage said to Connor. "You can take off whenever you want."

Giving them a nod and a smile, Gage walked over to join his wife, where she was sitting at one of the picnic tables.

"I thought you might want to see your family right away," Connor said softly. "Even if you don't know a spell to return their memories of you yet, we can go to Idaho so you can see for yourself that they're safe."

Kat tried to stop the tears, but it did no good. They slowly rolled down her face as she went up on her toes to kiss him again. "Do you have any idea how much I love you?"

"I have a pretty good idea." He grinned, resting his forehead to hers. "So, you up for a trip to Idaho?"

Kat kissed him again, sure her heart was going to explode with happiness. "Definitely! And I already have a spell to restore their memories."

"Then let's get out of here and book a flight."

She smiled. "Sounds good to me."

Going back to the apartment to book their flight was only part of the reason Kat wanted to leave. The other part involved letting him know exactly how much she appreciated what he'd done for her.

But halfway across the compound, Connor stopped. "Crap! What about Jenna? She came to the cookout to hang with us."

Kat glanced over at the grills, where Connor's sister was still talking with Trevor, both of them eating burgers and laughing, clearly enjoying each other's company.

She smiled at Connor. "Something tells me she won't mind if we go. We'll fill her in on what we're doing before we leave."

Connor regarded Jenna and Trevor for a moment, and she waited for him to scowl at them again, but instead, he gave her a quick kiss, then flashed her a sexy grin. "Okay, let's talk to my sister, make the rounds, and then go home."

Home.

Something warm and wonderful wrapped around Kat's heart and her lips curved. Home sounded perfect to her.

Keep reading for a sneak peek of the next book in Paige Tyler's thrilling SWAT series

NEW YORK TIMES AND USA TODAY BESTSELLER

PAIGE TYLER

LOVING THE WOLF

SWAT: SPECIAL WOLF ALPHA TEAM

THE TRAIL ENDED AT A SMALL, JAGGED HOLE IN the floor a few hundred feet later. Trevor would have thought someone made it with a jackhammer if it weren't for the claw marks gouged into the floor. Crap. The creature had dug this getaway hole through reinforced concrete. He knelt down and shoved his head through the hole in the floor, not sure how the creature had fit through it. But the strong smell of oily musk coming from the opening confirmed it had.

The passage below the sewer was narrow and roughly hewn out of stone, concrete, and dirt. Trevor would have fit but would have had to crawl on his hands and knees the whole time. Not the position he wanted to be in if that creature came at him again.

Knowing it would be stupid beyond measure to keep going after the creature in its own backyard, Trevor retracted his fangs and claws, then turned and headed back the way he'd come.

It took him a lot longer to get back to the alley off Winston Street than he would have liked. He hadn't realized he'd chased the creature for so long, and by the time he picked up Jenna's scent, it was surrounded by several others. Whoever they were, their presence made her heart beat faster. Trevor could almost feel her panic.

Adrenaline surging through his veins, he forced himself to keep his fangs and claws in check as he sprinted the rest of the way.

Four people were arrayed around Jenna as she knelt beside the injured woman. The new arrivals—two men and two women—were dressed like something out of a *Mad Max* movie, right down to the biker boots, leather pants, and heavy dusters that hung down below their knees. They were hounding Jenna and the woman with questions about what they'd seen as one of the men pointed a video camera in their direction. The panic was clear on Jenna's face, and she looked like she might start hyperventilating any minute.

Trevor didn't think. He simply reacted.

Closing the distance between them, he shoved the two men away from Jenna and the injured woman. Even though both men were clearly startled, the guy with the camera got himself together enough to point it at Trevor while the other guy shoved a microphone in his face, asking who he was and what his connection was to the *Skid Row Screamer*.

Deciding he really didn't like either of these guys, Trevor grabbed one of them, shoving him and his stupid camera toward the closest dumpster. He would have put him *in* the dumpster but decided at the last second that might be a bit much.

Turning, Trevor knocked the microphone out of his face and got a handful of the second man's duster, ready to toss the jackass across the alley, but then Jenna was by his side, putting a calming hand on his shoulder.

"Trevor, stop," she said softly, her voice immediately penetrating the shroud of anger that had enveloped him. "It's okay. I know them. They can be a nuisance sometimes, but they're harmless."

Trevor didn't release his hold on the man's duster. While he wasn't sure the guy and his friends were as harmless as Jenna claimed, he'd give her the benefit of the doubt. Loosening his grip, Trevor let the jerk go with just the slightest nudge backward. The man immediately lifted the microphone again, but Trevor stopped him with a single uplifted finger.

"Put that thing in my face again—or Jenna's—and I'll shove it up your ass."

The guy apparently got the message, dropping the mic and letting it hang from the strap around his neck. The two women moved over to help the other man off the ground near the dumpster. This guy was wise enough to turn off his camera before coming toward them.

Trevor turned to check on the injured woman when Microphone Man stepped in front of him. "I'm Owen Cobb," he said extending his hand and not really giving Trevor any choice but to shake it. "I run the HOPD team. You've met my cameraman, Isaac Callahan. His sister, Esme, is our lead researcher," he added, gesturing to the blond, then at the dark-haired woman beside her. "And this is Maya Griffin, our main equipment operator."

Trevor stared at the man for a moment, wondering if they were actors or something, because he was pretty sure Owen was wearing makeup. He threw a glance in Jenna's direction, ready to ask her if this guy was for real. Unfortunately, she'd moved over to help the unhoused woman, using the woman's scarf to wrap around the deep scratches on her leg.

"HOPD?" he asked, turning back to Owen, though he wasn't quite sure if he truly wanted to know the answer to the question.

The dark-haired guy looked at Trevor in obvious disbelief. "You've never heard of Hunters of

Paranormal Darkness? What, do you live under a rock or something? HOPD is the most recognized and respected team of paranormal investigators in LA. We're famous in a city full of famous people."

Trevor scanned the alleyway, looking for a hidden camera somewhere in the darkness. This guy must be trying to punk him. Right? No one could be that self-absorbed.

"What happened?" Esme asked, motioning toward the woman Jenna was still tending to. "We heard screaming and yelling from this direction. Did the *Skid Row Screamer* attack her?"

The excitement in Esme's dark eyes was downright disturbing. Trevor glanced at the other three members of HOPD and saw that they all looked positively giddy at the idea that someone had been attacked by a paranormal creature.

Trevor was about to ream them a new one for being a bunch of shallow, selfish jerks, but was cut off by Jenna clearing her throat.

"We didn't get a good look at the thing, but it definitely wasn't human," Jenna said softly, capturing everyone's attention. "Trevor challenged it and the thing ran off that way," she added, pointing into the darkness deeper along the alley.

Trevor wasn't sure what he expected Jenna to say, but it wasn't that. Then again, she had said she knew these people. He could only assume that meant she trusted them.

"Isaac, try and find a track. Esme, go with him," Owen said, sending the cameraman and his sister running off into the darkness, then turning to look at Trevor. "That was very brave of you," he said, reaching out to clap Trevor on the shoulder. "But you should never confront an unknown creature of the night. Not without proper training. And never ever chase one down a dark alleyway. That's a good way to get yourself killed—or worse. So, while it was brave, it was stupid. It's best to leave this to the professionals."

Before Trevor could say anything, Owen turned and motioned to Maya. "Let's hunt," he said before trotting off down the alley after his HOPD buddies.

Maya hesitated for a second, a guilty expression on her face as she looked back and forth between Trevor, Jenna, and the injured woman sitting on the ground. "I can stay if you need me to help. I know a little first aid."

Trevor supposed he was relieved to see that not all the HOPD contingent were worthless doofuses.

"No, we'll take care of her," Trevor said, moving over to scoop the woman gently off the ground. "You should catch up to your friends before they get too far away."

Maya nodded and started backing away, giving Jenna a wave and saying she'd see her later before turning to run after her friends.

Jenna motioned Trevor toward the entrance to

the alley. "Come on. We can take her to the mission on the other side of Winston. They'll make sure she gets the medical help she needs."

Trevor followed as she jogged ahead of him, biting his tongue on the dozens of questions that were spinning through his head right then. What the hell was that thing he'd chased? Had Jenna been looking for the creature when she'd taken him to this part of Skid Row, or was it merely a coincidence? And if she *had* been looking for it, why?

The questions continued to spiral in his head, one after another, each building on the last, until his head started getting fuzzy. When they got to the mission and turned the woman in his arms over to several of the people working there, no one asked how the woman had been injured or offered to call the cops. That wasn't too surprising. Unhoused people usually didn't report anything to the police unless they absolutely had to. Unfortunately, their interactions with officers tended to be negative, something he and his pack mates back in Dallas were always careful not to do whenever they interacted with anyone.

But since the people helping Rubi didn't even ask how she'd gotten hurt, he suspected there might be more to it than that. Yeah, there was definitely something weird going on here.

He and Jenna didn't say anything on the walk back to the rental car. Even as he opened the passenger door for her and then moved around to the driver's side, they both stayed quiet. But when he got behind the wheel and sat staring out the windshield, Trevor knew he had to ask at least one of his questions.

"Do you know what that thing in the alley was?" he asked quietly, turning slowly to look at her. "More importantly, have you seen it before?"

Jenna didn't answer right away, and for many long seconds, he wasn't sure if she would. But then she nodded, almost as if she'd made some kind of decision. "No, I don't know what that thing is. But I have seen it before. It's the same thing that kidnapped my sister ten years ago."

ACKNOWLEDGMENTS

I hope you had as much fun reading Kat and Connor's story as we had writing it! If you read the previous books in the SWAT: Special Wolf Alpha Team series, then you know they've been together for a while, only Kat was an actual *cat* in those books. It took some time to finally get them together, and I know everyone has been eager for their story, but I think it was worth the wait! Kat's character was inspired by a news story we read about a real-life SWAT team whose pet cat/team mascot had gone missing. While worrying about what had happened to the cat, the writers in us decided that the cat must be a witch and had gone off to change into her human form. That was the moment we realized we were going to add a cat to the SWAT series. Not only was she going to be a witch, but she was going to be *The One* for a member of the Pack. I've tried to find a follow-up to that news story to see if the cat is okay, but couldn't find anything. I hope it had a happy ending!

This whole series wouldn't be possible without some very incredible people. In addition to another big thank-you to my hubby for all his help with the action scenes and military and tactical jargon, thanks to the editors at Sourcebooks (who are always a phone call, text, or email away whenever we need something), and all the other amazing people there, including my fantastic publicist and the crazy-talented art department. The covers they make for me are seriously drool-worthy!

Because I could never leave out my readers, a huge thank-you to everyone who reads my books and Snoopy Danced right along with me with every new release. That includes the fantastic people on my amazing Review Team, as well as my assistant, Janet. You rock!

I also want to give a big thank-you to the men, women, and working dogs who protect and serve in police departments everywhere, as well as their families.

And a very special shout-out to our favorite restaurant, P.F. Chang's, where hubby and I bat story lines back and forth and come up with all of our best ideas, as well as a thank-you to our fantastic waiter-turned-manager, Andrew, who makes sure our order is ready the moment we walk in the door!

Hope you enjoy the next book in the SWAT: Special Wolf Alpha Team series coming soon from Sourcebooks and look forward to reading the rest of the series as much as I look forward to sharing it with you. Also, don't forget to look for our other series from Sourcebooks, STAT: Special Threat Assessment Team, a spin-off from SWAT!

If you love a man in uniform as much as I do, make sure you check out X-OPS, our other action-packed paranormal/romantic-suspense series from Sourcebooks.

Happy Reading!

ABOUT THE AUTHOR

Paige Tyler is a *New York Times* and *USA Today* bestselling author of action-packed romantic suspense, romantic thrillers, and paranormal romance. Paige writes books about hunky alpha males and the kickbutt heroines they fall in love with. She lives with her very own military hero (a.k.a. her husband) and their adorable dog on the beautiful Florida coast. Visit her at paigetylertheauthor.com.

Also by Paige Tyler

COWBOY WOLF OUTLAW

Cowboys by day, wolf shifters by night—don't
miss the thrilling Seven Range Shifters series
from acclaimed author Kait Ballenger

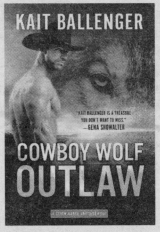

Grey Wolf assassin Malcolm Grey is set on revenge, and no one can
stand in his way. With the pack facing their most challenging battle
yet, his mission is simple: locate the perpetrators and destroy them.
Malcolm will do anything to keep his pack safe, especially when
sassy, southern belle Trixie Beauregard makes a proposal he can't
resist. But Trixie has problems of her own, and she knows better
than to run with the wolf. The smart thing to do would be to stay
away. Too bad she's always had a taste for trouble…

"Kait Ballenger is a treasure you don't want to miss."
—Gena Showalter, *New York Times* bestselling author

For more info about Sourcebooks's books and authors, visit:
sourcebooks.com